TH

HOUSE

Also by Caroline Mitchell

THE BONE HOUSE

CAROLINE MITCHELL

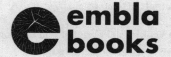

embla books

First published in Great Britain in 2023 by

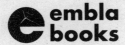

Bonnier Books UK Limited
4th Floor, Victoria House, Bloomsbury Square, London, WC1B 4DA
Owned by Bonnier Books
Sveavägen 56, Stockholm, Sweden

A CIP catalogue record for this book is available from the British Library.

ISBN: 9781471415401

1

This book is typeset using Atomik ePublisher

Printed and bound in Great Britain by Clays Ltd, Elcograf S.p.A.

Embla Books is an imprint of Bonnier Books UK
www.bonnierbooks.co.uk

To my diamond of a father-in-law.
You will always live on in our hearts.

The Reckoning: the avenging or punishing of past mistakes or misdeeds.

It whispers your name
In the dead of night,
In the silent spaces
Devoid of light.
Keep your babies silent
For it will take them too.
The bone house, the bone house
Is calling for you . . .

Prologue

2004

My husband is going to kill me.

The words crawled through Julia Osmond's mind as he pulled back the waffle blanket and helped her swing her legs off the hospital bed. A comet of pain erupted from her C-section scar, and she winced. 'Are you alright, sweetheart?' he said, so caring, so attentive. The nurse smiled and Julia bit back a scream. *Say it,* she told herself. *Say it now, before you lose your nerve.* But nurse Abeba was short, with boyish hips and skinny arms. Certainly no match for Richard should it come to it. Instead, Julia nodded, offering a well-trained watery smile. She watched her husband, with his broad shoulders and neatly cut sandy hair. A consultant at the hospital, he was offered much respect. Who would believe that someone so kind could develop such a macabre side?

'I should have brought slip ons.' He chuckled as he dropped to one knee and tied the laces of the trainers he had brought for Julia to wear. She forced herself to blink. Her pain meds were kicking in, and the edges of her world became blurry. *How much has he given me?* she thought. *I don't want to go home.* She could feel its evil presence, waiting for her to return. The antiseptic smell of the hospital brought back the stink of acid from the day she'd seen Richard in the bunker, stripping the flesh from a dead animal that he'd found on the side of the road. She'd always sensed a dark malevolence from the land on which her home was built, but the bunker wasn't just eerie . . . it felt alive, and it forged a strong connection with the man she used to love. Richard changed after they moved to that address. They all did. She thought of his morbid collection . . . all in the name of medical research. Then there were the skulls. She could still see their fleshless

1

faces, their teeth grinning in an eternal breathless smile. All legal. All paid for. All terrifying. Several houses in their village had World War II bunkers in the gardens. But none were quite like theirs. *I will have you and your bastard baby.* The words were dark and throaty. They visited her in her nightmares, which had flourished ever since she thought about having the bunker filled in. She glanced at her husband, sensing the same pull of darkness behind his smile. He had reason to hurt her baby – because Elisa wasn't his.

She told herself she was being dramatic. Richard didn't know, so everything would be OK. Their ten-year-old daughter, Cora, would be fine too. Her safety was part of an unspoken deal. As long as Julia was a good wife then Cora wouldn't be involved. Technically, she was Richard's stepdaughter, but he'd raised her from an early age. Richard eased Julia into the wheelchair and her vision was swamped with red as he handed her an oversized bouquet of roses.

'I couldn't wait until we got home.' He smiled at nurse Abeba; the display of marital affection was for her benefit, after all.

'They're beautiful,' Julia said automatically. She'd learned Abeba's name was a palindrome and meant 'flower' in Ethiopia. She was twenty-three years old and loved living in the UK. She talked a lot while she was caring for Julia in her private room. They spoke about everything, apart from what Julia needed to say.

'You're so lucky, Julia.' Abeba was unable to hide her admiration as Richard expertly scooped Elisa from her hospital cot. But she didn't notice his eyes were glazed, because his thoughts had turned inward – somewhere dark. Abeba gave Julia's hand a squeeze when she failed to respond. 'Dr Osmond is going to take such good care of you both.'

'Aw now, I'm the lucky one,' he replied. Julia's automatic smile faltered as she watched him dress her little girl in the clothes she'd brought in her hospital bag. She jerked as he roughly tugged on her baby's clothing, snapping the poppers into place. *Oh God. He knows.* Tears welled in her eyes as a wave of nausea rolled over her. *He's done a DNA test. Of course he has. Now he's taking us home to kill us both.* Picking up on Julia's anxiety, Abeba left to get her medication, enough to see her through the day. But not before she threw Richard a sad, sympathetic smile. *Poor Dr Osmond, putting on a brave face as he copes with his wife's mental illness. At least now she's had the baby she'll be able to go back on her meds.* Julia could read her thoughts because she'd heard it all before. Abeba was a little bit in love with him no doubt. Just like the rest of the staff here. Julia was like that once, but he was a different man then. Now she was sitting in a wheelchair, her body hiding recently healed fractures, her tongue stuck to the roof of her dry mouth. But this wasn't just about her. She had Elisa and Cora to think of. She forced herself to breathe. The walls were closing in and it felt like the oxygen in the room had thinned.

Within minutes, Abeba was back, and she pushed Julia down the corridor in the wheelchair while Richard took Elisa, who was wrapped up securely in her car seat. Elisa, with her black hair and olive skin too dark to be from either of them. Her father was from Cyprus. A much loved old flame who had given her comfort and the possibility of escape. He couldn't help her now. As they travelled down the hospital corridor, Julia examined the faces of the people walking by. Would any of them believe her if she told them her husband had become a monster? Her hand reached for the small gold crucifix on a chain around her neck. She glanced up at Richard. His jaw was taut, his knuckles white as they gripped the handle of Elisa's car seat. *When did he find out? Yesterday?* she wondered. *This morning?* She hoped that Cora was OK. Then she remembered she was staying with a friend and exhaled. She was safe, at least, until she returned home. A warning thought drove through the fog of her mind. It came with alarm bells and flashing lights. *Take the baby and run. Don't go back to that evil place, because it will have you both.* But she could barely walk unaided, and she'd never leave without getting Cora first. Because good wives didn't leave their husbands, and he'd kill her daughter out of spite. *Another skull for his wall.*

Nurse Abeba was listening intently to Richard as he told her he'd traded in his beloved Porsche for a sensible car. The automatic hospital doors parted, and Julia blinked as the sun stung her eyes. The car park was half-full but there was nobody around. The sight of their grey Volkswagen made her grip the arms of the wheelchair.

A family car for a family man. *He does know, doesn't he? Or is it all in my head?* Then she thought of the bunker in their garden and all the hours he'd spent down there. She remembered how he looked when she last saw him there, his lips stretched over his teeth in a grin.

A light breeze carried the familiar scent of his aftershave, and it made her stomach churn. He opened the car door and she watched, stupefied by horror as he strapped Elisa in. Abeba was chatting about how wonderful it was that men could take paternity leave. For a split-second Richard's smile wavered. Julia saw the darkness in his eyes as he examined Elisa's face. *He knows.* Milk rushed through Julia's breasts as the baby started to cry and her pads became soaked through. *I've got to get us out of here* she thought, as panic returned. *This is my last chance.* She opened her mouth to scream that he was going to kill them both. Then he was back, his fingers digging into her shoulder deep enough to bruise.

'Cora's so excited to see you both,' he said, and the warning silenced her. Within seconds, Richard lifted her out of the wheelchair and into the car. He pressed a kiss to her forehead, but the movement was hard and sudden, and his teeth bumped against her skin. She looked at her baby, her heart beating fast, her armpits damp with sweat. Then he was next to her and with a cheery wave, strapped himself in. He pushed a CD into the stereo system and her favourite song played. 'Here Comes the Sun'. It was artificially perfect. Her throat felt like it was closing in as she strained to take a breath. She wanted to cry out, but the words were stuck.

'I've got your room all made up.' Richard delivered a grim smile as the car engine purred. 'Yours and Elisa's. Your own special place.' Julia wrapped her fingers around the car door handle, but the doors were locked and Abeba had gone, and it was far too late.

Chapter 1

It started the day the crows fell from the sky. They labelled it an anomaly of nature, but some people knew better. Some knew exactly what it was. It was the start of the reckoning.

Cora was ironing Millie's dress when she heard about it. It was an impulse buy, made of silken material, with tiny blooms of flowers that made every day feel like summer. A season of hope. Of long sun-soaked evenings and clear starry nights. She was feeling positive. Her iron was on low so she wouldn't damage the delicate material. It wouldn't be long before Millie grew out of it. Cora was humming a tune while she ironed – a song from her childhood, buried deep in her mind. Like an old transistor radio, her brain would pick up on her mood and then the Beatles song would come. 'Here Comes the Sun . . .'

An image flashed on her television screen, and the tune on her lips died. There it was. After all these years. The reckoning. She didn't realise she was ruining Millie's precious silk dress until the smell of burning fabric tickled her nose. There was no time to mourn it. Hands shaking, she placed her iron aside and picked up the remote control. But she had thumbs instead of fingers as she tried to rewind the newscast that put her life on hold. She turned up the volume as Connie Bocsik from KCom relayed the news. It was an off-beat local channel, and until today she'd liked how the presenters bounced off each other with their jokey remarks. As always, thirty-something Connie was perfectly groomed, while Eamon, with his double chin and perpetually knowing smile, appeared more like a favourite uncle who spent too much time in the pub.

'Well, Eamon . . .' Connie flashed a set of unnaturally white teeth. 'It's a strange tale indeed. We've already reported on the phenomenon of the hundreds of dying and dead birds which fell into Slayton's lake two weeks ago. It's an incident which has frightened locals, as groups of conspiracy theorists claim it's the prelude to the "end of days".'

'Yet we're still here,' Eamon joked. 'So, what's changed since then?'

'We've not been able to find a reason for this anomaly, but it doesn't end there. Slayton's lake is a popular tourist attraction, and given the ongoing heatwave, many locals swim there too. But now the lake has turned into a festering cocktail which is driving people away.'

'I'm with you there, Connie. When I drive past Slayton, I keep the car windows up. It's quite a stench!' He waved his hand before his nose to drive his point home.

'Well, the good news is that the council has taken steps to dredge the lake, so we should return to normal soon.'

'That should be interesting,' Eamon winked. 'It's Slayton, after all. Who knows what they'll find?'

'No,' Cora managed to whisper before she retched. She clasped her hand over her mouth, swallowing the bile down. Her mind was a jumble of panicked thoughts. She couldn't think straight. She ran the cold tap and splashed water on her face. She surely couldn't be found, not now. Not after all these years. She'd been careful. She'd made a life here. Nobody knew who she was. But the words of a poem rebounded in her mind. One she'd known as a child.

It whispers your name
In the dead of night,
In the silent spaces
Devoid of light.
Keep your babies silent
For it will take them too.
The bone house, the bone house
Is calling for you . . .

Millie. Stumbling to her feet, Cora ran to her bedroom, her heart fluttering in her chest. She stared into her baby's bedside crib. At night Cora kept the side down so she could sleep with her hand resting lightly on Millie's chest. The warmth of her baby's body provided the reassurance she needed to keep the nightmares away. Right now, Millie was asleep, her fleshy pink cheeks moving rhythmically as she sucked her thumb. Cora's legs weakened with relief. Her baby was her life. Her reason to get through each day. She didn't deserve her, but she had been blessed with her just the same. She couldn't allow her daughter to become consumed by the evil threatening to come her way. It was hard to believe that Millie had only been with her for eight short weeks. Loved by all, she was a favourite in the bookshop on the days Cora brought her in. She had a presence about her that made the customers smile. But now the truth was coming out and soon the police would be knocking on Cora's door. Tears welled in her eyes as the foundations of her world crumbled. Millie wasn't safe. Neither of them were. The reckoning had begun.

Chapter 2

'We're all doomed! Doomed, I tell ya!' The homeless man waved his placard, much to the amusement of Slayton police front counter staff.

'Steady on, Alfred,' DC Sarah Noble raised a hand to lower his sign. 'You'll have someone's eye out with that.' In her other hand was a disposable cup of machine tea. 'How about we swap? A cuppa for a placard.' He'd been ejected from the busy police station twice already today and Sarah had come to give them a hand. A change of tactics was clearly needed to keep the old coot at bay.

Alfred raised a bushy grey eyebrow. 'Only for a minute, mind. I'm heading down to the town hall after this.'

'Deal.' Sarah exchanged the tea and guided him out, keeping his 'The End Is Nigh' placard held low. The smell of urine emanated from his baggy mackintosh as he walked in front. The air was thick with humidity, and it wasn't much better outside. You could still catch a whiff of the dead bird smell from Slayton's lake. As Alfred sipped his tea, Sarah gave him a dubious look. 'Why don't you get yourself down to the YMCA and have a shower first? I don't mean to be personal, but you smell like you've been swimming in sheep dip.' She'd known him long enough to get away with the remark without causing any offence.

A smile stretched on Alfred's lips, displaying a row of nicotine-stained teeth. 'That's the crow. I'm taking it down the vets, having it checked out.' He knocked back the dregs of his tea before crushing the cup and throwing it in the bin. Sarah watched as he slipped his hand in his coat pocket and pulled out the black feathered remains. Its head dangled to one side, its pebble eyes dried in their sockets. Sharp talons were pulled in close to its body.

'You're too late, Alfred. There's nothing the vet can do for him.' Sarah recoiled as she spotted movement within its feathers.

'I know that,' he said, shoving the bird's remains back into his coat pocket. I want him to do one of them . . . what do ya call it . . . where they take 'em apart and see what's wrong.'

'Post-mortems?' Sarah suggested.

'Yeah. That's it.'

'This is one of the crows that fell out of the sky last week, isn't it?' She wrinkled her nose. 'Throw it away. It's probably infested with maggots.' She took a breath, glad she hadn't had her lunch just yet. 'It's too late for a PM now.'

Alfred stood in a huff, pulled the bird's corpse from his pocket, and threw it in the bin. 'Why won't anyone listen to me? The world is going to end! That's why the birds fell out of the sky.' He gazed upwards at the darkening clouds. 'Can't you feel it? The time of reckoning is here.'

'OK.' Sarah sighed, seeing no point in arguing. 'Say you're right. What do you want us to do about it?'

His answer was immediate. 'Repent, of course!'

'Right,' Sarah replied, as a group of teens walked past. 'And what do you think a police officer's job entails?' She watched Alfred frown and decided to dumb it down. 'What do we do all day?'

The agitation left Alfred's face. 'You lock up bad people.'

'Yes, that's pretty much it.' Sarah smiled. 'You're preaching to the converted, fella. We spend all day telling sinners to repent. Best you get yourself down to that town hall. Your work here is done.'

Alfred shook his head, bemused. 'I hadn't thought of it like that.'

'I'm just saving your precious time. But go to the shelter first and ask for a change of clothes. That coat of yours needs to go into retirement.' Alfred looked a sorrowful sight as he lifted the lapel of the coat and gave it a sniff. 'They've nuthin to fit. I tried.'

Sarah checked her watch. She needed to get back to work. It was a typical Monday morning, being dragged away from her desk to deal with something bizarre. But she couldn't leave Alfred in this state. God only knew what was crawling in the pockets of his old mackintosh. 'Fine,' she sighed. 'What size shoe are you?'

'Eight,' he replied.

'Wait here – quietly. I'll see what's in our lost and found.'

She caught sight of her own reflection in the glass doors of the police station before going inside. She'd tried to improve her appearance, although her efforts at losing weight weren't quite paying off. If anything, the waistband of her linen blend trousers had become tighter during the week. She blamed M&S. Their sizing was all wrong, although the matching jacket seemed to fit her well enough. At least her black hair had been cut into flattering waves, although she resented having to get up early to style it.

Self-care was something Alfred didn't concern himself with, but in Sarah's eyes he deserved some comfort in his advancing years. Within a few minutes she was handing him a reasonably new woollen coat, a pair of trainers, and a custody tracksuit. The coat was a real find. It had come from lost property, seized from a raid two years ago and never claimed. 'Their loss is your gain,' she said, as she watched him shrugging on the coat, somewhat impressed.

'Sure enough,' Alfred agreed. 'I may as well see out the last few days on earth in style.' He shoved his hand into his pocket and pulled out a twenty-pound note. 'Well, look at this! It really is my lucky day!'

As he ambled off to the nearest café, Sarah's eyes flicked up to her office window on the second floor where her colleague Richie was shaking his head. The pair of them usually worked cases together, and he was a protective soul. Richie didn't just walk, he swaggered, and was a biker to the core. But he also had a soft side known to very few. He gave her a look which suggested he knew the cash that appeared in the coat pocket had originated from her. Sarah shrugged. She regretted nothing. Alfred was one of the few homeless people in Slayton who didn't beg for money. Sarah helped him whenever she could because she knew he'd spend it on food. But her colleague was wise to her ways, and would no doubt take the mickey out of her for being a soft touch. Still, with his full stomach and comfortable clothes she shouldn't have any return visits from Alfred today. She glanced at the sleeve of his old coat as it dangled from the bin. A shudder drove down her back as she thought of the poor dead crow. She was there when the crows fell, on a rare outing, visiting the lake. The memory of them slapping against the windscreen of her red Mini Cooper filled her with horror. She could still hear the children's screams as they clambered out of the water, followed by the rush of panicked parents to the shore. Sarah sighed, snapping herself back into the present day. The sun dipped behind a cloud, casting Slayton in gloom, but it wasn't enough to dampen the rising heat. Her beloved town had been through so much in the last year. She climbed the steps to the station, trying not to allow suspicion to influence her thoughts. *It's alright,* she told herself as automatic doors parted to allow her back inside. *Everything's alright.* But as her feeling of foreboding grew, she wasn't entirely convinced.

Chapter 3

Sarah was grateful for DI McGuire's air purifiers and plants as she returned to the office. CID was situated on most of the second floor, with uniform rows of wooden office desks and a view of the streets below. Gabby, her sergeant, sat like a teacher at one end of the office, her stern gaze bearing down on them. DI McGuire's office was situated at the other end of the room, but he spent most of his time either in meetings or floating around their desks. In the past few months, the wiry young DI had put his stamp on the place. A few of his ideas had been knocked back, such as the suggestion of a one-minute morning meditation and a Buddha indoor water feature. But it had been fun watching McGuire try to implement them. His stocks of green tea were pretty much untouched, but the homemade flapjacks went down a treat. Overall, McGuire was liked, despite his eccentric ways.

The energy in the office seemed different upon Sarah's return. McGuire caught her attention from his office with a wave. At least the blinds were open, which meant she wasn't in trouble, although Richie was in there too. It was the longest walk when you were called into any office when the blinds were shut. Today, slices of sunshine streaked across McGuire's desk. His corduroy jacket was hung on the back of his office chair, and he was wearing jeans and a Ralph Lauren shirt. His casual-but-smart style drove her sergeant mad. Sarah smiled to herself. If Gabby had her way, they'd all look like the Men in Black.

'I have a job for you both.' The lilt of McGuire's Northern Irish accent floated pleasantly over Sarah as she joined Richie at the desk. 'You two can partner up and head down to the lake.'

Richie exchanged a glance with Sarah. 'I'll get the keys for the job car while the boss fills you in.' He straightened his tie, a hint of a smile brightening his face. Why did he always look like he was up to something?

McGuire stretched across his desk to switch on his fan but all it did was circulate warm air. 'How's it going, Noble? Alright?'

Sarah nodded. 'Yes, boss. All good here.'

'Good, good.' He echoed the sentiment. 'The council called. They've dredged a rusty old pram out of the lake and now they've got it into their heads that there's something inside. I want you and Richie to go down there, take a look.'

Sarah's eyebrows rose. She had been half expecting something to turn up. The day had felt heavy with foreboding from the moment she awoke. The incident with the crows had really got under her skin.

'Sure thing, boss. We'll head down there now.'

'It's probably one of those weird collectable dolls. But I don't need to tell you that.' McGuire gave Sarah a knowing smile. 'Take a look and report back to me.'

Warmth spread to Sarah's face. He was talking about the Ashton-Drake dolls which had infiltrated Slayton thanks to a newly opened collectable shop, The Gift Boutique. The dolls were too lifelike for Sarah's liking, and she couldn't understand what grown women wanted with them. But the residents of Slayton were a law unto themselves, and if it wasn't dogs being pushed around in prams it was scarily lifelike collectable dolls. A couple of weeks ago, she had smashed the window of a Vauxhall Astra trying to rescue one strapped into a car seat on a boiling hot day. Richie had teased her mercilessly. She'd been fooled once. It wouldn't happen again.

'Oh, and, Noble,' McGuire said, as she turned to leave. 'I know you weren't gone long, but it's best to keep any personal visits to essential visits only this week. We're understaffed and the top brass are sniffing around.'

'Sorry? What personal visits?'

'McGuire wiggled the mouse on his desk to breathe life back into his sleeping computer. 'Richie mentioned you were in the front office talking to your boyfriend.'

Sarah stared, dumbfounded. 'Boyfriend? He's not my—' But the phone rang on McGuire's desk. 'Don't worry, it's fine,' he mouthed, picking up the handset. 'Hello, sir,' he said, giving Sarah a look to suggest she should be on her way.

Growling beneath her breath, Sarah joined Richie in the car park. She squinted fiercely beneath the midday sun. 'Thanks for nothing,' she said, as he unlocked the marked Ford Focus. 'I do one good turn . . .' But her words fell into mumbles beneath her breath. She could have put McGuire straight, but she didn't want to get Richie in trouble for telling fibs. Besides, Richie only joked with people he trusted, and she was grateful to be on that list.

'What?' Richie said innocently, starting the engine of the car. 'You and Alfred make a lovely couple. With his looks and your fashion sense, you'll both go a long way.'

'Don't think I won't get you back for this.' Sarah clicked her seatbelt into the buckle, making a mental note to come up with something later. The car was like a furnace, and she switched on the air con and turned up the dial. A fine film of dust blasted through the air vents, but it was a relief to cool down. As they made their way to the lake, her thoughts were consumed with the case.

'How are we playing this, Richie? Do you think they've found anything?'

'Nah. People have been jumpy since crowpocalypse. You know what they're like around here.'

Crowpocalpyse. Sarah chuckled at Richie's name for the event which had sent townsfolk into a flurry. Slaytonites were a suspicious bunch. Given the town's history, they had every reason to be. It wasn't that long since townsfolk were being murdered after answering the door. An involuntary shiver drove its way down her back as she recalled their last case. She could still hear the whispers of those poor lost children in her dreams.

Slayton was divided into two communities, thanks to investments from Irving Industries. Properties in Upper Slayton were luxurious and modern, but on the other side of the train tracks, residents of Lower Slayton battled hard times. But the town centre was the great equaliser, where people from both sides mingled and gossip spread.

'Your Facebook group must be having a field day with all this crowpocalpyse stuff.' Sarah could imagine the myriad of posts and responses since news of the birds broke. Richie had varied interests, from motorbikes to conspiracy theories, and he spoke with like-minded people online. He steered with one hand, pulling down the sun visor to shield his face.

'You should join in,' he said. 'We've had some sensible theories about the birds dropping out of the sky. It's not all woo-woo stuff.'

Sarah snorted. 'I get enough drama being partnered with you. I don't need to talk to your weird friends.' She had heard all the theories, from electrical currents in the air to feathered predators panicking the flock. Then there was the wilder speculation of the end of days and UFOs. There was never a dull moment in Slayton, and while she worried about the impact of these dark events, she needed the sense of purpose that her job provided. It gave her a reason to get out of bed. It wasn't that long ago that she was a shut-in who hated answering the door. She turned down the car's air con as they approached the lake. It would be a blessed relief when they rid the town of the rotting carcass stink.

Chapter 4

Dredging the lake was a huge undertaking and Sarah was grateful for the local Police Community Support Officers who kept back the onlookers who had come to watch. As she tried to accustom herself to the smell, Sarah pulled her shoulder harness on over her shirt and took the gravel path from the car park to the water's edge to join the workers at the scene. The machinery was stilled for now, and the area felt eerily quiet for the time of year. It was the town's most popular beauty spot, dotted with trees, benches and picnic areas and a jetty off the nearby hotel. For once, there wasn't a canoe or swimmer in sight. Old bicycles, shopping trolleys and inky-black crow remains were piled in a heap at the water's edge. Sarah flapped away a swarm of midges as she traipsed after Richie towards three men in fluorescent vests. They stood around a rusted pram and parted to allow her and Richie through.

Sarah introduced them both, but Charles Wilbur, the contracted foreman, spoke directly to Richie in a broad Yorkshire accent. As a female officer, Sarah was used to taking a back seat, unless she was with someone younger, then people usually turned to her. Mr Wilbur was a tall, robust man, his shirt armpits damp with sweat as he battled with the heat of the day. 'At first, we thought it were the head of a doll. But then we took a closer look and found what looks like a skull.' His face soured, relaying that their discovery had been grim. 'We were told to report anything suspicious. I 'ope this doesn't 'old things up.'

'We won't take any longer than we need to.' Richie gestured to Sarah. 'It's all yours.' Sarah wasn't surprised. He always left the grisly stuff to her. She braced herself as she stood over the pram which was rusted rigid. The hood was pulled up but torn. There wasn't much fabric left but the metal body of the pram was intact, along with the thin white straps which were designed to hold a baby in. She snapped on her thin plastic gloves. She'd already had a close encounter with a rotting carcass today and didn't want to take any chances this time. She peered inside the pram past the wet silt and dead leaves to see what was underneath. Steeling herself, she pulled aside the threads of a pink blanket, making out the remains of a rotted pink onesie. Whatever it was, it appeared to have been in the water for some time. Poppers were evident, detached from disintegrating clothes. She gently cleared away more debris to reveal what looked like a small skull, with a fine halo of black hair still attached. 'Guys,' she glanced back as everyone peered in. 'You're blocking my light.' Satisfied as they stepped back, she returned her attention to inside the pram. Only then did she notice a rock in a plastic bag which was fixed to the straps. She glanced down at the wheels, noting the remains of plastic bags which had been tied to the spokes too. The rocks that held them down must have detached when the dredger caught the pram. Whoever pushed this into the water didn't mean for it to resurface. 'Where did you find this?' She turned back to the foreman.

'It's 'ard to give an exact location but we started near the jetty today.' He pointed further along towards the Lakeside Hotel. Sarah imagined a dark figure wheeling the pram up to the jetty, weighing it down with rocks and pushing it off the edge. But she had to keep an open mind. She'd seen pretend skulls before, realistic casts which had been used during Halloween in the past. The youth of Slayton were more imaginative than most when it came to celebrating the day. But a sense of sadness descended as she leaned in and gently pulled the clothing and detritus aside. The remains of a tiny but complete skeleton were evident. It would have been difficult to replicate.

'Oh no,' she said softly, her heart plummeting in her chest. She turned back to her colleagues. 'We're going to need a forensic anthropologist to confirm it, but it does seem to be the remains of an infant, and it looks like it's been down there for some time.' Her mind immediately began running through missing baby cases from the last few years.

'So, it's not a prank?' one of the younger men said, no doubt hoping it was. He fiddled with his wedding ring, perhaps thinking of children of his own.

'I don't want to tamper with it any more than I already have.' Sarah delivered a sympathetic look. 'But it seems real enough to me.' She wondered about the value of a scene guard at this late stage. Protocol would have to be followed until they knew more.

'We'll put a police cordon in,' Richie added. 'I'm afraid you won't be doing any more work today.' Detaching her radio from her harness, Sarah turned away from the men to update control. It was happening again. Something dark was running through the lifeblood of Slayton. Its inhabitants were offered little peace. Who knew how long this tragedy had been hiding in the depths of the cold, black waters? What they might unleash by bringing the lake's dark secret into the light? As Sarah updated control about the incident, she wondered if some secrets were better left alone.

Chapter 5

'And if that mockingbird don't sing, Mama's gonna buy you a diamond ring . . .' Cora's voice trailed away as the nursery rhyme came to an end. Millie must have picked up on her discontent, as she had been grizzly since Cora heard the news. It was a relief to get her to sleep. How would Millie feel when she was old enough to understand the vile and unforgivable truth? She would never look at her in the same way. But since details of the pram were splashed all over social media, Cora had stopped picturing a future for them both. There was only now, interspersed with flashbacks of the past. She recalled her father's panicked face as she found him in the back room of his bunker. How his eyes had bulged from their sockets, the vein throbbing on the side of his forehead as he found her witnessing the aftermath of violence so great that it stole her breath away.

'What . . .' he'd gulped in a breath, the clang of his hammer assaulting the silence as it fell to the floor. 'What . . . are . . . you . . . doing . . . here?' Each word was a struggle as he tried to grip onto his sanity. Cora had watched, rooted to the spot as her father's blood-spattered fists clenched and unclenched. Now, with the eye of an adult, Cora realised an internal war had been taking place. He could have easily killed her then. Had she turned on her heel and run, he would have caught up with her before she reached the house. She would have left him no choice. Because there was one thing she knew about her father. Whatever was at the root of his violence, it didn't come from him. Evil seeped from the walls of the place where they lived. Much later, the newspapers would title it 'The Bone House,' and while the nickname was crude, it fitted. She saved her own life on the day her mother died, by staying quiet and still. She was a bird in the presence of a domesticated cat who was fighting every instinct to pounce. Then, when the worst of the danger had passed, she only needed to utter one word as her father advanced. She turned her wet eyes upon him, his image blurring behind a dam of tears. 'Daddy?'

She reached out her hand and guided him out of the back room. Even now, she didn't know how she'd remained so calm. But then she had lived beneath the shadow of darkness, which made her different from other children. She knew what part of her needed to retreat, and what part needed to stay. She'd watched her mother placate her father in the aftermath of his violence before. *Don't run, don't try to escape. Make no sudden noises. Accept whatever he says or does. Then, when his shoulders are shaking and his anger is spent, guide him to a chair where he can sit.*

Cora led her father to the table. She didn't see his collection of bones, or the life-sized medical skeleton in the corner of the room. It was just her and her daddy. Everything else fell away as her need for survival dictated her actions. Her father's eyes were vacant, his mind back in the room where he had done the awful thing. He was still on the cusp of it, his sinews tense. Anything could have made him snap – the ring of the phone or the sudden bark of a dog. Shrouded in shock, Cora felt like she was outside of herself as she waited for him to sit. Quiet sobs backed up in her throat as she monitored the movement of her father's chest. Finally, his breathing slowed. He blinked, coming to ground.

'She made me do it.' He spoke in a rough whisper. 'She left me no choice.' Each word dropped into the depths of the silence of the bunker. Then the consequences of his actions came at Cora with force. Her mummy wasn't walking away from this, like she had done before. And what about her baby sister? The silence from the back room was all Cora needed to know. The sound of her pounding heart swished in her ears. She was trembling now, her world lost in a torrent of violence. Her father stood, his face turning resolute. As Cora struggled for breath, it was his turn to extend his hand. 'Come with me. I need you to wait in the back room while I sort myself out.'

But Cora didn't want to go back to that room. She wanted to see her mummy, but not like this. The dam of tears she had been holding finally broke free.

'No time for that now.'

She felt the warmth of her father's hand as it wrapped tightly around hers. 'C'mon. You can stay here for now, while I sort everything out. It's going to be alright.' But there was dried blood on his skin, up his shirt sleeve and splattered in the creases of his handsome face.

Cora told herself it had been an accident. That Daddy hadn't meant to hurt her mummy or little sister. That maybe they were just sleeping, and everything was going to be alright. Sinking deeper inside herself, she allowed her father to guide her towards the room at the back of the bunker where her mother and sister lay. He was mumbling to himself. She had become his biggest problem because she had seen too much. As she stood in the doorway, Cora stared at her feet, unable to look inside. Then came the push – and her body jerked from the sudden unexpected force as she was propelled three steps forward. The door closed with a click. She pressed her face against it and cried to be let out, too scared to turn around. She could feel the aftermath of his violence. Smell the tang of freshly spilled blood. Blood that had patterned the windowless concrete walls.

She hated the bunker, and from the first moment she entered, it felt like a strange and desolate place. When they first moved into the old farmhouse, her daddy thought it was a wine cellar. But not only was the entrance boarded up with an inordinate number of nails, it was camouflaged beneath a garden shed. Back then, nobody stopped to ask why it had been so well hidden. It wasn't meant to be found.

It took more than a tightly nailed trapdoor to stop her father and as he climbed down the narrow cement steps, he discovered it was a World War II bunker hidden beneath the ground. The eleven by six feet space held more surprises. There was another room at the back. Her father made the space his project, putting in a new floor, electricity and heat. But Cora had always hated it. It wasn't just the complete absence of light, it was the creepy undercurrent it held. She had so many questions about it, but her father insisted that they keep it to themselves. The garden shed which was erected over the entrance to the bunker did a good job of camouflaging it. Even the estate agent hadn't known about it when he showed them around. Cora knew that nobody would find her now her daddy had locked her inside, but she was still too scared to fight.

* * *

A layer of sweat glistened on Cora's skin as she snapped out of her trance and came back to the present day. The room was growing dark. How long had she been standing here, lost in the past? When she was young, she used to lose chunks of time as she withdrew from the world. She stared at her daughter as she stirred. She needed to protect her – but from what? Time after time, she had tried to convince herself that the bone house wasn't awaiting her return. It took a year of counselling before she would contemplate that the darkness which inhabited her father didn't live on. Because not everything in life was black and white. Something had influenced her father on the day he committed murder. Something evil. It found him in the bunker and seeped into his soul. Her father was a kind man. Her mum wouldn't have chosen him otherwise. He'd never been a stepfather to her. He'd been Dad, the man who taught her how to ride a bike and encouraged her to be a doctor herself one day. He'd been there to help her practise her lines for the Christmas school play and cheered her on when her mother wasn't well enough to watch her perform. But he changed the day he discovered the bunker, and over the years whatever lingered there affected them all. It started off as a place for her father to store his medical books and study anatomy in peace. But soon shelves on the walls of the bunker were lined with bones. It didn't end there. Whatever haunted the bone house lived on in Cora's dreams, growing fat on her fears and anxieties. Something so powerful had become real. And now it was coming for her.

Chapter 6

Elliott's dark lashes fluttered as he fell into a hostile sleep. His room was cast in shadows, dimming his twinkling nightlight, and turning the stars on his ceiling into inexplicable black blobs. Given he was nine years of age, some would argue that he was too old for such a childish nightlight. But to Elliott, it was a lighthouse in the choppy waters of his dreams. His eyes darted beneath his lids as he was drawn deeper into a nightmare that felt all too real. His room was usually a happy place, with a thick blue carpet and a stack of soft toys on his dressing table in the corner of the room. Framed artwork of turtles brightened the walls, and a bookcase in the corner was filled with adventures stories and travel books that fuelled his imagination. But tonight, his comforters fell away. He cried out in his sleep as he turned one way then the other as he tried to escape the vision that had him firmly in its grip.

'Elliott.' The voice was kind and gentle. It didn't belong in the inky blackness, but he was grateful for it just the same. He was falling from the sky, the night air cold between his outstretched fingers. His movements were in slow motion, the ground rising to greet him.

'Elliott, it's OK. I'm here.'

He recognised the voice, but he couldn't name it. Not yet. The air had turned to water. He flailed, his sheets tangling around him, becoming long rotting reeds. Fear controlled his movements, his teddy falling to the ground as he kicked out. Sweat dampened his pyjamas as he fought for breath.

'Elliott, it's just a dream. You can make it stop.'

It wasn't Mummy. It was his friend and mentor. But he couldn't reach out to Miss Grogan, and the dream had changed again. He wasn't falling in the air, or deep under water, but standing in darkness so solid that it was hard to move. His eyes twitched in rapid succession as a slow, rasping breath entered his space. Something else was with him.

It was horrid and stinking, with breath that smelled like it was rotting from the inside out. Robotically, Elliott swung his legs from his single bed. The cuffs of his pyjama legs skimmed his ankles as he approached the full-length mirror in his room. He was caught in somebody else's thoughts. His movements were not his own. His hands by his sides, he stared into the moon-washed glass, his face haunted, his limbs stiff.

'Elliott.' Miss Grogan called his name once more. This time, her voice was insistent. She wasn't asking, she was telling. 'Listen to me. Pull up your drawbridge. Don't let it in.'

Elliott fought against the vision as he pulled up his internal drawbridge which kept the bad things at bay. But the reflection he saw in the mirror was not his own. And that stink . . . the grinning skull that stared back at him sucked the breath from Elliott's throat. 'No!' He screamed, shutting his eyes tight. He balled up his fists and stood strong before his mirror. He knew what to do. He wasn't alone. He felt Miss Grogan's presence as she guided him to safety. Deep in his mind, he pulled up his mental drawbridge, then sent a series of internal shutters slamming down. Curtains were closed, boxes snapped shut, again and again he continued snapping, shutting, slamming, and closing until the darkness went away. He blinked, seeing nothing but his own pale reflection. He touched his face, his skin cool beneath his fingers. As he returned to bed, the remnants of his friend faded in the night air. He picked his teddy from the floor and fixed his duvet into place. On his ceiling, the starry projection offered comfort as he slipped beneath the covers. But there was an echo of his vision that remained. The words of a poem which lingered in its wake.

It whispers your name
In the dead of night,
In the silent spaces
Devoid of light.
Keep your babies silent
For it will take them too.
The bone house, the bone house
Is calling for you . . .

It would play on a loop until the morning sun filtered through his windows. But Elliott knew how to keep himself safe. Whatever was coming from the bone house, it wasn't here for him.

Chapter 7

Sarah stifled a yawn as she approached her front door. She'd left at 7 a.m. and now the moon was high in the sky. Her calves ached from being on her feet all day. She'd spent hours down by the lake and had the insect bites on her summer tanned skin to prove it. She had been kept busy since returning to work full-time. Now her restrictions were lifted, she was a fully-fledged detective. She was thankful to her friend Maggie and her son Elliott as they looked after her cat, Sherlock, when she worked late. Sarah's corner house had once doubled as the town's old post office and it was handy having her friend right next door. The street was quieter now that the police had put a stop to joyriders, and not many ventured down at this hour apart from the pack of stray dogs who raided the bins at night.

'You look done in.'

Sarah jumped as Maggie's voice rose from nearby. A low fence divided their gardens, and she hadn't seen her friend standing in the shadows outside her front door. Maggie exhaled a stream of smoke, her mint green dressing gown wrapped around her slim waist. Sarah was convinced that had Maggie grown up anywhere else she would have lived a charmed life. As a teen, her charismatic presence was impossible to ignore and with her ash blonde hair and striking blue eyes, she was popular in school. She should have been on stage or ridiculously famous. Or even the wife of a top politician who did no wrong. But over the years Slayton dimmed her sparkle, doling out misfortune at every turn. She was the same age as Sarah, but she should have had so much more.

'You frightened the crap out of me.' Sarah spoke on the exhale as she leaned on the fence for support. 'What are you doing out here?' The street lamp flickered in the dim light – something else in Lower Slayton which needed attention.

Maggie delivered a wry smile. 'Elliott's asleep. Sneaky cigarette time.' She lifted a beat-up cigarette packet from her dressing gown pocket. 'I should smoke roll-ups. These things are crazy expensive now.'

'Or you could give them up altogether?' Sarah knew she was wasting her breath.

'And you could give up pizza and ice cream but hey, everyone has their vices.'

Sarah couldn't argue with that. 'I take it Sherlock is inside?'

'He is. He's had his supper and an evening of cuddles from Elliott and is ready to go home.' She raised her cigarette to take another drag but paused, taking in Sarah's face. 'I heard about that pram they pulled out of the lake. You OK?' But Sarah didn't get the chance to reply. Maggie stubbed out her cigarette and waved her over. 'Come, I've got half a bottle of red inside.'

Within minutes, Sarah was at Maggie's kitchen table, a glass of wine in hand. She liked Maggie's new kitchen which was like her own but more homely, with Maggie and Elliott's artwork on the walls. Sarah clung to the stem of her wine glass, barely knowing where to start. 'I was going to FaceTime Elsie,' Maggie said, phone in hand. Their friend currently lived alone and didn't go to bed until late.

'Do, give her a call.' Sarah smiled. She was glad to see her friends getting along. Elsie was a playful character, and while she knew most people in Slayton, Sarah and Maggie were her closest friends. As the FaceTime call flickered into life, Elsie seemed delighted to see them both. 'Well ain't this a treat, seeing y'all at this hour.'

'What have you been up to?' Sarah said, enjoying her friend's Southern American accent.

Elsie shooed her cat as he blocked the screen. 'I've been busier than a one-legged cat in a sandbox. This morning, I went out to do my shopping, and I spent my evening with Adrian Williams. Broke into quite the sweat.'

Maggie raised a questioning eyebrow, but Sarah was in the know. Last year, after coming into money, she bought Elsie a Peloton treadmill to help her in her quest to lose weight. Her friend couldn't resist the attractive instructors who encouraged her on screen.

'Do you know what Adrian says?' Elsie continued, her cheeks pink. 'That we should never give up because great things take time. Man, I think I'm in love.'

'I'm glad one of us had a nice day,' Sarah countered, filling in her friend about the discovery in the lake.

'Oh lordy,' Elsie replied, the smile fading from her face.

Sarah sipped her wine. 'It was awful. The bones are being checked but I'm pretty sure they're real.'

Maggie was listening intently. 'I saw it on the local news. Who would do such a thing?' The women exchanged a glance. Slayton had plenty of troubled inhabitants. 'Imagine . . .' Maggie continued. 'If those crows hadn't died, nobody would have known.'

'Makes you wonder where the mother is now, after all these years.' Sarah took another sip of her Merlot. Its warm cherry tones provided a level of comfort after a long day.

'I take it you don't know who she is?' Elsie enquired. There was nothing she liked more than a good mystery.

'Not yet. There wasn't a lot left. That poor baby must have been there for years. We don't even know if it's male or female, although the remains of a pink onesie suggests it was a little girl.'

Maggie shook her head in disgust. 'I hope they throw the book at them, whoever they are.'

'It's a cold case so there's no sense of immediacy like before. I'm the officer in charge of the case.' Sarah was pleased to have been designated as the OIC.

'I'll put some feelers out,' Elsie said, stroking a ginger cat. 'See if anyone knows anything.'

'As long as you don't repeat what I've said.' Sarah turned to Maggie. 'How's Elliott?' She had a special affinity for her friend's little boy, who reminded her of her little brother. Unlike Elliott, Robin would stay forever four.

'He's spark out,' Maggie replied. 'His class went on a nature walk today. He had a lovely time, but it wore him out.'

'And he's not been having nightmares?' Sarah asked. Elliott had a sixth sense when it came to bad things.

Maggie arched an eyebrow. 'If you're asking about the crows or the pram, then no. He's sleeping well. He seems to have a handle on it now.' Maggie swirled the last of her wine before finishing it off. 'Moving house helped. There were too many bad memories in our old place.'

'I'm glad you're settling in.' Sarah was warmed by the thought of helping her favourite little boy. Having recently come into money, Sarah had bought the property next door and rented it out to Maggie at a low price. Sarah never had children of her own, so she was grateful to have Elliott in her life. But talk of Elliott's insights always shut Maggie down. Sarah gripped the stem of her wine glass a little tighter. Elliott had been helpful in their last big case and she wasn't ready to let the subject of the recent strange occurrences drop yet.

'If Elliott ever wants to talk, he knows where I am. But promise not to say anything. Yvonne's out for my guts as it is.'

'Yvonne?' Maggie's features tightened. 'You want me to have a word with her? Because I will. I can't stand that bitch.'

'Me neither,' Elsie said. 'She really dills my pickle.'

'You haven't even met her!' Sarah chuckled.

'No matter,' Elsie replied. 'I don't need to stroke a skunk to know that it stinks.'

She had a point. DC Yvonne Townsend did not make life easy and Maggie had encountered her sour disposition when she interviewed Elliott in the past.

'I'm a big girl,' Sarah said. 'I can stand up for myself.' But she appreciated her friend's protectiveness. Their history would keep them forever entwined. Reassured, she continued.

'Everyone's freaking out about the crows. Everything seems . . .' she searched for the right word. 'Heightened. Have you noticed that?'

Maggie nodded. 'Things do feel different. It's like that gap between lightning and thunder when you can feel the electricity in the air. Elliott's picked up on it too. He's edgy but he's managing.'

Sarah inwardly smiled as her friend contradicted herself. She had said he was fine just moments before. She didn't blame her for wanting to protect him. Elliott was too young to take on the weight of Slayton's problems. Maggie blinked, realising she'd been caught in a lie. 'You won't say anything to him, will you? He's been sleeping so well and now this . . .'

Sarah cupped her hand over Maggie's and gave it a quick squeeze. 'You forget that Elliott's always been the one to approach me. The last thing I want is to upset him, especially now he's standing on solid ground.'

Suitably admonished, Maggie stared into her glass, as if she could find answers there. After a little while, Elsie bowed out. Her exercise regime was taking it out of her. Silence passed as Maggie and Sarah became lost in thought. Sherlock slinked towards Maggie and curled his tail around her legs. Maggie wasn't hugely fond of cats, but Sherlock was slowly winning her around. 'Oh, here you are, your highness.' Sarah greeted her pet. 'Ready to come home after your evening of pampering?' She bent to pick him up and he replied with a resounding 'miaow.' She glanced at the door, half expecting Elliott to appear. She was being truthful to Maggie. She would not approach him about the recent strangeness in Slayton, but if he came to her then she would not turn him away.

Chapter 8

Cora, you are back inside my head, and how you have affected me. I stagger to the back door of my house, barely able to catch my breath. I told my wife I was putting the bins out for the morning – anything to buy me some time alone. Grateful for the darkness of our narrow side alley, I try to compose myself. But I'm shaking. I can barely think. After all this time . . . I never thought I'd see that pram of yours again. Facebook will be alight with armchair detectives speculating on where it came from, or why the police are involved. But we know, don't we? I recognised it immediately – even after all these years. It was called The Balmoral, a luxurious Silver Cross pram worth thousands of pounds. But you didn't have to worry about the cost, did you, Cora? Not when you were so gifted at stealing. It was the jagged remains of the logo that confirmed it. You'd tried to remove it in a vain effort to make it unrecognisable. But instead, it had snapped in half. The detail came at me with the force of a punch. You didn't know it at the time, but I was watching you closely back then.

I grasp the wheelie bin and drag it to the end of our close. Its wheels rumble on the pavement. There are ten bungalows on our development, mostly inhabited by people who have too much time on their hands. I keep my head down as I walk my small suburban street. I don't want to see Mr Chatterjee from next door, with his irritating Highland White Terrier which barks day and night. Neither do I want to hear the wispy voice of Silvester Herbert from number seven complaining about the birds defecating on his car. I bet you can imagine it, can't you? Me, smiling and waving at my neighbours, all the while imagining what their skulls would look like on my wall. Remember when you used to do your homework at the kitchen table, and I'd catch you staring into space? You'd tell me that you were in your 'mind palace' and I'd laugh and recommend you hit the books. Well, I have a mind palace too, and I've slowly been making it a reality. In my palace there's a special place for each of my neighbour's skulls. But the pride of place goes to you. I wouldn't call it a shrine as such, but the glass cabinet I've assembled is big enough to house all of you.

Sigh. I'm doing it again. Another internal conversation with you. I had them all the time after you left. I was so angry, I used to go somewhere remote, fill my lungs with air and shatter the countryside silence with my screams. I used swear words I dare not utter in company. I think I even made up a few. On bad days you'd answer back, but clozapine quietened that in time. My meds helped me to progress with my life, but closure never came. It wasn't as if I could visit you where you were holed up in the psychiatric unit. That was far too risky. I tried to forget you, and everything you put me through. And now you're here, climbing back into my head. But you know what? It makes me feel alive. I hadn't realised just how numb I'd become until I saw the image of the pram online.

I leave the bin in the designated spot and keep walking. I'm wearing my slippers, but I can't go back to my wife. Not yet. I know exactly where I need to be. I raise my hand to wave as a neighbour drives past. Everyone around here knows me – or at least, they think they do. I'm not the same person I used to be. My shaggy beard and wild curly hair only disguises my outer shell. My other half calls me her Viking man. Only you know what I'm capable of because you've seen all the way inside. I never thought I'd see you again. But now you're firmly in my thoughts, thanks to the recovery of the pram. My special girl. No . . . you're a woman now. I gasp. I shudder. I laugh at the prospect of meeting up. I'm on a Jekyll and Hyde high. I can barely contain the emotions running wild as compartmentalised memories break free. My slippered feet plod quietly away from my sleepy little village and down the grassy tree-lined lane where people walk their dogs. The small, broken-down cottage sits on the edge of a misty fishing lake which has turned into a polluted swamp. Funny, how both of us have been drawn to water, isn't it? But I'm not laughing, and you certainly won't be. A flutter of wings erupts above me as I disturb sleeping pigeons in their nests. I slip my hands into my cardigan pockets, feeling like I'm wearing someone else's skin. You must know that I've seen it. That I will come for you. The sensible part of you will deny it, but deep down, you're expecting it. Because that pram wasn't empty. And its contents belonged to me.

Chapter 9

Sarah wrapped her hair in a towel, knowing that within minutes of getting out of the shower, she would be hot and sweaty again. 'Alright, matey?' she said, finding Sherlock in the kitchen. He responded with a miaow, pressing his face against her pyjama leg. An evening with Elliott had done him good. Now if only she could teach him how to tidy up the house. The carpet needed hoovering, and the microwave smelled of last night's reheated curry. But she was weary from being on her feet all day. 'I'll give you a good clean tomorrow,' she promised beneath her breath, continuing in her long-practised habit of talking to inanimate objects. She pottered around the kitchen, looking for something to eat. 'Good old Mr Warburton. You never let me down.' After sliding a giant crumpet into the toaster, Sarah hunted for butter and jam in the fridge. She was getting used to eating at odd hours and moved on autopilot as she prepared her food. Her mind was on work, and she wondered if it would always be this way, riding the merry-go-round of good against evil as she fought to keep the residents of Slayton safe.

The image of the rusted pram left her uneasy in her skin. She had swum in those waters, the air sweet with fragrant water lilies and the warmth of the sun on her skin. Now every memory of her time there was tainted with the knowledge that a baby's lifeless body lay beneath. She decided that she would attend the burial, as soon as the bones were released, and lay a posy of baby's breath on the grave. Someone needed to be there. Someone needed to care.

Sherlock loudly protested the indignity of being ignored. 'You've already eaten,' Sarah said, opening her fridge just the same. The light flickered on, putting her to shame. It was time she did a food shop, but most of her day was spent at work. She cast her eyes over the contents: half a carrot, some questionable-looking cheddar cheese, a pack of bacon and a slice of chicken. 'Alright then, you've worn me down.' Smiling, she picked out the slice of chicken before presenting it to her ginger cat. The funny little sod. With Sherlock, you never knew what you were going to get.

Her thoughts wandered as she settled down with her crumpet in front of the TV. She needed time to decompress. As tired as she was, it would be at least another hour before she took herself off to bed. She listened as KCom news reported on an impending electrical storm. No wonder it was so humid outside. But it would be more than the weather keeping her awake tonight. She flicked through the channels, stopping at a rerun of her favourite docudrama, *In the Bones*. The presenter, Sophia Hudson, was discussing her latest case, which involved a body found in unusual circumstances. In tonight's episode, they discussed how Sophia handled being an expert witness in court. Sarah admired her ballsy attitude and extrovert nature but mused that there was power in quietness too. Finishing the last of her crumpet, she brushed away the crumbs and pulled a blanket over her knees. The sofa cushion bounced as Sherlock decided to join her. His head held high, he chose to sit on the furthest end. 'Here, puss,' she coaxed, reaching out to stroke him, but her cat gave her sticky fingers the side-eye before settling down. The corners of Sarah's mouth twitched in a smile.

Not that long ago, Sherlock couldn't stand to be anywhere near her and the only thing Sarah worried about was herself. She'd felt incomplete after her husband died, as if she had no right to carry on without him. For a while, she'd had little intention of doing so. She'd been so wrapped up in grief and sorrow, she'd barely made it through each day. Now she had real friends, and a job where she was valued for who she was. But something dark was looming. Whatever was coming for Slayton, she wouldn't allow it to threaten the life she had built, or the people she loved.

Chapter 10

Yawning, Cora tugged on her old T-shirt as dawn broke through her blinds. Black was the worst colour to wear with a new baby in the house, but regurgitated milk stains would wash out and she needed the comfort of old clothing today. The 'M' for Metallica was faded from years of use but the T-shirt was from a rare time in her past that she took comfort from. The first night she'd worn it, she met awkward, skinny, cute-as-hell Josh. It was one of those nights that made you feel happy to be alive. She'd gathered up all her courage and gone to the indoor music festival alone. She was just about to leave when she'd slipped on a puddle of beer. Josh caught her before she'd hit the deck. They were inseparable after that. For the first couple of weeks, they discussed music and movies, and vented about people who pissed them off. It wasn't until they'd been dating for twenty-eight days straight that she told Josh about her past.

She smiled as she recalled the picnic. The air was thick with humidity and there were thunderbugs everywhere, but Cora treasured the simple memory of the past. Their feast consisted of crisps and chocolate, and a huge bottle of orange pop that Josh had taken from his parents' fridge. As he cracked it open, it fizzed all over her white Converse trainers that she'd saved so hard to buy. Then Josh had laughed and said her parents could buy her a new pair. But when her tears kept coming, he didn't understand. That's when she told him that she didn't have any proper parents. Once she started talking, she couldn't stop. She spoke about her mother and the baby, and how her father had lost the plot. How she'd witnessed the aftermath of their murders and what happened afterwards. 'I come from the bone house,' she'd said, feeling like she'd thrown up poison that had been sitting in her stomach for years. But her relief evaporated as soon as she took in Josh's face. He'd stopped blinking. He couldn't comprehend her words. Then he let go of her hands and raked his fingers through his hair. She knew from the moment that he withdrew his touch that it was over for them. She was tainted by something so awful, it didn't belong in his world. Josh tried to be nice after that, but he was too sweet for such horrors and things were never the same between them again. She still kept the T-shirt and sometimes imagined where their life could have gone had the bone house not come between them. 'The bone house' was a crude and absurd nickname given by journalists to the tragedy of her life, but it had stuck in more ways than one.

She dated a few more times over the years but soon learned that she was better off on her own. Which was why she wore her mother's wedding ring when she went on a night out. The sort of guy who didn't care if she was married was the sort of person who wouldn't bother her afterwards. The day she discovered she was pregnant with Millie, she laughed out loud. Not a gasp of shock or a sudden intake of breath but a proper shrieking laugh so loud that it felt like it was coming from someone else. She'd clasped her hand to her mouth, scared someone might hear. It wouldn't have been so bad if she hadn't been in the loos of her local Tesco at the time. She'd picked up her bags of frozen pizza and chunky chips and walked home. By the time she reached her front door, she'd decided she was keeping it. The father didn't need to know. The last thing she needed was a man interfering in her life. Her mistrust of men was deeply ingrained.

She thought she'd had all she needed with her bookshop and the friends she'd tentatively made. Her efforts at fundraising had been well received. It was her dream that every young person from Slayton's lower income households should receive at least one free book a month. She knew first-hand how books could transport you to another world. She hadn't realised what a hole there had been in her life until Millie arrived just a couple of months before.

She stared into her baby's cot. Millie was sleeping in a starfish position, with her limbs flung outwards. She looked so safe and secure, a picture of innocence. Cora gazed at those precious plump cheeks, pink with sleep. The gorgeous folds of her skin. The wavy tuft of black hair. Her lips moved in a sucking motion, her eyes tightly closed. Her long black lashes were enough to make Cora's heart melt, and she felt a surge of protectiveness towards her beautiful child.

Then the question came, as it always did. *How could anyone hurt a precious little baby such as this? How could she?*

Chapter 11

Sarah hadn't expected anyone to be waiting for her when she got to work. She pushed through the door to reception, hoping the enquiry wouldn't take too long. The name rang a bell. She'd heard of Grogan from somewhere. She glanced around the police station reception area but failed to recognise any of the faces. To the left, a bearded man clutched a holdall close to his chest. A couple of seats down was a bored teenager scrolling through his phone, and across from him sat an older woman with young blue eyes and a kindly face framed by silver blonde hair. Her sleeveless crimplene dress and heeled Mary Jane shoes reflected a unique vintage style. 'Miss Grogan?'

'That's me. Are you Detective Noble?' the woman said, rising to her feet.

'Call me Sarah. What can I do for you?'

'Well, um . . .' The woman glanced around the space. 'Is there somewhere we can speak in private?'

'Of course,' Sarah gestured to a side room and ushered her in. 'Sorry for keeping you waiting,' she said, shooting the woman a warm smile. 'What can I do for you?'

'I'm Elliott's teacher.' She took a seat behind a small desk in the windowless room.

Sarah pulled back a chair. At least the room smelled of lemon now the cleaners had finished their morning rounds. 'I thought I recognised the name. He talks about you a lot.' Her smile faltered. 'Is he alright?'

'Oh yes, perfectly fine,' Mrs Grogan replied. 'Sorry, I didn't mean to worry you. I expect you're wondering why I'm here so early. I needed to see you before class.'

Sarah delivered a reassuring smile. She knew that for some, visiting a police station was a difficult step to take. She only hoped that it didn't involve Elliott in a negative way. Miss Grogan cleared her throat before taking a breath to speak.

'I need to tell you something. It may not make a lot of sense, but it's important. Given how much you mean to Elliott, I take it you're open-minded?' She chuckled to herself. 'Then again, living in our queer little town, how could you not be?'

'Policing in Slayton does bring its own set of challenges.' Sarah exchanged a knowing glance.

'The thing is . . .' Miss Grogan hesitated, her penetrating blue eyes fixed firmly on Sarah. 'I see more than most. It's always been that way, for as long as I can remember. I was fortunate to be born to parents who understood my unique insights. Others are not so lucky, which is why I take them under my wing. I've been doing it all my life. Elliott is a very special boy.'

She reached into her leather holdall and produced various childish drawings. Resting them on the table, she leafed through each one. 'These belong to my students. They provide insights on how the children were feeling at the time.' She smiled as she pointed to the image of a creature which appeared to have been crossed with a giraffe. 'Tommy Young drew this picture of his new dog.' Her eyes roamed over another picture of a family dwarfed by a big house. 'At first glance Lucy Mayweather's picture seems ordinary, but the stickman holding the suitcase is her father walking away. It's no wonder the girl can be a bully, given her difficult home life.' Her words trailed into a sigh. Sarah checked her watch. As touching as this was, she had more pressing matters to deal with.

Miss Grogan set aside the pictures, keeping one for last. 'I shouldn't have a favourite pupil, but Elliott is head and shoulders above the rest. One day, his insights will be stronger than mine. It's important that he doesn't get overwhelmed.' She smoothed the picture across her desk, taking in every facet Elliott had brought to the page. 'This wasn't drawn from imagination like the others,' Mrs Grogan stated. 'It came from his mind's eye.'

Sarah stared at the drawing. It did not project a happy scene. By the look of it, Elliott had taken a wax crayon and lain it on its side, covering two-thirds of the page in black. He'd worked in a circular motion, before taking his brown crayon and drawing a table in the centre of a gloomy room. On that table was a lit candle and next to it was a round ivory object. Sarah peered closer at the image.

'Is that a skull?' she said, the temperature cooling for the first time that day.

Miss Grogan nodded. 'His visions are getting stronger. I'm doing all I can to protect him, but sometimes in sleep, when his mind is open, they filter through.' She folded up the picture and slipped it in her bag along with the others before checking the time.

Sarah was sorry to hear that Elliott's bad dreams had returned. This sounded like a conversation that Miss Grogan should be having with his mother, but Maggie was too closed-minded to deal with talk of visions and premonitions. Sarah would support Elliott in any way she could, but she didn't want to get carried away. 'Elliott's been through a lot. Surely it's only natural for him to have bad dreams every now and again. We don't want to go putting ideas in his head.'

'I agree.' Miss Grogan's brow creased in concern. 'Like you, I'm in a position of authority. All I can do is listen. These images . . .' She cast a hand over his picture. 'I've not influenced his thoughts. They come entirely from him. But he's not alone in his feeling that something bad is on the periphery. You've listened to Elliott in the past. I hope you'll offer me the same courtesy.'

'Of course,' Sarah said, intrigued. 'What do you want me to do?'

'Be vigilant. There is someone, no, some*thing* coming. They possess a dark energy, and the ability to move outside their periphery. Slayton is on their radar. They're powerful, with the ability to influence. They'll kill whoever gets in their way.'

Sarah tugged at the neck of her shirt as her skin began to prickle. 'How do you know all this?'

'As I said, I sense things. But so does Elliott. If he knows the message has been passed on, he's less likely to feel the need to get involved.'

Sarah was never one for psychics. But living in Slayton had broadened her mind. 'Miss Grogan, you're not giving me a whole lot to go on. This energy that you're describing. What do they want? Are they male or female? Can you describe them in any way?'

Her gaze wandered to the corners of the ceiling before resting on Sarah again. 'I haven't seen them as such. It's a sense, a very bad one. It makes me feel quite ill. I see the same dark room as Elliott, with a desk and bones hung on the wall.' She paused as the image seemed to come through. 'Bones and skulls of every shape and size.'

'I've seen first hand what Elliott is capable of. His visions ... they're very powerful,' Sarah began. 'But are you sure about this? I mean ... it's not a bad dream perhaps? So many awful things have happened in Slayton, and with the crows dying in the lake ...'

'I wouldn't attend a police station at this hour of the morning to discuss a dream.' Miss Grogan seemed resolute. 'Elliott's picture prompted my visit. I wanted to speak to you before he did. He needs to be protected from such things.'

'What things?' Sarah replied. 'You're not giving me any straight answers.'

Miss Grogan paused to compose her thoughts. 'Imagine walking home alone in a strange place.' Her voice lowered to a whisper. 'It's dark, so dark you can barely see your hand. You're holding a cold metal torch in your hand. The light keeps you safe. But there are footsteps in the gravel behind you. You can almost feel the person's warm breath on the back of your neck. But your torch, it keeps you safe.' Sarah became invested, her shoulders creeping up an inch. She didn't know it yet, but she was an empath. She absorbed the emotions swirling around her and made them her own.

'Imagine all that,' Miss Grogan continued. 'Then picture me asking you to take the torch batteries out. Because that's what you're asking of Elliott, and of me. We can sense danger, from both the living and the dead. But if you want us to delve deeper, it puts us at risk too.'

'I see.' Sarah cleared her throat. 'Well, if anything else comes to mind then you know where I am.'

Mrs Grogan nodded. 'Please, if Elliott comes to you, tell him it's all under control.'

'That little boy is family to me. You don't need to worry.'

'I know,' Mrs Grogan paused, looking thoughtful. 'And perhaps in another life, he was. Goodbye, Sarah. Thank you for your time.' She picked up her bag and left.

Sarah squinted as the morning sun beamed through the glass reception double doors. Anyone else may have been concerned for Miss Grogan's mental health. They may have even made enquiries about her suitability to teach. But there was something about the woman's presence of mind that completely drew Sarah in. The comment about Elliott being a family member in a past life should have angered her. The woman could have known about her little brother and the tragic set of circumstances which claimed his life decades before. But Sarah didn't doubt Miss Grogan's sincerity and Elliott was thriving under her care. People were entitled to their own beliefs, no matter how outlandish they seemed. She only hoped her concerns about a house of bones were nothing more than a bad dream.

Chapter 12

'Look at you, grinning like a Cheshire cat.' The voice was that of DC Yvonne Townsend. She was sat across from Sarah, her desk offering a view of the streets below. It wasn't what she said, but the way she looked down her nose when she said it, that annoyed Sarah. Sarah tried to like Yvonne, but the woman wasn't happy unless she was lording it over someone, so the pair of them had never gelled.

'Better than coming to work with a sour face,' Sarah countered, pulling up her desk chair. Once, she would have entered the room, head down. But today she happily worked to the backdrop of ringing phones, printers, and the occasional burst of a police car siren exiting from the car park below.

Yvonne flicked her straightened black hair over her shoulder. She was well dressed, in her silk blouse and black pencil skirt. Sarah watched her scan the room while crossing her legs beneath her desk. She was ready to snipe at someone, but today their colleagues had their heads down.

Sarah glanced over at her sergeant, feeling the heat of her gaze. Gabby was dressed in her usual cheerless black trouser suit, her afro styled in a side parting which suited her high cheekbones. Her face stony, she watched the interaction. She was no fan of Yvonne but tended to keep out of office banter. 'I've set you some tasks on the system.' Gabby clicked her mouse with a red varnished nail. Given it was tourist season, Slayton's population had doubled – and so had the level of crime. Each officer had their own case workload. CID dealt with a variety of serious offences. Sarah was fortunate in that her work hadn't built up yet which made her the next in line for this case.

'I'll get to them right away.' Sarah spoke with a smile which had yet to be reciprocated.

'How are you doing?' Gabby asked. It wasn't unusual for her sergeant to check in on Sarah every now and again.

'I'm good, thanks. You?'

'Jahmelia's got a boyfriend.' Gabby rolled her eyes. 'It's completely harmless, but try telling her mum that.' Sarah was flattered that Gabby was confiding in her, Elliott was good friends with Jahmelia, who was Gabby's granddaughter. 'Anyway, the Dalai Lama wants to see you,' Gabby continued, before Sarah had the chance to reply. Gabby had yet to warm to their new DI and his efforts at encouraging the team. Sarah enjoyed his pre-briefing pep talks, but given Gabby was a staunch pessimist, it was hardly any wonder that McGuire's cheerful nature got under her skin. Sarah opened her drawer on its runners and slid out a pack of double chocolate biscuits. 'I won't tell if you won't,' she winked, sliding them onto her desk. According to McGuire, chocolate was an unhealthy option and bad for concentration, but he didn't need to know. As Gabby slid the biscuits beneath a folder, Sarah could swear she saw the tiniest of smiles.

'Right, Noble,' McGuire said cheerfully, as Sarah took a seat in his office. It was a narrow space, much smaller than the one their last DI had occupied down the hall, but McGuire preferred to be near the team and had plans to extend. Sarah sniffed at the smell of incense. It wasn't a stick, but a plug-in air freshener that emitted the same sweet, spicy scent. 'Do you like that?' he said, as Sarah wrinkled her nose. 'Reminds me of a trip to the Himalayas. Smell evokes such great memories if you let it.'

'You've done a lot of travelling.' Sarah folded her hands on her lap, wondering how he'd fitted so much in to so few years. There were images on the wall of a younger McGuire with what looked like his little sister, arms around each other in a goofy pose. Other images portrayed him in far-flung countries from a young age upwards.

'My parents were nomads,' he said, his eyes resting on a family photo. 'We travelled the world.'

Sarah liked her new DI, but she wished he'd get to the point.

'Anyway,' he continued. 'I brought yous in here to talk about your baby in the lake.' The wheels of McGuire's chair squeaked as he rolled it in an inch. 'This won't be a huge operation. Not like before. Judging by the age of the pram, you're effectively working on a cold case.'

Sarah nodded. The team may have been busy, but everyone was talking about the discovery. Just because the baby was abandoned years ago, it didn't make him or her any less important in Sarah's eyes. Of course, she didn't say any of this. She sat quietly in McGuire's office, taking it all in. McGuire watched her fidget, a slight smile playing on his face.

'But a smaller operation doesn't mean it's any less important. I've called in someone to help. You're going to like this . . .' He threw her a wink as his office door creaked opened another inch. 'Noble, may I introduce Sophia Hudson, *New York Times* bestseller, star of *In the Bones* and world class forensic anthropologist.'

'Sophia, meet Noble, detective and all-round good spud.'

Sarah's mouth dropped open. It couldn't be. She spun around to see five feet eleven inches of glamour standing at the door. The red lipstick, the wry smile. The scent of Chanel No.5. Sarah couldn't believe her eyes. Sophia Hudson was in her mid-fifties and came with a wrinkle-resistant face, thanks to Jackson Foley, cosmetic surgeon to the stars. Her clothes were high class, her smooth skin crowned by a head of glossy brunette hair. She was a featured expert in true crime documentaries and Sarah had watched her long-running docudrama *In the Bones* for years. But her personal life was closely guarded. What was she doing here?

'I've read all of your books!' Sarah exclaimed, jumping up from the swivel chair. 'And I saw you on TV just last night.' Heat rose to her cheeks as she realised she was fangirling in front of her DI. She couldn't help herself. The woman before them reached out a manicured hand.

'Thank you, darling. Aren't you a delight?' She squeezed Sarah's hand tightly, her rich New York accent filling the room. 'Now, what crime did you commit to end up with this washed-up hippy as your boss?'

Sarah exhaled a nervous laugh. She wasn't sure how to take that. 'Ach, don't pass any remarks on her,' DI McGuire countered with a wave of a hand. He turned his attention to Sophia, his arms outstretched as he stood. 'C'mere.'

Sarah watched as they hugged, then cleared her throat. This all felt very surreal.

'Right,' Sophia said, parting from McGuire. 'Enough of all that. Down to business. I need a shower and a change of clothes to help me battle this jet lag then we'll get to work. That sound OK with you, Noble?'

'Please, call me Sarah,' she replied. She had given up trying to get McGuire to use her Christian name months ago. Sophia nodded in acknowledgement before thrusting her open hand towards McGuire. 'Key?'

Sarah couldn't believe the scene playing out before her. Was *the* Sophia Hudson staying with her DI?

'We go back a long way.' McGuire glanced at Sarah, before pressing a key into Sophia's palm.

'Right, well, I'll get back to work,' Sarah mumbled, before shuffling out of the door. She almost bumped into Richie, who was holding a wad of papers while peering in through McGuire's door.

'Is that . . . ?' he began.

'It is!' Sarah squeaked, squeezing his arm as she dragged him away. 'She's working on my case. Imagine, me rubbing shoulders with a real-life celebrity. I've been watching her show for years.'

'She's nothing special,' Yvonne snorted, watching them both. This was her opportunity to shine. She had been concerned about making a fool of herself but the coroner had agreed that the bones were those of a human baby. The question was, however: how on earth had McGuire managed to get someone as famous as Sophia Hudson to come to Slayton?

Chapter 13

Sarah almost didn't answer her mobile phone. Clutching a mug of tea, she wrestled with her file, slipping it under her arm as she checked her caller display. It was Cora, the owner of their local bookshop. Sarah could buy books cheaper elsewhere, but she liked supporting local businesses and appreciated the personal touch. Cora was a real bookworm, pleasant and personable. The bookshop was a cosy nook, where everyone was welcome, and Cora was on hand to personally recommend reads. She was most likely ringing about a book Sarah had ordered, but the investigation was calling, and Sarah didn't have time to chat today. But as her phone rang for the fifth time, she didn't have the heart to switch it off. The call would only take a second anyway.

'Hello,' Sarah said. 'I'm afraid I'm a bit busy right now.'

But it was as if she hadn't spoken at all. 'Sarah? I . . . I need to talk.'

The panicked voice didn't sound like Cora and Sarah checked the caller display before returning her phone to her ear.

'It's not about your book,' Cora continued, her breath ruffling the line. 'I . . . I need to talk to someone in the police and you're the only one I trust.'

Sarah rested her mug and file on her desk before taking a seat. Her colleagues were too busy with their own work to notice her. 'OK,' she replied with as much reassurance as she could muster. 'I'm listening. What's wrong?'

'I can't talk about it over the phone. Please. Can you come?'

Sarah sipped her tea as she tried to decipher the motives for her call. 'OK, what about this evening? I can pop over to the bookshop after work if you don't want to come here.'

'It's about the baby,' Cora blurted. 'The one they pulled out of the lake. I can tell you where it came from.'

Sarah sat back as her words sank in. 'Then come in. I'm at the station. We'll talk in the witness suite. It's got sofas. There's a kettle too, and biscuits.' Silence fell. Sarah shook her head at her own ineptitude. *Biscuits?* As if the promise of chocolate digestives would make her come in. It was obvious the woman was distressed.

'I don't know . . .' Cora replied. 'Can you come to me? Alone? This is . . . well, it's sensitive.' Sarah could hear her swallow. Every word she spoke was tense. From what Sarah knew, Cora had only moved to Slayton a couple of years ago. Whatever they dragged from the lake had been there for some time. Perhaps Cora was calling to tell her it wasn't a baby at all. She worked in a shop and may have overheard people gossiping between the book aisles. Sarah chewed on her bottom lip. It was wrong to hope that the bones were real, but the appearance of Sophia Hudson had put a whole new slant to the case. Either way, she had to follow up on the lead. 'OK. Where would you like to meet?'

Sarah could have informed her sergeant of the visit, but she wanted to see where it would lead first. So, when Richie mentioned making enquiries in town, Sarah persuaded him to drop her off at Cora's bookshop, Turn the Page. It was part of a parade of shops with flats overhead, situated in Slayton's old town. Cora had worked wonders with it, painting the frontage a cheerful duck egg blue and installing pretty lights and soft furnishings between the bookshelves to create a welcoming space.

An old-fashioned bell tinkled above the door as Sarah entered. Timothy, Cora's assistant, sat on a high stool behind the counter, his head in an Angela Marsons book. He was a stout man in his forties, his auburn hair parted at the side to camouflage a bald spot. Sarah liked his bubbly personality, and most days his campness was only outdone by his flamboyant shirt. A warm welcome was guaranteed when Timothy was around.

'Well, if it's not my favourite police officer.' He slipped a bookmark between the pages before closing the book. He had arrived in Slayton not long after Cora and it seemed the pair of them had hit it off.

'Hi, Timmy,' Sarah returned his smile. 'Is Cora about?'

'She's out back.' He gestured towards the door at the end of the shop. 'But tread lightly. She's just got little Millie-belle to sleep. She's got the lungs of Pavarotti, that one.'

'Will do,' Sarah said, before heading to the small stock room. The room held boxes of stock, along with a filing cabinet, a small desk and two chairs. Piles of books rested on a counter next to a microwave, kettle and small fridge. Cora was standing over Millie's pushchair, watching her daughter intently. Sarah peeped in at the baby's sleeping form and felt her heart melt. 'She gets more beautiful every time I see her,' she whispered. Millie's cheeks had a rosy glow, her long black lashes fanning her face. Sarah glanced at Millie's tuft of black hair, her smile fading as an image of the baby from the lake invaded her thoughts.

Cora's jitteriness was palpable as she stood, wide-eyed. 'You didn't say anything to Timmy, did you?' She took two quick steps towards Sarah. 'I told him you're giving security advice.' Sarah's heart sank because her behaviour pointed to one thing: the baby in the lake was Cora's and she had put her there. She didn't want to believe it. Not Cora. Please, no.

'Don't worry. Mum's the word.' Sarah tapped the side of her nose, masking her concern. She looked the new mum up and down. Cora's face was haunted, with dark shadows circling her eyes. She was wearing an old Metallica T-shirt and leggings, her hair hanging limply around her face. It was only natural that a new baby would knock the stuffing out of her. She was a striking young woman, with her ice blue eyes and platinum blonde hair. The crescent moon-shaped birthmark over her right eyebrow only served to enhance her looks. When she ran the bookshop single-handed, she was always smartly dressed, in brightly patterned dresses and skirts. At least now she'd managed to keep the place open, by extending Timmy's hours to full-time. Sarah imagined it was tough, running a business while being a single mum.

Sarah declined her offer of refreshments, taking a seat next to a small fold-up table. The air was thick with the smell of old books and leather-bound journals. They were Sarah's favourite scents. But her time was precious, and she couldn't afford to delay. McGuire was keeping tabs on her, and she was expecting a call from Sophia

Hudson soon. 'What's wrong, Cora? You sounded upset on the phone.'

'The pram you found . . .' Cora took a deep breath, her eyes swimming with emotion. 'It's mine. I mean . . . it's my baby. I put her in the lake.' Each word seemed to cause pain as she spoke in the cosy little back room. Cora fidgeted with her hands, fighting back tears. Sarah sighed. This didn't feel right but it was safer to caution Cora at this stage. She followed through with the words that she had known by heart since her first week in the job. Sarah calmly opened her police issue notebook and wrote down the time, date and place. Satisfied procedure had been complied with, she told Cora to proceed.

Chapter 14

Do I ever enter your thoughts, Cora? Have you wondered what happened to me? I'll tell you. I live in an insipid little house on an insipid little street. Every day is a battle and so far, I've won. For years, I've managed to keep the best side of myself in its proper place. I give to charity. I live in a neighbourhood of neatly manicured lawns, where the rubbish goes out on time and every item in my recycling is washed and in the right colour bin. My nasal hair is trimmed, my nails clean. My moles are checked every six months and I see a dental hygienist three times a year. I keep myself fit, my muscles are defined as I make use of my gym membership three times a week. My life is orderly.

But you are affecting me. You, the last page of a book I have yet to complete. Already, my perfectly constructed façade is crumbling. I skipped my medication today. I stood over the sink, tap running, empty glass in hand. Then I watched the pills disappear down the plughole, as if all by themselves. Sometimes my limbs feel like they're moving with no conscious effort from me. There are also moments when some of the thoughts entering my head seem alien at first. I'm sensible enough to know that by skipping my meds, I'm making things worse. But when it comes to you, I can't help myself. I've always hated taking tablets, and while I'm being truthful, I suppose I miss your voice.

Now I'm walking with an extra bounce in my step. I'm almost there when my phone buzzes in my pocket. It's my other half, asking if I'm free for a pub lunch. It's part of our weekly ritual. Doesn't every married couple have them? Pub lunch on Wednesdays to break the monotony of the week, if I can spare the time. Three times a week we watch Coronation Street *with tea and chocolate digestives before bed. I've always been an early riser. I do a lot before the break of dawn. My footsteps steady, I keep walking, because I cannot turn back now. I text to say that I'm sorry, but I can't make it for lunch. I imagine* them sighing in disappointment because they must make their usual sad offering of a ham and cheese on rye.

My thoughts are distracted as I cross the railway track. I head down the narrow lane towards Willow Cottage, swiping a cloud of midges away. The place is swarming with them as they migrate from the nearby lake. The earthen path to the cottage is arid and cracked beneath my feet. It's bordered by three-foot-high nettles which seem to thrive, despite the drought. It's already been a long, hot summer and not many people venture this way. I received the keys to the dilapidated cottage over three years ago. I'd befriended the old fool who lived there. Betsy, her name was, with her crooked teeth and one eye that was looking at me and the other looking for me. I smile to myself, I can almost hear you laughing at my cheesy joke. Do you remember that special bond we had? You were everything to me. But I digress. We'll talk about that soon enough. I was telling you about Betsy, wasn't I?

Local children feared the stinking old recluse, which was why they called her a witch. With her yellowed teeth and cataract eyes it was easy to see why. She offered me a biscuit once and there was a mouse in the tin. She didn't see the mouse droppings on her kitchen counter. Nor did she realise how dark the place was because she kept her curtains closed most of the time. She didn't socialise. She had little awareness of how she appeared to the outside world. But I saw potential. There are several lonely people in our village that I keep an eye out for. I do a little bit of shopping, mow their lawns if they can't manage it themselves. I target the ones without family, who aren't too needy of my time. I think Betsy had a crush on me as I was the only person she allowed inside. When I got called to the reading of her will, I wasn't thinking of her money. I was thinking of how her cottage would make the perfect base. A place where I could be myself.

The surrounding trees offer ideal cover and I check over my shoulder before darting into the overgrown garden. I recover the key from my secret hiding place. I can't risk bringing it home. Everything inside is how Betsy left it, apart from the infestation of rodents which I swiftly dealt with. I manage the heating and council tax bills for my little bolthole online. Where is your bolthole, Cora? Because I know you're not far from that lake. Do you have a hideaway? Or are you in plain sight?

The Bone House

A waft of sweet, rotting carcass tang hits me as I push open the door. I walk down the narrow corridor, taking care not to bang my head on the cobwebbed ceiling beams. In the kitchen sink lie the remains of some of the rats I killed. I use the bath to clean my bigger treasures, mainly roadkill. Such sounds, smells and textures offer their own special gifts. And now I'm entering the back room – the most secure in the house. It used to be Betsy's bedroom, but I cleared it ages ago. This room is kept under lock and key. The hinges of the thick wooden door groan as I force it open, and my hand automatically reaches for the light.

Rows of china cup-white skulls stare back at me, silent in death. I reach out to the frail vertebrae resting on the table, my thoughts firmly with you. My fingers skim their dry surface, and a soft moan escapes my lips. Peace descends. I can almost feel the presence of hearts that no longer beat. Carefully, I pick up a skull from the table. Her name is Charlotte; at least, that's the name I gave her. I told my wife she was once used for medical purposes, but I bought her privately from a collector. I caress her bloodless bone before bringing her skull to my face and slipping my tongue between her teeth. It's a strange, cold sensation that makes me tingle all over, because what I'm doing is so wrong. I expect to hear your voice in my mind, even a gasp of disgust, but there is nothing. I can wait. A tingle of excitement runs through me at the thought of seeing you again. Not in my dreams, or through disembodied voices, but the real you. The one who's aged. The one who thought she was safe. If it wasn't for those crows falling into the lake, I would never have known where you were. Which is why this is meant to be. For a moment, I question myself. I'm older now, settled. Can I go through with it? But then I look around and imagine the possibilities. I wanted this, and the urge is strong. It may have taken years but now I'm calm, measured, and in control. I open my notebook, flicking the pages past scribblings and sketches of my plans. I'm due some time off. I can make it work. I glance up at the glass case, a satisfied smile stretching my face. I can't wait to caress your pretty little bones.

Chapter 15

A level of discomfort grew as Sarah's pen touched her notebook and she recorded every faltering word. She knew what was coming. She could feel it in her blood. It was ugly and tragic, and she'd been called here as a friend. It wasn't her job to console, no matter how remorseful the confessor. She was here to ensure justice for the baby in the lake. A life had been snuffed out. But while Sarah spoke in comforting tones, she still felt like a betrayer. Cora's confession could land her in prison, taking her away from the baby she obviously doted on. Given she relied on Timmy to babysit, it seemed she didn't have much in the way of family. So much time had passed. Lives had been rebuilt. Now their meeting felt like an old bomb buried in the ground, about to detonate.

'It was a navy blue Silver Cross pram. The Balmoral, it was called.' Cora stared into the middle distance, a sad smile playing on her lips. 'It was the most perfect pram I'd ever seen. I had one when I was a child, a smaller version for my dolly.' She smiled wistfully. 'Mum bought it for me for my birthday.' Her face clouded over as she finally met Sarah's eye. 'So, when I saw it on the shop floor, I couldn't help myself. The shopkeeper was distracted with a customer and her baby, who was screaming the place down. I took off the sale tag and wheeled the pram out of the shop. I even grabbed some blankets and a onesie on the way out. I couldn't believe it when I got outside. Nobody even noticed me leave.'

Sarah didn't reply. She didn't want to break her flow. After taking a deep breath, Cora continued. 'There was this place I used to go to, a derelict old barn belonging to a rundown farm. Nobody went that far down the fields. I hid the pram under some tarpaulin. I couldn't risk it being found. Not just because I stole it, but because questions would be asked. Nobody knew I was pregnant back then. It's weird . . .' Cora continued, taking another shaky breath. 'The whole time I was pregnant I was in denial. It felt like the pram would make everything alright. Of course, something that expensive would be spotted straight away, especially with a children's home teenager pushing it. I had to rough it up a bit.' Her eyes flicked up to the left as she beckoned the memory. 'I tried to rip the logo off, but it broke in half. Then I bought some spray paint and painted it black. The next night, I went back to the shed and . . .' She sighed. Sarah delivered an encouraging nod. In the privacy of the stock room, the outside world melted away.

'I wasn't expecting the baby to come so quickly. Back then, nobody knew I was pregnant. I wore baggy clothes and was always moody so that was nothing new. I was in and out of homes from the age of eleven.' She glanced at Millie's sleeping form before shaking her head. 'I gave birth to my first child in a rundown barn. I'd stowed away some scissors to cut the cord and a piece of string to tie the end until it fell off.'

'I can't begin to imagine it.' Sarah was unable to stay silent any longer. 'How on earth did you know how to do that?'

'One of my foster families ran a farm and I used to help with the lambs. Oh God . . .' Cora blinked, snapping out of her narrative. 'What must you think of me?'

Sarah grasped her hand. 'Cora . . .' She sighed as conflicted emotions battled for precedence. 'A lot of time has passed, and it's obvious you're sorry for what happened that day. Are you sure you want to continue? I have a duty to report whatever you say.' She waited for her to withdraw. To comprehend the seriousness of the situation. But instead, she delivered a slow nod. 'I need to finish. You're going to find out anyway.'

Sarah felt a weight lift. At least Cora knew where she stood.

'I didn't know what to do with her,' Cora continued, shifting in her chair. 'It was freezing in the barn, so I wrapped her up in blankets and put her in the pram. She was so little, she barely cried. I thought maybe I could leave her outside the hospital, but I was scared the shop might have CCTV and trace her pram back to me.' She rubbed the back of her neck, her movements stiff as she recalled the painful moment in time. 'A little later I tried to breastfeed her and she fell asleep in my arms. I was woozy. I fell asleep and the next morning . . .' She heaved a tearful sigh. Watching Cora confess was like witnessing a wounded animal trying to drag itself to the side of the road. 'The next morning . . .' she repeated, 'my baby was dead.'

Sarah used to think that Cora had life all sussed out. How wrong she had been. Slayton truly was a home for troubled souls. She turned the page of her police issue notebook as she documented her words. Cora described how she'd cleaned herself up and placed the baby back in her pram. 'I took a train to Slayton. Then I walked through the night in a daze, and when it was almost dawn, I came to the most beautiful lake.'

Sarah could picture the scene. A haggard young girl, tired and confused, pushing a pram by the side of the road. Why hadn't anyone stopped to help? Surely someone must have seen her.

'I must have sat there for hours, by the edge of the lake. I didn't want anyone else to have her,' Cora continued. 'And I didn't want anyone to know. The sun was rising. It was so peaceful and the birdsong . . . it was beautiful. I wanted to walk off the end of the pier with her. But when I got there, I pushed the pram and let it go.'

Sarah's brow furrowed as she recalled the bag filled with rocks in the body of the pram. Cora hadn't mentioned that, or the plastic bags tied to the wheels. But Sarah could not impart such sensitive information. Not yet. Cora sat back in her chair, spent. There were gaps in her account. What was she leaving out?

As Cora tended to Millie, Sarah's mind raced ahead. Had her baby really died of natural causes? Was any of her account true? Sarah's phone vibrated with a text from Sophia Hudson. Another part of the puzzle would soon be revealed.

Chapter 16

Sarah didn't usually visit the coroner's office. Until now, it hadn't been part of her remit. As a detective constable, she was happy in her local community, but in her job no two days were the same. Today she stood in an ominous brick building, one with a brass nameplate on the front. She stood behind the swing doors, a powerful scent of disinfectant rising from freshly mopped floors. The air was cool, in the name of preservation. A wrapped cadaver was wheeled past on a gurney by a young man in scrubs. Sarah fidgeted, feeling strangely out of place. She was grateful when Sophia Hudson appeared, an entirely different character in her scrubs. 'Come,' she gestured, showing Sarah into a separate room. It was modestly furnished, with a steel sink, a paper towel dispenser and a bin. In the middle of the room beneath fluorescent lighting was a steel table. The muscles in Sarah's throat constricted as she took in the sight of the tiny, decomposing remains. Their backstory made them all the more tragic.

The sweet scent of Sophia's perfume rose as she joined her. Sarah watched, enthralled, as Sophia educated her on a subject she was clearly passionate about.

'In utero, a baby's skull starts to form towards the end of the second month of pregnancy. By the time the baby is born, the skull consists of almost forty different bones. Some are only a few millimetres. It's that flexibility that gives it safe passage through the mother's birth canal.' She waved a hand over the remains on the table as she proceeded to explain. 'Thankfully, her skull was recovered pretty much intact.'

'It's nothing short of a miracle,' Sarah replied. 'Given how much the lake is used.' But Sophia didn't appear to be listening as she stared at the fragile remains.

'You know, no matter how many times I work with bones this

size, I never quite come to terms with it.' She shook her head. 'She should be a young lady now, with a life of her own. Who knows what she could have become.'

This was what Sarah admired about the woman beside her. She humanised each case she dealt with, emphasising the tragedy of a life unfulfilled. 'She could have been a librarian, or an author, maybe.' Sarah received a curious look and took a breath before she explained.

'I spoke to Cora Osmond. She's the owner of a bookshop in town. She's responsible, reliable, and the mother of this baby, according to what she had to say.'

'And what *did* she have to say?' Sophia arched a defined eyebrow, her expression inscrutable.

As she basked in her undivided attention, Sarah felt like she was in one of Sophia's dramas. It felt both sad and surreal. 'She hid the pregnancy. She said she gave birth in a barn on a cold night with no medical intervention. She was completely on her own. She fed the baby, then fell asleep. When she woke up the next morning, the baby had passed away.'

'Hmm,' Sophia said. It was as if the cameras were upon her as she paced the length of the table. 'I know how this baby died. Even from a brief examination it's obvious.'

'Oh,' Sarah replied, wondering how it was possible to determine a cause of death so quickly with so few remains. She glanced at the tiny skull. At the set of bones laid out in order on the table. So tiny. So fragile. A flicker of light snuffed out in a barn in the middle of a desolate field.

'I'm afraid Cora lied to you.' Sophia's voice broke into her thoughts. 'This baby suffered numerous fractures and broken bones. She did not die peacefully in her sleep.'

Chapter 17

Usually, Sarah and her colleagues ate on the go, if they got time to eat at all. Meals were often missed as cases unfolded before them and paperwork piled up. Gabby tried to ensure that everybody got a break. According to her, it wasn't out of any great concern for their welfare, but merely because sustenance would help them to carry out their tasks. Sarah knew better. Gabby's brusque exterior was a front. She cared about her team more than she would admit. Now they sat in the uncomfortably warm office to a backdrop of whirring fans, with sandwiches or tubs of salad in hand. Sarah fanned a piece of paper before her face, listening intently as Gabby summarised each of their cases in turn. This was an informal catch-up to keep everyone abreast of the latest goings-on. Her case had gathered surprisingly little media attention, despite the omen of the birds dropping from the sky. Apart from featuring on the local news, there was little national attention given to the remains dredged from the lake. People were more concerned about inflation and rising fuel costs. Perhaps after the last big case, Slayton had had its fifteen minutes of fame.

After a discussion concerning a spate of millennium burglaries in Upper Slayton, Gabby turned her focus to Sarah. 'What's the latest on the cold case?' Once, Sarah's cheeks would have reddened when put on the spot. She'd not received the warmest of welcomes when she first joined the team and had felt their animosity each time she spoke up. But she had worked hard to integrate herself and had gained her colleagues' acceptance over the last few months. She could not afford to mess up now. With a slice of yesterday's leftover pizza in one hand, Richie gave her an encouraging smile. He had been her rock since learning of her background. She wouldn't have got this far without him.

Sarah unconsciously picked at a mayo stain on the leg of her trousers as she relayed her visit to Cora, and the admission that had followed in the back room of Turn the Page. She continued, describing her subsequent visit to the coroner's office. The room fell silent as she spoke of the tiny baby's fractured bones. 'Sophia . . . I mean, Ms Hudson . . .' Sarah cast a guarded eye over her DI as she corrected herself, 'believes the fractures were deliberate due to the nature of the breaks. It was a girl, believed to be premature, under six pounds in weight. But we've no way of knowing if she was dead or alive when the fractures were sustained.'

'And they couldn't have come from the pram being pushed into the lake?' Gabby asked.

'The baby was strapped in and padded with clothing and blankets. The pram offered a level of protection too. Ms Hudson said the breaks would have required brute force. Either deliberate, or if the baby was dropped from a height.'

'What about timings?' Gabby asked. 'Any clues there?'

'Further tests on the skeletal remains are ongoing but I've made enquiries with the manufacturers about the pram after checking the sizing of the tyres and frame. That particular model is believed to be around ten years old. Ms Hudson agrees that seems to fit.'

'And you've not arrested Cora Osmond yet?' Despite it not being her place, Yvonne was quick to point out Sarah's perceived flaws. She spoke in a nasal voice, her expression relaying her disapproval. 'Because if it was me, I would have nicked her the second the admission was made. Her murdering feet wouldn't have touched the ground.'

'It's not as simple as that,' Sarah replied, trying to get a word in edgeways.

'Why not? You're too soft, Sarah, that's your problem. You care too much about the people who live here when most of them are a bunch of . . .'

'If you familiarised yourself with the case then you'd know an arrest wasn't necessary,' Richie interjected.

'It's not my case,' Yvonne said indignantly. 'I have enough of a workload of my own.'

DI McGuire stood as the atmosphere sharpened. 'Cora Osmond can't be arrested because she was charged with concealment of the birth of a child and infanticide almost a decade ago.'

Yvonne's features tightened. She had spoken too soon and been pulled up about it in front of the team.

An amused smile played on Richie's lips. 'I've spoken to social services. It turns out they've been monitoring her for years. But the story Cora gave Sarah is contrary to the evidence recovered from the lake.' He looked to Sarah, waiting for her to pick up the reins. She held everyone's attention as she stood.

'According to Cora, her baby died in her sleep. But when I caught up with social services, they said Cora handed herself in to the police and said she'd smothered her. She was so traumatised by the birth, she said she'd buried her in a field but couldn't remember where.'

Sarah couldn't believe how she'd been taken in by Cora's lies. The sight of the tiny, fractured bones had made her blood boil. 'She had clearly given birth, but no amount of therapy or persuasion could make her reveal what she'd done with her baby. Police were suspicious as she kept changing her account, and she was charged.' Sarah had studied the act of infanticide in her probationer days and the details rang clear in her mind. Not only was it an offence, but it could also be used as a partial defence. Only a biological mother who killed her own child within twelve months of its birth could be charged. The death could be an omission of care as well as an outright violent act, so it appeared that Cora had been charged correctly. 'She was given a twelve month conditional discharge and spent a year in a mental health unit. Due to her family history her defence had a strong case.'

'And so, the plot thickens,' McGuire added. 'You've got yourself quite a juicy case there, Noble. Tell them who our bookshop lady really is.'

'She's Cora Osmond, daughter of Dr Richard Osmond, who murdered his wife and baby over eighteen years ago.' A low rumble of murmurs carried around the room as her colleagues absorbed the news. 'Cora was kept in a bunker with their remains until she managed to escape.' McGuire gave them a potted version of the case, telling them about the fire which had taken place. 'Osmond's body was found at the scene, Cora was lucky to get away.'

'And she's been living on our doorstep all this time,' Richie continued the story.

'Why weren't we aware? I mean, like father like daughter...' Yvonne found her voice.

Richie seemed happy to explain. 'The offence happened in Rutland, which comes under the jurisdiction of Leicester police. Cora entered the care system when she was eleven and was placed with foster carers in Lincolnshire. We weren't to know that she came to Slayton to dispose of her baby. The next day she walked into a police station in Oakham and confessed.'

'But social services...' Yvonne spoke again.

'They never lost track of her,' Sarah interrupted. 'She should have been on our intel system. I'm not sure why she wasn't flagged up but we're looking into it.'

'I remember when they disappeared,' Yvonne remarked. 'There was a big manhunt at the time, then it seemed to fizzle out.'

'The tsunami disaster hit that year,' Richie said. 'It was all over the news, so lots of cases went unreported. What I'd like to know is what brought Cora here.'

'Seems Slayton is the place to go if you want to reinvent yourself.' Yvonne raised an eyebrow as she delivered the barb aimed at Sarah.

Gabby took a sip of Diet Coke. 'Cora is going to need safeguarding. If news about the baby's injuries gets out, there will be a lynch mob on her door. I want everyone to be vigilant. We can't afford any more unease in the town.'

By the end of briefing, Sarah felt wrung out. 'You alright?' Richie said, borrowing a pen from the holder on her desk. The colourful clay pot had been a present from Elliott and a reminder not to sweat the small stuff.

'I can't believe it,' Sarah said. 'I feel like an idiot. She gave me this big sob story when all the while she put that poor little mite through hell.'

'We've all been there.' Richie twiddled the pen between his fingers. 'It's easy to get taken in.'

'The thing is...' Sarah sighed. 'If she was up front from the start, I could have accepted it. I know what it's like to witness the death of a parent. It changes you as a person. But to hurt your own flesh and blood...' Her words fell away.

'She's been through the system. Everyone was taken in.'

'Yes, she has. One look from those big doe eyes and she gets away scot free.'

'She could have had postnatal depression. She *was* mentally ill.'

Sarah couldn't help feeling that she'd been taken for a mug. 'But she's not ill now. Or so social services say.' Sarah drew in a sudden breath as another gloomy thought occurred. There was Millie to consider. 'What if she does it again?'

Richie didn't seem concerned. 'Social care will be all over this, but Cora has served her time. It's not like on TV. They don't take children from their mothers unless they're in real danger. All we can do is safeguard them both.'

'Safeguard them from who, when the danger is close to home?'

'Sarah, I thought you of all people would have some compassion for her.'

'What do you mean?'

'After everything you've been through . . . I mean, you hid your identity when you came back here. Why?'

'Because I didn't want to be judged. I wanted a normal life.' Sarah's husband had killed himself in highly questionable circumstances which had made Sarah burn with shame. Given he was sergeant of her team, it had taken time for Sarah to be accepted again.

'Perhaps Cora wants peace too,' Richie countered. 'What happened is horrific. It's easier for her to glaze over the truth rather than face it all over again.'

'I can't argue with your reasoning.' Sarah glanced up at him as he leaned on her desk. A moment passed between them, and not for the first time. Sarah would never tire of his company. He was always there to reassure her, or just to listen when she needed to vent. As always, he was right. When it came to being in denial about the past, she'd been riding that dragon for years.

Chapter 18

Wednesday 19th July, 2023

You are getting to me, Cora, and there is a part of my brain reserved solely for you. As I bend my head to enter Willow Cottage, I exhale a breath of relief, sweeping a cobweb from the low wooden beam. The pretence of being someone I'm not is becoming exhausting to maintain. I never realised how much I needed Willow Cottage until now. I thought I was happy, honing my true self to fit in. Lately, I feel like I'm squeezed into a skin suit that doesn't fit.

Do you remember the first time I helped you with your English homework? I said some silly joke and you emitted a soft giggle, crinkling your cute, freckled nose. That was the first sign of real acceptance, and I watched, transfixed while you implemented my suggestions and rewrote your essay. You weren't interested in shopping with your mum or hanging out with friends. You were quite happy sitting at the small desk in our kitchen with me. On days like those, when it was just the two of us, I could have stayed there forever. It's a shame you grew up into such a bitch.

I know I've hurt you, Cora, and I'd like to say I'm sorry but the truth of it is that I'm not. Things happened. You had your part to play too. It took a long time for me to reconcile how everything turned out. There's another side to me that you could never understand. That's why I have my own special place. I come alive when I'm down here, with my collection to hand. My interest in bones sprung from an early age. I was digging in the garden when I came across some remains. My parents were fairly open minded, and they helped me clean them off. I became fascinated with their origin and we discovered that they once belonged to a cat, buried in the garden by the previous owner after their pet passed away. I dug up all sorts of stuff after that. My parents didn't mind, as long as I kept my collection in the shed. I even got into taxidermy for a while. But then my teenage years hit and I realised that my hobby was repulsive to girls my age. I was older and settled when I attended a modern art exhibition and a piece involving a human skeleton caught my eye. It wasn't hard to find like-minded enthusiasts and so my collection began. Just like before, I kept them out of the house, in my own special place. I saw the beauty of what lies beneath the skin. Sometimes I'd see right through people, imagining their jawlines while I shook their hand tightly so I could feel the sturdiness of the bones beneath. There's nothing nicer than caressing a smooth clavicle or stroking the outline of a woman's spine. My girlfriends thought I was an attentive lover, but it was me who was receiving the thrill. My collection has grown over the years, as has my fascination. Because I'll tell you something, Cora. If I didn't get to let off steam, I'd claw off my own skin.

I'll let you into another secret. Today is a good day because I have a new toy to play with. Many toys, to be precise: scuttling, wriggling, hungry little things that smell like graves. My dermestid beetles are settling nicely into their new home. I watch their black oval bodies scurry around in my glass tank. I can barely contain my excitement as I drop the remains of a dead rat inside. I've starved them so they're extra hungry. Soon the carcass will be stripped clean. A beetle climbs the inner wall of the tank, making a bid for escape. Gently, I lower it back inside and place the lid on top. Even a speck of dirt on the glass wall of the tank is enough to give him a leg up. Not only are they great climbers, but in time and with the right temperatures they can fly. A strong colony like mine will strip a human skull in under three days. It's the gentlest way to get a carcass clean. Only the best for you, Cora. I'm thoughtful like that. My precious beetles can eat their way through anything, as long as it's not metal or glass. I watch my pets feast, my mind wandering free from morals or judgement. I imagine what you'll say when I open your eyes to my world. Justice has been a long time coming, and as you can tell by now, I have just the punishment in mind.

Chapter 19

Cora rested the heavy handset of the rotary dial phone back into its cradle. She had an identical one in her bookshop. They were genuine seventies phones, not like the plastic replicas that Argos sold. She'd bought them as a set in one of Slayton's second-hand stores, a steal at ten pounds each. Today her phone call had not delivered good news. The police were coming back to speak to her tomorrow. They didn't know everything, but they knew a lot more. Already, she could hear the judgement in Sarah Noble's voice. Out of all the people in Slayton, she thought she would understand. Especially as Cora had given her a sanitised, more palatable version of the truth.

It was said that the people of Slayton were a strange, unwelcoming bunch, but from the moment Cora opened Turn the Page, she'd felt like she belonged. A sob hitched in her throat as she thought of her little business. It would never make her rich, but with a town full of readers, and no other bookshops, it had provided enough income to get by. With Timmy's help, she thought she had life all sorted out. They became good friends after she'd employed him and he'd seemed happy to work for a minimum wage, which was all she could afford on the bookshop's earnings. What would he think of her now? As soon as details of her first baby's injuries got out, she would be finished in this town. If even kind-hearted Sarah Noble couldn't hold off her judgement, then she had no chance against the rest of them.

But it was only what she'd expected. Ever since Millie was born, she'd been waiting for her perfect life to come crashing down. She looked around her flat, at the rug she'd purchased from the nearly new store, and the fairy lights around the fireplace that twinkled all year round. At the television she barely turned on, preferring to settle down each night with a book. In the corner was her snuggle chair, one of the few purchases she'd made from new. Next to it was the bookcase which was made from scratch by a tradesman in Slayton who had taken a shine to her. She loved the comforting scent of oak that still lingered in the air, and the floor lamp in the corner which cast the perfect soft glow. Each piece of furniture was chosen and assembled with love. She planned to decorate the spare room with an *Alice in Wonderland* theme for Millie when she was old enough to appreciate it. But like Alice, Cora had lost her footing and now she was tumbling down the rabbit hole.

She thought she'd put the past behind her, but ever since the discovery of the pram, memories of her childhood were returning with alarming force. She used to be a normal little girl, who went to school and spent time with friends. Then, bit by bit, her happy life crumbled away. It started just weeks after they moved to their house in the country, and her dad discovered the dark space beneath the ground. Nightmares soon followed. She couldn't remember the details but she either woke up crying or drenched in sweat. The longer her dad spent in the bunker, the more her mother withdrew. It was a slow but steady decline. It took years for things to get as bad as they did. It was only when Cora visited her friends that she noticed just how depressing her own home was. The dark energy that settled on her shoulders felt like a physical weight. Her place seemed washed out and faded compared to everywhere else. Then the unthinkable happened, as everything came to a head. She recalled her sleepover at Becky's as if it happened last week.

Becky was a short, freckled girl, with thick, wide-rimmed glasses and owlish hazel eyes. She came from a blended family, with six people living in their countryside three-bedroom home. That night she'd filled Cora in on what it was like to be a sister, and the hell of a constantly crying sibling when teething was underway. The cries of Joseph, Becky's baby brother, seemed to prove her right but Cora was still so excited to see her baby sister that she counted the minutes until she got home. Back then, she had so much love to give. Her mother was suffering from depression and her father's time was taken up between caring for her and being at work. Had they known what lay ahead, Becky's parents would not have allowed Cora to walk the short distance to her house. But nobody could have foreseen what was about to occur. Giddy with excitement, Cora skipped down the sunlit countryside lane, her head filled with idealistic plans of how their lives would improve. Her mother would smile again. Her father would love Mummy more, and things would go back to how they used to be. As she imagined a brighter future, Cora smiled so much that her jaw ached. The car was parked in their gravel drive, which meant they were home. She'd let herself in through the front door, treading quietly in her black Converse across the kitchen floor. Her eyes crept over the steriliser and the bottles, and the tubs of SMA on the counter. She couldn't wait to give her sister a feed.

But the house was so quiet, and the air felt so still. A prickle of unease made her skin creep. It was hard to put her finger on it, but something felt wrong. The house felt so different from the one she had just come from, a quarter of a mile down the road. She'd always thought that Becky's home was a chaotic loud mess, what with the laughter, and her siblings and the blaring television that seemed to be on all day long. Her home was so quiet in comparison, and not for the first time she wondered if *her* family were the weird ones, and loud and messy was the norm. She'd crept through each room, experiencing the strangest feeling of being watched. Instinct brought her into the garden and led her to the bunker. The shed door was open. A part of her wanted to go back to Becky's and wait for her father to pick her up. She didn't like her daddy's bunker and his weird collection of bones. She stepped into the garden shed, absorbing the heavy silence. It seemed like any other shed at first glance, with plant pots, gardening tools and wellington boots. But today the bunker door was gaping open, exposed for the world to see. She didn't want to descend the cold cement steps, but she could hear her father's voice. Perhaps Daddy was showing Mummy something new from his collection. But what? She forced each foot downwards, her eyes flicking to the solid concrete wall in the search for spiders. The steps were steep and precarious, and on the rare occasion she was allowed in, her father warned her to be careful due to the lack of handrail. Her steps echoed around the bunker. She felt the hollow stare of her father's collection of skulls lined up on wall shelves. As she silently ventured towards the back room, it felt like the place was alive. That's when she heard the tail end of a groan. But it wasn't the cry of a baby. It was her father. 'You made me do it,' he whispered beneath his breath. 'Both of you. This is all your fault.'

Then Cora's heart gave a funny little jolt because it didn't sound like her daddy at all. Goosebumps broke out on her arms. What were they doing down here? She felt like she was walking through treacle and her heart was skittering all over the place. 'Daddy?' She stood at the open door, eyes wide, her mouth dry. What she saw made her scream. Scream so hard that she couldn't stop. Even when a strong hand was clamped over her lips.

Overwhelmed by her thoughts, Cora snapped back into the present day. She had to stop torturing herself about a past she could not change. It was the present day she should be scared of. Her stomach lurched as she imagined social services taking her baby. She couldn't comprehend life without Millie because there would be no reason to go on. She turned to check the screen of the baby monitor that she'd set up in Millie's room. It was so sensitive that she could hear her soft snore. Her baby lay on her back, her face to one side. A mixture of love and anxiety felt like a solid weight on Cora's chest. The police were coming for her. But what would she tell them? Because there was one thing she knew for sure – they would never believe the truth. Her daddy didn't kill her mother and sister – the bone house did.

Chapter 20

'Nobody saw you leave, did they?' Sarah eyed Richie up. 'I mean, if this gets out . . .'

'You've asked me that already. Don't worry. I covered my tracks,' Richie replied. 'I have my street cred to think about. I'd never live it down.'

'Gee, make a girl feel good about herself.' Sarah enjoyed the light-hearted ridicule as she grabbed at the blanket which had fallen to the floor. Their secret rendezvous had been her idea. Richie was teasing, and she wouldn't have him any other way. At first, it took them time to get used to seeing one another outside of work, but now it was a once-a-week guilty pleasure. Not quite friends with benefits, more like friends helping each other unwind.

Sarah mooched on the sofa and stared at the board in front of her. A smile curled on her face as she laid the letters on the Scrabble board. C-H-U-T-Z-P-A-H. 'Chutzpah. Meaning insolence, the unbelievable gall.'

Richie harrumphed. 'That's not allowed.'

'Go ahead, check. You've only yourself to blame. If you were a little nicer then I wouldn't have been inspired to come up with it.' Sarah loved their weekly get-togethers. Richie had learned of her love for words, and one night when he'd had too much to drink, he'd let it slip that he had competed in championship spelling competitions and Scrabble games as a child. Sarah didn't think he would turn up when she invited him over to her place to play. It suited her to keep things quiet. If Yvonne found out about their gatherings, she would either make a meal out of it or invite herself along. It felt good to get close to Richie, although sometimes Sarah felt a little *too* close. Her feelings for Richie had developed into something she wasn't ready to act on yet.

J-E-Z-E-B-E-L. 'Jezebel,' Richie said with some satisfaction. 'A shameless, scheming woman.' Sarah laughed as he gave her the beady eye.

'And promiscuous,' she smiled. 'So if you're getting at me, you're way off the mark.'

'And you're a sore loser. That word gives me seventy-five points which means I win.' Picking up his iPhone, he took a photo of the board. 'There,' he said smugly. 'Proof I'm better than you.'

'At least I don't need to worry about you sharing that on Facebook,' Sarah laughed. 'How about a rematch? We'll soon put that right.'

Richie stretched in a yawn. 'Not tonight. I'm bushed. We'll have to do it another time.'

He picked up his motorbike helmet, slid on his leather jacket and made his way to the front door. 'Goodnight, Danger Mouse. See you in the morning. Lock up after I go.'

'Will do.' Sarah smiled, touching his arm. 'And you be careful riding home.' She opened the door. The air was still and warm, and a dog's bark echoed in the distance, most likely one of Slayton's strays.

'Will do.' Richie stood, gazing down at her. Sometimes, when he looked at her like that, it felt like they were the only two people in the world. But the moment was broken as Sherlock made a break for the door.

'Hold it, you.' Sarah scooped her cat from the floor. 'Not out the front door, Mister.' There was still a chance the joyriders could reappear.

She gave Richie a quick wave as he turned his motorbike ignition before closing and locking the door. She kissed Sherlock on the forehead. It had been a good day. Her world felt warm and comfortable – for now.

Chapter 21

Sarah leaned against her car bonnet, the heat of the late afternoon sun warming her skin. She felt sticky from the heat, despite topping up with deodorant throughout the day. The tar on the roads was almost at bubbling point as waves of heat rose. The atmosphere felt unsettling in Slayton today. Townsfolk exited their cars, sweaty and red-faced. Their shoulders slumped, they appeared blinkered to the rest of the world. They passed, lost in thought, burdened by the gloom which had descended after the crows fell from the sky. Even the sun wasn't a friend to Slayton as rising humidity levels made the day too hot and sticky to bear.

Sarah waited in the car park to meet Maura, Cora's social worker. The job car was being serviced, and this was the safest place to leave her beloved red mini during their rendezvous. She couldn't stop thinking about Cora and what she'd been through. She may have had mixed feelings, but she was pleased to be entrusted with her case. It made sense that she visited her with Cora's social worker as they often worked hand-in-hand. She had spoken to Maura Milner on the phone, but this was the first time they'd met in the flesh. She was a friendly woman, whose hair carried a plum tint that caught the light.

'Sarah, I presume?' Maura hooked her handbag strap over her shoulder as she approached. In her hand was a zipped leather document holder. Sarah admired her linen dress and tan leather slingback shoes.

'The one and only.' Sarah held up an identical document holder. 'And snap.' It held every kind of form, from MG11 statements to domestic abuse safeguarding forms.

'I thought it would be better if we met beforehand,' Maura

explained, as they walked the short distance to Cora's flat. 'So we're working from the same page.'

'God, yes,' Sarah delivered a sideways smile. 'But I don't understand how we weren't already up to speed, given Cora's history.'

Maura replied with a shrug. 'She should be on your intel system, but to be fair, Cora served her time years ago. It's our job to safeguard her baby, not hang her out to dry.' She exchanged a look as Sarah's eyebrows rose half an inch. 'Don't worry . . .' she added. 'We've been monitoring her closely throughout.' She pressed the button at the pedestrian crossing as they waited to cross the road.

Sarah admired Maura's passion for her job. It made her wonder as they waited for permission to cross. How many other troubled souls were going under their radar in Slayton?

'So, what do you know?' Sarah waved her thanks at an elderly driver as he stopped to allow them to cross. 'Because the baby in the lake didn't break its own bones.' She filled her in about Sophia Hudson's findings as they reached the other side. Full reports would be made on both sides and exchanged.

The streets were mercifully quiet as the women walked, side by side. Children were in school, and most people were either at work or at home, now the lunchtime rush had passed. Slayton's high street was wide and clean, and waves of heat rose from the concrete as Sarah fell into step next to Maura, grateful for the ability to speak frankly without being overheard.

'Cora had a traumatic upbringing.' Maura spoke in a low voice. 'Richard, her stepfather was a consultant at the hospital, a popular man by all accounts. But behind closed doors, he turned into a narcissistic bully who gaslighted his wife, Julia, for years. Apparently, she'd made enquiries with a solicitor about a divorce. But then she fell pregnant, and he persuaded her to give their marriage another go.' Her face grew serious as she recalled the story. 'Then Richard discovered that the baby wasn't his and well . . . you know the rest.'

Sarah's thoughts went to the victims of domestic abuse she had safeguarded during her career. The deadliest time was not when the victim was with the abuser, but when they tried to leave. Throw a baby or a love triangle into the equation and things got a whole lot worse. Abuse didn't always equate to violence. There were many ways power could be taken, leaving the victim wholly dependent as the perpetrator created a prison without bars. 'And nobody suspected anything from this upstanding member of the community?'

'He put on a good front.' Maura sighed. 'He had an old World War II bunker in his home in the countryside. A few houses had them back then. It's not uncommon but most are filled in. He used it as a modern-day man cave, a place to decompress.'

'Ah yes, the good old man cave,' Sarah said. Her husband used to sit for hours in the shed at the bottom of the garden. Nobody knew what he was getting up to in his secret space until it was too late. It had brought her untold relief to have it taken apart. She tuned back into Maura's narrative, pushing thoughts of her husband away. She couldn't compare herself to Cora. They were worlds apart.

'Richard had a fascination with skeletons, but then again, he was a doctor so it's not unheard of.' Maura slowed her step as she turned onto Cora's road. 'He had some medical books down there, with some bones and skulls. All legit. It was quite a big space; it even had a separate back room.' She shuddered at the thought. 'Then one day, he told his neighbours and colleagues that Julia had left him, taking both the children. Gossip had already spread about his wife's infidelities so most of the sympathy went to him. In their eyes, the esteemed doctor could do no wrong.'

'So everyone believed him?' Sarah glanced at the bookshop as it came into view. She had come to love the small business, but would Cora stick around to run it now?

'You tell me.' Maura delivered a smile of recognition to a teenager as she pushed a buggy down the street. 'I'm sure it's all on the police files once you get a hold of them. After Cora escaped, police did the usual house-to-house enquiries. Neighbours said that his wife was planning to leave. He was apparently distraught, said it was all his fault for working such long hours at the hospital. Nobody knew about the bunker. Not until Cora got out.'

Sarah shook her head. 'That poor girl.' After Cora witnessed the aftermath of the murders, her father panicked and kept her captive in the bunker while he figured out what to do. She was forced to live underground with the remains of her mother and sister in the next room. 'I don't think he wanted to hurt her,' Maura continued. 'Apparently he'd idolised his stepdaughter since meeting her mum eight years before.'

The more they discussed Cora's backstory, the more Sarah realised that nothing was black and white. Cora had been through a horrific experience long before she gave birth in her teens. No wonder she had a distorted view of the world. To feel so isolated that you had to give birth on your own . . . How could the sweet young woman who ran the bookshop in Slayton be capable of breaking her baby's bones? Just what was the truth behind the baby in the lake?

Chapter 22

Sarah frowned at the sight of Turn the Page's cracked storefront window. The mindless act of vandalism was the last thing Cora needed now. She followed Maura down the side alley to the flat.

'I prefer to meet Cora at home,' Maura said, pressing the buzzer for access. 'You get a measure of how someone is coping judging by their surroundings.'

Sarah quietly nodded. It wasn't that long ago that she had lived a lonely existence, barely venturing outside her front door. Her cottage had borne the evidence of her difficulties, with wine stains on the rug, dirty dishes piled high, and empty crisp packets shoved between sofa cushions. Not to mention the pills she had stockpiled in case it all got too much. Her job had been a lifesaver in more ways than one. Now, thanks to her rekindled friendships, she felt like a new person. Like her, Cora had suffered from a traumatic childhood, but it didn't mean that history had to repeat itself again and again. *Three babies,* Sarah thought. *Cora's little sister, Cora's firstborn and now Millie . . . would she also meet a tragic end?*

Cora seemed different as she nursed her baby, holding her tightly to her chest. Her two-bedroom flat was summer warm, and as clean as you could expect for a new mother. The atmosphere was pensive as Maura complained about the hot weather and how busy she'd been at work.

Small talk dispensed with, Sarah steered the conversation towards more serious matters. 'What happened to your shop window? That crack wasn't there before.'

Cora's eyes darted towards her own flat window. She had the look of someone ready to jump out of her skin. 'Someone threw a bottle at it last night. It bounced off the window. Timmy's called the glaziers. We didn't see the point in reporting it.'

'You should always report criminal damage,' Sarah said swiftly. 'Have you got any CCTV?'

Cora gave a tight shake of the head. 'There's some across the street but it doesn't stretch this far.'

Sarah sighed. Upper Slayton was monitored by CCTV but businesses in the lower end of town had to provide their own. Pawnbrokers, charity shops, off licences and gambling establishments were all located in the poorer end of town. But there were other businesses such as the bookshop and street cafés that gave a much-needed lift to the street.

'How have you been?' Maura said, moving things on. Like Sarah, she had other tasks to deal with that day.

'Fine,' Cora said tightly. 'Millie's feeding well. She's been an absolute angel. There's no issues here.'

'I mean in yourself,' Maura replied. 'It must have upset you, hearing about the pram again.'

'I've already spoken to you about this . . . and the police,' Cora looked at Sarah pointedly. 'I don't understand why you're back.'

'We're back because we're concerned,' Sarah replied. 'You lied to the police, Cora, and I'd like to know why.'

'It's all so long ago. I don't want to think about it anymore.' Cora cast a wary glance at Maura as she held her baby close.

'I know,' Sarah replied. 'We don't want to upset you. Social services are here to offer support, and I'm here in a safeguarding role.'

'I've said all I'm going to say. I'm fine. Millie's fine. That's all you need to know.' Cora stared at her child, softly brushing a hand over her fine black hair. Sarah spoke about safeguarding, and the importance of transparency, but as Cora finished feeding her baby it was as if she hadn't spoken at all.

'Cora . . .' Maura began. 'We're not here to take your baby away. That's the last thing we want.' But Cora was humming 'Here Comes the Sun' as she began to pace the floor. Millie was on her shoulder now, and Cora rubbed her back in a circular motion.

'Cora?' Maura said again.

'I've nothing more to say,' Cora said, turning her back on them both. 'Millie's due a sleep. Please go.'

After an uncomfortable silence, Maura scribbled some notes. 'Alright, Cora, I'll be in touch again soon.'

But Sarah wasn't ready to leave. 'I just need five more minutes. You go ahead.'

As Maura saw herself out, Cora turned away. 'Millie needs a nappy change.' Sarah followed her into the bedroom. It was decorated in warm neutral tones, with linen curtains shielding the window and a Laura Ashley duvet cover on the double bed. Sarah handed her a Pampers nappy from an open pack on the bed.

Her eyes fixed on her baby, Cora lay her down as if she was made of glass.

Sarah watched the new mother. There was more to this case than Cora was letting on.

'You didn't hurt your first baby, did you, Cora?' Sarah sensed a shift in the atmosphere and knew she was on the right track. 'Who was it? Who killed your little girl?'

But Cora's lips pressed tightly together as she changed Millie's wet nappy. Sarah handed her a nappy bag. 'Cora. You know me. I'm just trying to help.'

Cora finally met her eye. 'The last time I told people what happened, I ended up in an institution. Nobody believed me then. Why should you?'

'Is that why you changed your story and said you hurt her yourself?'

Cora didn't deny it.

Sarah watched her hand tremble as she fixed her baby's clothes. 'I've seen things. Things that shouldn't have existed but yet, they did. But then I've had to bite my tongue because I've been categorised as "wibble" by my peers.' The out-dated police slang word for mental health issues was still doing the rounds.

Cora dressed her baby, looking at Sarah with new eyes. 'It's a knowing,' she said. 'I felt it the moment the pram was pulled from the lake. It's out there, and now it knows where I am, it's coming for me.'

'What? Who?' Sarah said. 'The father of your baby? Is he responsible for this?'

'Whatever possessed my father is still out there.' Cora scooped her baby from the bed and rocked her in her arms. 'You can't help me. Nobody can.'

'I can safeguard you . . .' Sarah began, but when Cora turned to face her, she had tears in her eyes.

'You can't.' Cora swiped away an errant tear from the corner of her eye. 'It's the bone house, or its essence. How can you stop that?'

'Are you talking about your stepfather?' Sarah said, trying to make sense of it all. But Cora shook her head.

'I'm talking about the thing that made him that way.' She flinched as a car horn beeped outside. Clutching her sleeping baby, she turned towards the window and pushed the net curtain aside. 'It's still out there, watching and waiting. Nobody is safe.' She spun around, her face a maelstrom of emotion. 'Just leave. I know you don't believe me, and even if you did, there's nothing you can do.'

'Cora, wait. Are you being stalked? Have you had any unwanted contact? Phone calls? Threats? I'm on your side, however unbelievable this stuff is.'

'There's nothing,' Cora said miserably. 'Nothing but a feeling of dread that won't go away.'

Sarah stared at the young mother, encompassed by a feeling of helplessness. She was right. Safeguarding had been put in place, intelligence updated, and her address flagged, but it made no difference. Sarah rubbed her arms as a sensation of creeping evil tickled her skin. How could she protect Cora from something that didn't physically exist?

Chapter 23

Sarah couldn't help but feel guilty for having a day off. Like everyone, she needed rest, and given she was working on a cold case her sergeant wouldn't authorise overtime. But Cora's situation consumed her every waking thought. It was why she'd arranged to meet her old school friends in Craig's Coffee and Cakes. It beat sitting at home, with visions of a skeletal baby haunting her thoughts. It was difficult to get away from it. When she turned on the television, Sophia Hudson was being interviewed on Sky and BBC. The media could not get enough of the star of *In the Bones*. Sophia had even appeared on *Loose Women*, talking about women in the field of forensic anthropology. At least she hadn't spoken about the baby found in the lake. Cora was upset enough as it was.

Sarah's meeting with the distraught mother had not ended well when Sarah suggested that she speak to her doctor about postnatal depression. Cora had insisted she leave, after begging her not to mention her outburst to social services. The young woman was clearly terrified that her baby would be taken away. It was as frustrating as it was mystifying. The crows . . . the pram . . . and now that damned itchy feeling of bugs creeping on her skin. *Formication*, Sarah thought, spelling the word in her mind to bring herself back to ground.

The barista was busy dealing with a stream of orders, especially now they were also taking orders online. The hiss of the coffee machine and waves of background chatter was better than the ticking clock on the wall at home. As Elsie and Maggie sat across from her, she could see they felt the same.

Thanks to her regime of sensible eating and exercise, Elsie had lost over eight stone in weight. Her sixteen stone target was beginning to look like a reality. She wore a floral print dress and black leggings, her brown hair pulled into a plait that reached halfway down her back. She beamed as she spoke about her writing but soon changed the subject to Sarah's work. Elsie was an armchair detective who usually grilled Sarah for information, and thanks to their recent FaceTime call, she was already in the know.

'There's a lot of talk around Slayton about the baby in the lake.' The hum of chatter dipped in the coffee shop at the mention of the grim discovery. Townsfolk really were on edge.

'I'm saying no more about it,' Sarah whispered, resting her teacake on her plate. 'So don't even ask.'

'Don't need to.' Elsie tapped the side of her nose. 'I know exactly who left her there.'

'Who?' Maggie leaned in as they spoke in conspiratorial tones.

Elsie's eyes flicked from side to side before she leaned in. 'That poor little critter was dumped by the woman who runs Turn the Page.'

'Seriously?' Maggie's eyes widened. 'Where did you hear that?'

'I have my sources. Folk round here are as jumpy as fleas on a hotplate. First the crows and now this.' She exhaled a low whistle. 'Slayton's brewin' up a storm.'

Sarah prickled as Elsie shared her knowledge, which was surprisingly accurate. Was that why Cora's shop window had been targeted? 'Keep your voice down, Elsie. Cora's been through enough.'

'Not as much as that poor baby, by all accounts.' Elsie sniffed, lowering her tone just the same. 'I wouldn't be surprised if folk round here boycotted her store.'

Sarah groaned. This was all she needed. 'Where are you getting this from? What else have you heard?' But as Elsie gestured pulling an imaginary zipper across her mouth, it was her turn to be tight lipped. Sarah stirred her coffee. She would need to keep a close eye on things. The mood of Slayton was on a knife edge as it was.

As their conversation turned to Maggie, Sarah watched her pull a folder from her bag. 'What's that?'

'It's a printed portfolio of my art.' Maggie's face brightened in a smile. She rested her hands over the folder. 'I've been thinking . . . it's time I stopped wallowing and got back on my feet.' The binder crackled as she parted it. 'I've been selling a picture a month from my website, but it's time I upped my game.'

Sarah watched Elsie tilt her head to one side as she took in the colourful pictures of landscapes, seascapes and woodlands. 'Darn,' Elsie said in her rich Southern American accent. 'Y'all are good.' The pictures were bright and distinctive, each featuring a lone figure walking away. There were lots of artists in Slayton. The place seemed to draw all sorts of creatives in. But never, in all the landscapes Sarah had looked at, had she seen anything like this. 'She looks like she's just stepped into the picture,' Elsie said, leaning in for a better look.

'She's right,' Sarah agreed. 'These are amazing.'

'They've been selling really well,' Maggie smiled. 'If I put more effort into it, I can give up my job in the hotel and paint full-time.'

They watched Maggie light up as she talked about her paintings. It was how Elsie felt about her writing, and how Sarah felt about work. They all had something to cling onto when things got tough. Sarah sat back in her chair as she heard the tinkle of the bell over the coffee shop door.

'Well, hello, tall dark stranger,' Elsie murmured beneath her breath.

'Who is it?' Sarah whispered. She had her back to the door and was resisting the urge to turn around.

'I don't know,' Maggie's gaze flitted over Sarah's shoulder to the door. 'I've not seen him around here before.'

'He's a bit wiry for my liking.' Elsie continued with her analysis. 'But he *could* fit into one of my books.' Sarah watched as her friend unashamedly looked him up and down as he ordered a takeaway coffee. She'd seen her do this before, talking to herself as she plotted potential characters. Every person that appeared in Elsie's books was based on someone. Sarah had even recognised herself.

'He looks more like a suit man,' Elsie continued, as Sarah and Maggie exchanged a smile. 'His jeans are too pressed to be worn every day. Clean shaven, neat hair, possibly works in an office. Judging by the shadows under his eyes he doesn't get much sleep. A doctor maybe? Oh Lordy,' Elsie said quietly, averting her gaze. 'Don't look now but he's coming over here.'

'What?' Sarah turned around in her chair and inhaled a sharp intake of breath. 'Boss,' she said, banging her knee against the table and almost upending their cups.

'Noble!' he replied. 'What's the craic?' McGuire's presence felt like an invasion. This was *her* place.

'Boss?' Elsie repeated, an eyebrow raised.

Sarah watched as Elsie's face flushed. His northern Irish accent was clearly making her tingle in pleasure. McGuire was definitely going in her next book. He seemed cheerily unaware of Sarah's toe-curling embarrassment at encountering her boss not long after discussing her latest case.

'Excuse my rude friend,' Maggie graciously held out her hand as Sarah dithered. 'I'm Maggie, and this is Elsie. We're Sarah's friends. She's told us all about you.' Her eyes sparkled with mischief and Elsie grinned gleefully as she watched.

'All good, I hope!' McGuire said, cheerily.

'Why don't you join us?' Elsie gestured at an empty chair.

'Oh, no I couldn't possibly . . .' he started to say, until his attention was drawn to Maggie's portfolio.

His gaze lingered over her work. 'I own that painting. Amazing, isn't it?'

'Oh, thank you,' Maggie's smile broadened. 'It's a small world.'

'Don't tell me you're . . .' His face lit up as he took the chair next to Maggie. 'You're not the artist?'

'The one and only,' Maggie beamed.

McGuire rested his drink on the table. 'It's so good to meet you! I've been following your work, waiting for you to produce more.'

'But you're not a local. How did you find her art?' Sarah sipped her coffee, recovering from the intrusion. McGuire seemed in awe of Maggie, who was basking in his attention.

'My nan originated from Slayton. We used to visit when I was young. I searched online for some local landscape art as a way of remembering the area. But this . . .' he flicked through the portfolio. 'This is something else. The way you've captured the essence of the character walking through the woods . . . and here . . . the blend of light and shade as it highlights her hair.'

'Do you paint?' Maggie watched his face, immersed in her work.

'Och, I dabble.' McGuire flapped a dismissive hand. 'Nothing like this.'

Elsie and Sarah exchanged a look. It was lovely to see Maggie so animated as she chatted with her new friend. It was as if the rest of the world had melted away and it was just the two of them. The sudden ring of McGuire's phone interrupted their blossoming friendship.

'Damn. I've got to go.' He looked regretfully at Maggie as he silenced the call. 'Perhaps, um . . .' He patted his pockets, as if realising he wasn't wearing his suit. Chortling, Elsie reached in her bag for the pen and notebook she carried everywhere. 'Here. Borrow mine.' She gleefully passed it over, forever the matchmaker.

'Cheers.' McGuire beamed. He scribbled down his phone number. 'Perhaps we could meet again. I'd love to take yous out to dinner . . .' His gaze flicked towards Sarah as he seemed to remember she was there. 'To discuss art, of course.'

'I'd like that.' Maggie accepted the slip of paper. 'I'll text you my number.'

Sarah couldn't believe what had just taken place before her. After saying goodbye, McGuire was gone.

'Oh my God!' Sarah gasped. 'Look at you, flirting with my boss!'

'I was not flirting,' Maggie reddened. 'He's years younger than me.'

'A toyboy! This gets better!' Elsie enthused.

'He *is* cute, isn't he?' Maggie wrinkled her nose. 'Fancy him owning one of my pictures. He probably just wants to pick my brains.'

'Girl, I seen the way he looked at you. He's after way more than your brains.'

Sarah didn't like the sound of this. A dalliance with McGuire could upset the dynamics of their group. But Maggie was positively beaming as she leafed through her portfolio, touching the images McGuire had remarked on moments before. If her friend was happy, then who was she to stand in their way?

Chapter 24

Cora, I can't believe that you didn't recognise me. After all this time, mind you, I almost passed you in the street before I realised that it was you. You're taller than I imagined, and your freckles have disappeared. But the birthmark above your right eyebrow is still there. I've changed since our last encounter too. You didn't see me behind my sunglasses. Had you looked up from your phone you would have noticed that my beard now masks half my face. I sucked in a breath at the sight of you, thinking my cover had been blown. But you kept walking, head down, all your attention on your phone. You didn't pause. Didn't blink. Not a flicker of recognition. You should have felt me, surely? We shared the same energy for so long.

Now my emotions have swerved from relief to the sting of your oblivion. You may as well have slapped me in the face. I turn on my heel to follow you. I hadn't expected to find you so easily. But now my heart's pumping hard because you're out of sight. Shit. I walk a little faster, slowing as I turn the corner to see you standing outside a bookshop. Of course. You always enjoyed the quieter pursuits.

You step inside, and I wonder how long it is reasonable to stand on the corner waiting for you to come out. I won't lose you again. Five, then ten minutes pass, and I scroll on my phone. But I can't stay here all day. Neither can I afford to draw attention to myself. Beads of sweat break out on my forehead as I notice the police car from the corner of my eye. It's crawling along, its occupants looking up and down the street. I turn to face the shop window, watching the bookshop through the glass. Maybe you did recognise me after all and called for help. My jaw clenches as the old fury returns. You're not having one up on me again. The police car has passed, the bookshop door opens and my stomach clenches as I see you pushing a pram. My God. No. It can't be. For a second, I'm lost in limbo as I'm transported to the past. My shirt is damp with sweat, and I pull a tissue from my pocket to wipe my brow.

I must be seeing things. It can't be true. You? A mother? Again? I blink, expecting the image of you pushing the pram to disappear behind the waves of heat vapour rising from the road. I feel like I'm walking on stilts. I don't care if you see me now. I need to know. What the fuck are you doing pushing a pram out of a bookshop?

My plans change by the second. Should I follow you home? But now you're walking down the side alley next to the bookshop. I watch you fumble with your bag before you produce a set of keys and push them in the door at the back. I'm crossing the road now towards you, profusely sweating, feeling physically sick. Maybe you're babysitting. But what mother would trust you with her child? Then you pause at the door as the baby is screaming and I listen at the corner as you lean into the pram and say 'Shh, shh, shh. Mummy's here'. Then you glance over your shoulder, and I draw back. In a matter of minutes, I've discovered that you have a baby, and you live in the flat over the bookshop. Now I'm ambling into the store, trying to hold my nerve. The fat man behind the counter is talking on the phone and despite the ringing bell over the door, he doesn't even glance my way. He's wearing a salmon shirt, gold rings glinting from his beefy fingers. As I listen to him talk, I realise he is hired help.

'Sorry, dahling, I can't help you,' he gushes over the phone. 'I'm afraid my boss has just left. Give her a ring in the morning, although I think she's happy with our existing till.'

So that's why you live directly over the shop. Your assistant was the one babysitting, not you. I imagine you parking the pram and carrying your sleeping baby upstairs, all cosy in the little world you've created for yourself. I slip out the door before his conversation comes to an end.

Ideas turn over in my mind, little black pebbles glinting beneath the sun. I'd need bottles, a steriliser, baby milk. I'd also need nappies and somewhere for it to sleep. I cross the road, thinking of Willow Cottage . . . nobody would hear your brat crying there. And it's not as if she'd be noisy for long. I came here looking for you. I will leave with much more. I take one last, long glance at Turn the Page. A line of crows are perched on its roof, keenly watching the streets below. Slayton is such a strange, macabre little town. I can see why you chose to settle here. But any chance of your happy ever after ended the day you pushed the pram into the lake.

Chapter 25

Saturday 22nd July, 2023

Elliott stood in the hallway, resting his hand on the door frame. The eighties channel was playing from the radio in the kitchen and the smell of their cooked breakfast still carried in the air. Maggie had told him to get changed into something smart. He smoothed over his favourite short-sleeved check shirt. Sometimes when he dressed like a grown-up it reminded him of his daddy. The hurt that came when thinking about him didn't feel as bad today. He slipped his hand into the pocket of his red Benetton shorts and touched the ten-pound note. He'd finally saved enough money from his chores to buy a new tortoise book. He'd read everything in the library. The librarian said that there wasn't much demand for tortoise books so she couldn't order too many in. But that was OK because today was a sunny day, and Maggie was singing in the kitchen as she worked on a pretty picture of a woman sitting on a rock near the edge of the lake. She turned up the radio, singing along to 'Last Night A DJ Saved My Life'. She plopped her paintbrush into a jar before dancing around the room, her blue dress catching the light. She caught sight of Elliott as she spun, gesturing at him to join in. He shuffled forward two steps before she took him by the hand. Then they were both dancing as she twirled him around and around in the middle of the kitchen floor. Elliott giggled, almost losing his balance as his head spun. Maggie caught him before he crashed into her easel, scooping him up in her arms and making a funny snorting noise in his ear that tickled and made him laugh some more. Elliott loved days like these, when the bad things seemed so far away that they may as well not exist. Then, too soon, the song was over, and Maggie was turning the radio down.

'Are you ready to go into town?' Breathy from dancing, she brushed her blonde waves off her face. 'Go get your shoes. I'll buy you an ice cream.'

Elliott ran to get his trainers. Last night Maggie had sat him down to say she was going out on a date. She'd told him that she was lonely and needed other grown-ups in her life. Elliott said that she had Sarah and Elsie, but she told him that it wasn't the same. That the friendship she'd had with Daddy was different from the one she had with her lady friends. Elliott had tried to understand. He didn't mind his mother having a man friend too much, as long as they didn't make her cry, like Daddy did at the end.

Elliott skipped along the pavement, feeling all sunny inside. He hadn't realised that he was smiling until he turned the corner and the muscles in his face grew slack. Suddenly, he wasn't enjoying his day anymore. He reached for his mother's hand, and she smiled as she took it, too caught up in her good mood to notice something was wrong. That was the way it had always been. He could be facing monsters while Maggie was staring at rainbows, unaware of the world behind his eyes.

A chill hugged him tightly as Turn the Page came into view. The growing sense of dread felt like it was alive, finding its way beneath his clothes and raising goosebumps on his flesh. But his mother took his stiffness as reluctance as she stood outside the arts and crafts shop. It was directly across from the bookshop and Maggie wasn't able to pass it without popping in. 'We won't be long,' she smiled, guiding him inside. 'Then we'll get your book.' She let go of his hand as she turned to speak to the owner, a wizened man with frizzy white hair. Elliott stood near the shop window, wanting to scream, to run, to cry for help. Only now did he realise that the bad feeling he'd been picking up on was just a taster of what was to come. It felt like a giant fist was squeezing his body. *The shutters*, he thought, bringing them to mind.

Then he saw it . . . and his thoughts of self-protection fell away. He stared through the pane of glass as the tattered and rusted black pram wheeled down the middle of the street all by itself. Nobody seemed to notice. Nobody apart from him. Cars passed, their drivers looking straight ahead. A woman crossed the road but didn't give it a second glance. Elliott stared at the frayed plastic bags caught up in the rusted spokes, and lake reeds hanging from the frame. The cry from within was high pitched and shrieking. His gaze flicked to his mother. How could she not hear that? But now it was getting louder as it approached the shop, and he couldn't bear to listen. Whatever lived in the bone house was near. Its dark wandering energy turned his blood cold. It came from a black room with a rotting smell and thick, heavy air. A place where the sun didn't shine. A place of bones. The pram came to a halt in the middle of the road. Something black was moving from within. The cries had silenced, and all Elliott could hear was the beating of his own heart. Then he realised that the black substance wasn't any one thing, but lots of things, wriggling and writhing: beetles, what seemed like hundreds of them, scuttling from the body of the pram. Elliott forced his eyes shut, but that brought the dread inwards, and he could barely breathe.

He blinked as a ray of sunlight skewed his vision and suddenly the pram was gone.

'Elliott?' His mother's voice infiltrated his thoughts. 'Sweetheart, are you alright?'

The pram had disappeared, and he exhaled a long breath. 'Yes, Maggie.' He blinked three times, just to make sure. Maybe he had imagined it. Miss Grogan said that sometimes that could happen too. But he could still hear the baby crying in the back of his mind and he really, really wanted to shake it away. 'Can we go?' He looked at Maggie hopefully.

'Yes.' She lifted a small brown paper bag with two paintbrushes poking out of the top. 'We can visit the bookshop now.' But Elliott shook his head. He didn't want to be here anymore.

'Not today,' he said. 'Can we get an ice cream?' The parlour was way down the street.

Maggie's face fell into a frown. 'But you were looking forward to buying your book. Are you sure you don't want to pop over and get it now?'

Elliott gave a tight shake of the head as he opened the shop door. 'I'll get a comic instead.' Unspoken words passed between them. As she glanced up at the bookshop and back to Elliott, Maggie understood.

'OK, sweetie.' Her smile wavered only for a second. 'Ice cream it is.'

Chapter 26

Cora blinked as she tried to concentrate on the book resting on her lap. She was meant to be working, but Timmy had insisted she close early. 'The place is dead,' he'd said. 'Has been all week. Go upstairs with Millie and relax.'

He had a point. Turn the Page had been doing exceptionally well, despite the energy crisis and Covid fallout. But they had barely taken a penny during the last couple of days. Even the customers due to collect books weren't answering their phones. Her brow furrowed at the thought. People weren't avoiding her, were they? No. Surely not. Word couldn't have got out already . . . surely not. It wasn't as if the police or social care could break confidentiality. But it *had* been strange, how quiet the store had been when the streets were bustling outside. And then there was the shop window. Was it mindless vandalism or was there something more sinister afoot?

Her thoughts drifted until the words of the book she was reading became a blur. Her hand rested on the page as she became lost in time, seeing but not absorbing a word. Her past was knocking on the door, and these days it didn't take much to drag her back there.

On the first night Cora's father had locked her in the back room of the bunker, she had whimpered her mother's name. Taking baby steps, she'd approached her mother's body which was lying on its side on the ground. She'd found the baby at her feet, still in her car seat, crusted in blood. Cora had wrapped her up in her blanket and placed her in her mother's cold, lifeless arms. Their essence had long since departed. Cora had whispered her goodbyes before turning from them both. She had lain at the door, her throat raw from wailing, her fingers sore from scratching at the door for release. While her jagged nails had healed, her mental scars ran deep.

Three days after the murder, Cora's father allowed her out of the back room into the main part of the bunker. The stench had been overpowering, and she had fallen into his arms. He had lifted her to the new fold-up bed, stroked her hair and said that everything would be alright. His collection of bones had been packed away; a fold-up bed, books and a set of fairy lights were in their place. The sight of it was horrific to Cora's young mind, because she knew that it meant her father wasn't letting her go. Her screams came involuntarily, she couldn't stop the howls. But when her father squeezed her slim throat, there was madness behind his words. 'If you don't shut up this instant, I'll drag you into that back room and never let you go.' But it wasn't her father speaking, a darker force was driving him – and that terrified her the most.

Cora remembered the scruffy blue dungarees she wore every day, and how her hair fell loose from her ponytail because her hair bobbin had lost its elasticity weeks before. She could almost smell her own staleness rising from her clothes after months in the bunker, with nothing but a basin of water and a sponge to keep her clean. It was all coming back to her now, as past sights and sounds felt so real. Her father was sitting across the makeshift table as they played a game of Monopoly, neither of them daring to speak about the horrors which had brought them there. The lines on his face were deepened by the artificial light, but Cora could smell the aftershave on his clothes. At least he got to bathe, to speak to other people and be part of the real world.

'I'll buy it,' Cora said, as her Monopoly boot landed on the Liverpool Street square. They had been playing the game for days, but then, everything took longer when her daddy only visited for an hour at a time. She lived for that one hour a day. The other twenty-three stretched out far in front of her, each one feeling like an eternity. She wasn't living in the bunker, she was surviving, one day, one hour, one breath at a time. Looking back, Cora couldn't fathom how she'd done it, but then she'd had little choice at the time.

Darkness didn't fall in the bunker. But night came in the stillness, when she was weary from crying and her pillowcase was damp with tears. Each night after her father left, cold fingers of silence touched her as all hope disappeared. She wanted to beg for her freedom, but any emotional outburst cut his visit short because he couldn't manage his guilt. She saw it on his face when he glanced over his shoulder right before he locked her in. He had been used as an instrument for evil and the blackness that enveloped him was now waiting for her. Even after she escaped, she knew it wasn't over. Evil could be quick and brutal, but it was patient too.

She couldn't begin to think about her mother and sister. She'd locked that part of herself – the broken part – away. Cora hadn't known it back then, but her father had planned to turn the bunker into a grave. He must have wrestled with his conscience, but the influence of the bone house was strong. Some nights Cora heard mumbling, as he paced the confines of his shed. When the hatch door was open, his angry whispers filtered through. His arguments left her in no doubt: he was fighting his possession. It was the only way Cora could come to terms with what he'd done.

Sometimes she saw the battle taking place behind his eyes. Instead of clawing for escape, she'd placed her palm against his cheek. The soft, warm contact of a child was all he needed to bring him back to himself.

But it wasn't enough to keep the darkness away.

Chapter 27

Tiffany Rigby crossed her arms over her ample chest as she eyed Sarah up and down. A broad, muscular woman, she had wild red curls which it seemed no amount of hair clips could tame. Sarah stood on her doorstep offering a smile, but it was not returned. Tiffany came from an armed forces background, her father having retired as a Lance Corporal from the RAF. Sarah had gleaned her family history from an old article about fostering which had found its way online. It had gone on to describe how Tiffany and her husband Ross had taken in countless children since they began, thirty years ago. But the loving foster mum portrayed in the online article did not appear happy today. Tiffany's lips thinned further when Sarah produced her warrant card. The meeting had been pre-arranged, but it didn't stop Tiffany from voicing her discontent. 'Come in. This is messing with my schedule. You'd better not keep me long.'

Tiffany lived in Archer's Crescent, a close just off Slayton's Brewery Estate, made up of three- and four-bedroom two-storey homes. It seemed the ideal spot for Tiffany's family, given the nearby playground and parklands. Sarah had thought that Cora was a stranger to Slayton until she opened Turn the Page, but according to a report from social services, she'd spent six months being fostered by Tiffany and her husband. Sarah had not been able to ignore her hunch that further secrets were waiting to be unearthed, even after all this time. She sidled past the bicycles leaning up against the wall in the wide hallway, stepping over a pair of roller skates as she followed Tiffany into the kitchen. The house was warm and reasonably clean, with evidence of children everywhere you looked: crayon drawings on the fridge door; toys strewn on the floor; sandals, shoes and football boots in various sizes lined up near the back door. The sound of children's laughter rose through the open kitchen windows and, in the background, a radio played low.

From what Sarah had learned from social services, Tiffany packed the rafters high with foster children to receive a decent income from the state. It wasn't against the law to take in children for financial purposes and Tiffany had been doing it successfully for many years. But what about the children who desperately needed love? Sarah had considered fostering, but given the hours she worked, she couldn't afford the time.

'Is it OK if I take a seat?' She pulled a chair from the large dining table which was set for six.

'Knock yourself out. Oh, my bloody back . . .' Tiffany groaned as she bent to grab a giant bag of frozen chips and some chicken nuggets from the freezer. Two air fryers were running, as well as a large saucepan of boiling water on the stove. Her back turned to Sarah, she pulled a bag of carrots from the fridge and emptied it on to a chopping board.

Sarah rested an elbow on the red chequered vinyl tablecloth, wishing the woman would turn around. 'Can you tell me about your relationship with Cora? She stayed here for six months, didn't she?'

'It's all in my notes, which you have.' Tiffany rubbed the small of her back. She emptied the chips into one fryer before doing the same with the chicken nuggets.

The clinical lists of Cora's movements had offered little insight into her mental wellbeing at the time.

'Can you remember anything else?' Sarah asked. 'How Cora was in herself, if she talked about her feelings, or if anyone was bothering her.'

'It was years ago. I can't tell you any more.' Tiffany gave Sarah a withering look. 'I've lost count of the kids I've had here since then.'

'I know,' Sarah said, 'and it's amazing, what you're doing for them. But if there's anything you can remember . . . anything at all.'

Tiffany glanced out of the window as a wail rose from outside. Tutting, she returned her attention to Sarah. It seemed the disturbance had not been worth her time. 'What did you ask me again?'

'Cora. You mentioned in your notes that she had nightmares.' Sarah crossed her legs, clinging on to her patience as Tiffany turned to chop the carrots.

'Yes, she was a bit of a pain.' She glanced up at the clock, chopping and peeling the vegetables. 'Those nightmares of hers kept everyone in the house awake.'

'How often did she have them?'

'Every blooming night, to start with. I could see why she'd been moved from place to place. She threw the place into chaos. These kids need routine.' Every movement seemed regimented as Tiffany kept an eye on the clock on the wall. Another wail rose from outside and a red-faced little girl in a denim dress ran in, her face framed by a tumble of wild blonde hair. 'Bradley won't let me on the swing and he told me to eff . . .'

'Out!' Tiffany silenced her immediately. 'It's not time yet.' She pointed at Sarah. 'This lady's a police officer. She's come here to check if you're being good.' The child's eyes widened. Dilemma forgotten, she spun on her heel, her sandals slapping against the tiles as she bolted out of the door. Sarah tilted her head to one side.

'You know, it's better if children learn not to be afraid of the police, but to see them as somebody they can go to if they need help.'

Tiffany snorted. 'Given where most of these kids have come from, I'd say it's a bit late for that.'

'The nightmares . . .' Sarah sighed, trying to get her back on track. 'Cora had some bad ones, didn't she?'

'If I wrote it in the notes then that's what she said. There's always something with these kids. The Bogey Man, The Midnight Man, or Freddy Krueger himself. She wouldn't speak to counsellors, so it took her a long time to shake them off.' As Tiffany finished preparing the vegetables, she kept an eye on the children at play outside the kitchen window. 'I can't tell you any more than that.'

'Is your husband about?' Sarah said. According to the online article, both of them cared for the children full-time.

Tiffany snorted. 'That waste of space?' She finally faced Sarah. 'We split up ages ago.'

'Oh, sorry, I didn't know. It must be tough, coping on your own.'

'I manage.' Tiffany turned to wash her hands.

'What happens if you get sick?'

'Jade, my daughter, helps. She works part-time in Claire's.'

'And do you see much of Ross?'

A frown creased Tiffany's face as she took plastic tumblers from the cupboard and began to fill them with Ribena. 'He's shacked up with Miss Fake Tits down the road. No skin off my nose. I dumped him first.' She glanced at the clock and paused, resting her hands on her generous hips. 'Why have you really come here? Because if Ross is in trouble, then it's nothing to do with me.' The air became thick with the smell of air fried food.

'I'll be straight with you, Tiffany. Cora's not giving us the full story, so I'm speaking to everyone who has crossed her path.'

'Police visits are part and parcel of this game.' Tiffany checked the vegetables before returning to set the table for her brood. She lowered her voice as she approached Sarah, knives and forks in hand. 'He started sniffing about some of the older girls, so I gave him the heave-ho.' She shook her head in disgust.

'Were any allegations made?' Sarah had already spoken to social care about Tiffany and no concerns had been raised.

'Nah.' Tiffany's hoop earrings danced as she shook her head. 'It was just a feeling. I didn't like the way he looked at them when my back was turned. It was weird though . . .' She chewed the bottom of her lip as she worked it over in her mind. 'He never used to be like that. We started fostering when we were in our twenties. I was always able to rely on him. But when he hit his fifties, he changed.' She shrugged. 'Mid-life crisis I suppose.' The air fryers chimed in unison as the timers went off. ''Scuse me,' she said, taking a whistle from the drawer and going to the back door. Sarah watched as she blew three sharp blasts. Four boys and two girls marched inside, throwing Sarah a cautious eye. 'Upstairs. Wash your hands. You know the drill.'

Tiffany watched proudly as they obeyed. 'My dad was a Lance Corporal in the RAF.' She spoke with a hint of pride. 'A bit of discipline is what these kids need. And if they step out of line their privileges are taken away. They've been so good this week that we're going to the beach tomorrow. Some of them have never been.'

As the children marched downstairs, hands clean and hair brushed, it seemed that Tiffany's methods were doing the trick. 'I won't keep you any longer.' Sarah rose from her chair as Tiffany began dishing out food. 'You have my number. If you think of anything else, get in touch.'

Sarah had mixed feelings as she left Tiffany's house. That's what it was, a halfway house for children urgently in need of care. But it wasn't a home. She imagined Cora being shunted from one place to another, but never in the company of someone who cared enough to listen. But wasn't it better for Tiffany to rehome lots of children than one or two at a time? She hoped that whatever their situation, these kids could begin again. As for Cora, tragedy had followed her from a very early age. Sarah slid into the front seat of her car and rested her hands on the steering wheel. The sky had clouded over, bringing a little relief from the unrelenting sun. A flock of crows passed her eyeline, bringing a sense of foreboding. Was someone out to get Cora or was it all in her head? Cora wasn't the only one at risk of being hurt. Sarah could not shake off the feeling that Millie was in the eye of a storm.

Chapter 28

'Thanks for coming.' Sarah glanced at the couple across from her. 'I appreciate you taking the time.'

Richie had been tasked with speaking to Tiffany's ex-husband while Sarah dealt with another family who had crossed Cora's path. They were sitting in one of the newly refurbished witness suites. She could have taken them to one of the downstairs interview rooms, but a more informal setting usually helped people relax. Father Duffy and his wife seemed unaccustomed to the police station and they sat together on the blue foam sofa, almost glued at the hip. The room was deathly quiet, apart from the ticking clock marking each precious second passing away. 'Duffy, that's an Irish name, isn't it?' Sarah said, trying to break the ice.

Like many respectable people unacquainted with police interviews, they were smartly dressed. Mrs Duffy reminded Sarah of Lynda Bellingham, the Oxo advert lady from many moons ago. Her husband seemed a soft-spoken man of the cloth. They weren't holding hands, but they were sitting leg touching leg. Father Duffy spoke first. 'My father was Irish. He moved to Yorkshire when I was just a boy.'

'How did you get into fostering?' Sarah was grateful for their undivided attention. The interaction was worlds away from her previous visit with Tiffany Rigby.

'I was working as a tour guide for Lincoln cathedral when Peter was transferred here,' Mrs Duffy added.

'That's how we met.' They exchanged a brief smile at what was obviously a happy memory for them both.

'Peter's son lived with his mother, and I hadn't been blessed with children of my own. We thought we'd do something worthwhile and foster.'

'And Cora was your first foster child?' Sarah replied.

As the couple nodded in unison, Sarah guessed that they finished each other's sentences too. She envied their relationship as they spoke in sync.

'We flew through the process,' Mrs Duffy continued. 'We had a settled family life, a clean and comfortable home and were committed to caring for our foster child.'

Her husband nodded in agreement. 'We also specified that we were happy to take an older child. With many people requesting infants and babies, we wanted to be available for school age children too.'

'Do you remember when Cora came to us all those years ago?' Mrs Duffy tutted as she recalled the memory. 'Those big wide eyes. The smell of that bunker was on her clothes . . . in her hair. I stayed up with her all night, because she couldn't bear to be left alone.'

'I bought a nightlight.' Father Duffy continued the story. 'It was more of a projector. It lit her room up with pictures of the ocean, with dolphins and whales . . . I was worried she might think it was babyish, but she wouldn't sleep without it in the end.'

Sarah thought of the starry nightlight in Elliott's room and warmed to the man. You sought comfort in light when the dark invited monsters in.

'We had her for six months the first time,' Father Duffy continued. 'Slowly, she came out of her shell.'

'That's when she was adopted?' Sarah consulted her notes. The couple nodded in unison. 'You didn't want to adopt her yourself?'

Mrs Duffy shook her head. 'Cora was a sweetheart the first time around. But the plan was always to foster. Adoption meant we could only help one child instead of lots.'

Sarah understood their reasoning. She was fortunate that her grandparents took her in after her parents died. Had she ended up in the care system, she might not be sitting here now. 'Do you still foster?' Sarah said, more out of curiosity than anything else. Father Duffy lifted one of his hands mid-air, and only then did Sarah notice his trembling limb.

'Parkinson's disease put a stop to that,' he said sadly. 'I can just about manage to do my job these days.'

'Sorry to hear that,' Sarah said, watching Mrs Duffy give her husband's hand a squeeze as he rested it on his knee.

'God doesn't give us any more than we can cope with,' Father Duffy said with a gentle smile. Sarah held back the words. No child should have to cope with what Cora had been through.

'It's a shame Cora's adoption didn't work out.' She skimmed through her notes. The couple had since emigrated to Canada and Sarah had been unable to get in touch. Cora's history was confidential as far as the couple before her were concerned.

'We never forgot Cora,' Father Duffy added. 'When we were asked to foster her for a second time, we couldn't say no.'

'More like they begged us,' Mrs Duffy chuckled. 'Social services said ours was the only home where she'd settled, so we were happy to take her back.'

'And soon we found out why,' Mr Duffy removed a loose thread from the sleeve of his cardigan. 'We couldn't believe how much she'd changed. Nightlights couldn't fix things the second time around.'

Sarah watched the couple as they co-narrated the story. She'd never seen two people so perfectly synchronised. Only now did she notice they were wearing the same colours: navy and black clothes, and tan leather shoes.

'I tried to counsel her,' Father Duffy continued. 'But she was a teenager by then, and very hard to reach.'

'It's frightfully sad. She never got over the death of her mum,' Mrs Duffy continued. But Sarah wasn't so sure. What had happened with Cora's adoptive family to create such a turn for the worse?

'Then she got pregnant.' Sarah kept her tone level. It wasn't an accusation. She needed to move the narrative on.

'I'll never forgive myself for that,' Father Duffy shook his head. 'I've worked with troubled teenagers. We should have picked up on it. Why she thought she couldn't come to us, I don't know.'

'It was awful to find out after the event,' Mrs Duffy chimed. 'We both felt like we'd failed her.'

'Any idea who the father was?' Sarah directed this question to Mrs Duffy in the hope Cora had opened up to another woman. But she shook her head. 'We struggled to control her. There were a couple of different boys she was seeing back then but she wouldn't tell us who.' The clock on the wall loudly ticked the seconds away as Father

Duffy gave his wife a knowing look. 'You're very conservative with that figure. There were several, from what we heard. My parishioners were . . . vocal about it. That's when we began having our doubts that Cora was best placed with us. Especially when Abel moved in.'

'Abel?' Sarah raised an eyebrow as she returned her attention to her notes.

'My son,' Father Duffy replied. 'His mother remarried, and Abel felt like a third wheel. He asked if he could stay with us for a while.'

'Then Cora had the baby and well . . . you know the rest.'

Sarah did know the rest. It was documented in the lengthy social services report. 'Can I speak to Abel? Just to get his take on things.'

'I suppose we could ask . . .' Mrs Duffy began to say, but Father Duffy was already shaking his head. 'Sorry, but I'd rather not involve him. He has a lot on his plate right now.'

'It would just be a quick chat,' Sarah hastily replied. 'Ten minutes of his time?'

But Father Duffy's expression tightened. 'He and Cora barely exchanged two words. I'm not putting him through it.'

'I'm not that much of an ogre, am I?' Sarah chuckled, loath to let the subject drop.

Mrs Duffy leaned forward, speaking in a conspiratorial tone. 'Abel suffers from anxiety. The very thought of speaking to the police would send his blood pressure through the roof.'

'I see.' Sarah couldn't force him to speak to her unless she had just cause. She scribbled his name in her notebook and made a note of what they'd said. Cora's past was key to the investigation, but she was met by a wall at every turn.

When she next saw Richie, it seemed he felt the same way. After their interviews, they met in the police station's main kitchen, which consisted of a fridge, a boiling water tap, recycling bins for leftovers, tables and chairs and not much else. A diverse array of posters graced the walls, declaring war on domestic abuse and the danger of one-punch-kills. They were preaching to the converted as far as Sarah was concerned. She preferred to drink coffee at her desk, but it was nice to have Richie all to herself, if only for a minute or two. Today was a training day for many officers in uniform and the room was empty for once. Sarah filled him in on her encounter with the Duffys. 'They seem like nice people, but I need to follow up with a visit to their son. What about you? Any joy?' Sarah wondered if Tiffany's ex was as regimented as his former wife.

'He seemed decent enough. A bit chavvy, living with this brassy sort.'

'Miss Fake Tits.' Sarah smiled, recalling Tiffany's nickname for her.

'You're not wrong there.' Richie's mouth jerked up in a half smile. 'I didn't know where to look.'

Sarah liked that about Richie. Unlike some of the officers she worked with, he wasn't the leery sort. 'Tiffany hinted that Ross was a bit of a perve.'

'I didn't get that vibe from him. He said he genuinely wanted to help those girls. He tried talking to Cora a few times, but she always freaked out.'

'It's hardly surprising that she was wary of men.' Sarah stifled a yawn. She hadn't had a proper night's sleep since all of this began.

'Tired?' Richie enquired, making her melt a little with his enquiring brown eyes.

'Nothing a coffee won't fix.'

'If only all of life's problems were so easily solved,' Richie said. But things weren't so simple when it came to this tangled case. What secrets would Sarah unearth next?

Chapter 29

'Elsie,' Sarah hadn't expected to find her friend waiting at the police station upon her return. She was expecting to go home within the next hour, but she could hardly dismiss her friend. 'What are you doing here? Is everything OK?' Slayton police reception was relatively quiet as evening crept in. It felt strange to see Elsie out without her motorised scooter, and today she was dressed in a pink linen dress with leggings underneath.

'Everything's fine. Don't you fret. But I do need to speak to you in private.'

Sarah leaned in close. In the police station, walls had ears. 'This isn't a social visit, is it? My boss doesn't approve.' She detected the faint smell of apples from Elsie's glossy long brown hair. Her friend was a fan of fruit-scented shampoos.

'Relax. It's about Cora and it won't wait. Now do ya want me to spill the beans or not? Cos it took a lot of energy for me to get down here today.' She blotted a tissue on her brow. The heat had been hard on her friend.

'Where's your mobility scooter?' Sarah glanced through the glass double doors of reception at the empty steps leading out into the street.

'I took the bus.' Elsie spoke with some pride. 'I've been depending on that scooter for too long. I may just get a taxi back mind, my knees are giving me hell.'

'Follow me.' Sarah pressed her security tag against the security panel before escorting her friend down the corridor. She could have brought her into a room off reception to sit on a hard plastic chair, but the sofas in the vulnerable victim suite were more comfortable. They took the lift to the upper floor and Sarah made her friend a glass of orange squash from the tiny kitchen leading from the suite. Elsie's eyes danced around the room as she took everything in, no doubt plotting the setting for a future romance book. She'd been signed by an up-and-coming London agent, and it was only a matter of time before she bagged a book deal.

'What can I do for you?' Sarah said, conscious of the time. She had turned on the fan and was glad to see her friend's skin turning a healthier shade of pink.

'Hang on a second.' After making herself comfortable on the sofa, Elsie reached into her backpack and pulled out a slimline MacBook Air. 'Nice, ain't it? I figured I needed something portable, now I'm getting out a bit more.' She tethered the MacBook to her phone's 4G and worked at getting Facebook up. Sarah was impressed. Since her son had moved out, Elsie had worked hard to gain her independence, starting by getting to grips with technology.

'I thought it was better to show you rather than try to explain over the phone.' Her fingers moved swiftly as she brought up a group called 'Slayton Residents Only'.

'I've not seen this group before.' Sarah frowned. She was a member of the Friends of Slayton group which welcomed members from far and wide.

'It's a secret group,' Elsie said. 'And it's strictly monitored, which is why I haven't told you about it before. One whiff of me sharing with outsiders and I'll be kicked out on my considerable butt.'

'Can't you invite me in?' Sarah looked over Elsie's shoulder at the list of members.

'Nope. There are rules. No police. No outsiders, and members have to be vetted and approved by vote. But don't worry about all that. This is what you need to know.'

She turned the screen towards Sarah. It was alight with a conversation about Cora. 'So this is where you get all your inside info,' Sarah whispered, as if somehow the members could hear.

'Not all of it,' Elsie replied. 'But it's good to know the mood of the town.' She wasn't wrong. The residents of Slayton weren't quite a torch and pitchfork baying mob, but there were times when Slayton seemed like a living, breathing entity of its own. Sarah speed read the comments and drew a worrying conclusion. The town was turning against Cora Osmond.

'Who instigated this?' She searched the page for the source of their disgust.

'An anonymous poster,' Elsie replied. 'It's a new Facebook thing. It could be any one of our members. You can post anonymously and then reply to yourself in your own name so people don't suspect you.' She gave Sarah a look which suggested she had done it before. 'I mean . . .' she cleared her throat. 'So I've heard.'

'*You* didn't post this, did you?'

Elsie's mouth dropped open. 'Why, Sarah Noble, what in tarnation do you take me for? I, more than anyone, know there's two sides to every story.'

'Of course. Sorry. I was just making sure.' Sarah smiled at her friend. 'You smell lovely, by the way. New shampoo?' She hoped her words would ease the sting of her accusation. Elsie was a lovely person, but sometimes she acted on impulse.

'Apple and mango.' Elsie smoothed one hand over her hair. There was a time when Elsie didn't smell quite as good, but that was behind her now.

'I'll have to get myself a bottle,' Sarah muttered, while reading the original Facebook post.

Anonymous: It is with great sadness that I have shocking news to share. The proprietor of Turn the Page, our beloved local bookshop, is a baby killer. Not only is she the daughter of murderer Dr Osmond, she took a leaf out of his book (no pun intended) and killed her own baby before dumping it in our lake. Her baby's remains were found this week. But that's not all. It seems every bone in the poor lamb's body had been broken.

'How the hell did they know about the fractures?' Sarah read the stream of shocked responses. This was not good.

Eva Steel: To think that a baby killer has been living in our town. This can't be allowed to continue.

Claudia Irving: How can she just get away with it? Justice needs to be served.

Elsie Abraham: The poor girl should repent. She needs our prayers, not our judgement.

Claudia Irving: She'll be judged alright. She's a monster. That store should be burned down.

John Church: But she lives in the flat with her baby, doesn't she? How does she still have custody of that kid?

Eva Steel: She has custody because the police are useless. This should never have been allowed to happen. What other monsters are living in our town?

Helen Piper: It makes you scared to venture out the door. My children were in that bookshop. I can't believe it.

And so the comments went on and on. It was the type of reaction she would expect from the less than tolerant townsfolk of Slayton. But who had lit the fuse in the first place?

'Can you give me a list of members?'

'I'll email it to you right now. But for heaven's sake keep me out of it. If I'm kicked out again I won't get in a third time, and I need to be in the know.'

'You've been kicked out before?' Sarah couldn't help but smile.

Elsie scowled at the memory. 'All that stuff with Christian, my boy, cast a shadow over my name. They took me back once I was exonerated.'

'That was very gracious of them.' Sarah doubted any of the ninety people in the group were perfect themselves. 'Thanks for coming down. If you find out who's behind this let me know.' A thought struck. 'Why isn't Cora in the group? She seemed pretty harmless until this all kicked off.'

'She ain't a local. I grew up 'round these parts. She's only been here two years and she ain't got no family ties.'

'Well, I don't like the tone of some of these comments. I mean, talking about burning down her business? That's concerning.'

'That's why I came to you. I'd never forgive myself if anything happened to little Millie. She's as pretty as a peach, that one. Some of these folks don't have the brains they were born with.' Elsie rose. 'Well, I'd best be off. Take care. I can see this getting a whole lot worse before it gets better.'

As Sarah saw Elsie out, her concerns grew. There were only a handful of people who were privy to the information that the anonymous poster had shared. Police weren't allowed in the group so that ruled them out, and Elsie would never put up such a hateful post. That only left one other person – Cora's one and only friend. He was the closest person to Cora that Sara knew of and from what Sarah had heard, an incurable gossip prone to listening in on private conversations. He had to be responsible. She scanned the list of names that Elsie had emailed her. 'Bingo,' Sarah said, as Timothy's name appeared. Cora employed him to assist her in the bookshop. A native of Slayton, he had recently returned after living in Brighton for the last ten years. He was the closest person to Cora that Sarah knew of. He had to be responsible for leaking the news. But why would Timmy betray the woman who had taken him under her wing?

Chapter 30

Cora watched her daughter's clothes swish around in the washing machine. She'd been tempted to pack a bag, take Millie and disappear. But where would she go at this late hour on a Saturday night? She had a home for them here. Not to mention her business. She had fought so hard to buy her little bookshop, outbidding a competing offer at the last second. She had even knocked on the door of the vendors, begging them to sell to her. There weren't many places that she felt safe in, but her flat above the bookshop had felt like home the moment she'd stepped inside. Cora felt safest well above the ground, with a clear view of the populated streets and with the windows open all year around.

The machine began to whirr as it spun the clothes, and she was brought back to a moment in time that she'd rather forget. She was in care, shunted to yet another foster home. Tiffany had half frightened her to death, blowing that stupid whistle every five minutes as she trained them to jump through hoops like a bunch of circus poodles. The woman was cold and demanding, and her husband didn't say a lot. Cora was in the laundry room when he came and stood at the door. The washing machine was in the garage, along with the dryer and indoor clothes racks. It had been Cora's turn to do the washing, and she found solace in time away from Tiffany's army of foster kids. Ross watched in silence from the doorway as Cora folded the clothes from the dryer. He was a big man, with strong calloused hands from years of manual labour as a bricklayer. Since injuring his back, he spent all day at home. Cora had never felt intimidated by him, not until that day. She'd waited for him to speak, but he just stood, his dark beady eyes making her turn cold. She picked up the plastic basket filled with clothes, her pulse racing as she approached the door. Ross cast a long shadow as he blocked her exit, his thumbs hooked into the belt loops of his jeans.

'I heard you last night, thrashing about in your sleep.' He paused, his gaze lingering as he looked her up and down. 'You can talk to me, you know. If it all gets too much.'

It wasn't what he said, it was *how* he said it. Cora's throat clicked as she swallowed the lump which had formed. All she could think of was her father as he stood in the bunker, his fists clenching and unclenching, his face spattered with blood. She clung to the plastic washing basket, her limbs trembling. She was back there, in the dark space, screaming to be let out. A sharp whistle from the kitchen shattered the moment and Ross stood aside. Then Cora ran, socks and underpants spewing from her basket into the muddy grass where the boys had been playing football moments before. There had been hell to pay that day.

Cora jumped as her mobile phone vibrated on the kitchen table, bringing her back to the present. Why was that moment in time returning to haunt her now? She didn't recognise the number flashing up on her screen. Her hand hesitated. Should she answer? She accepted the call.

'Hello?'

'Hello, Cora? This is DC Richardson from Slayton CID.'

Cora rested a hand on her chest, rubbing in slow circular movements as her anxieties rose. 'Yes?'

'There's been a development. We've just made an arrest. We'd like you to come to the station and see if you can identify the suspect.'

'Suspect?' Cora's mouth dropped open. 'I . . . I don't understand.'

'A team of officers have been monitoring your address. They arrested a man trying to break into your flat. We'd appreciate it if you could come in and see if you can identify him.'

'Breaking into my flat?' Cora echoed. She hadn't heard anything.

'He's admitted to stalking you, but that's as much as he's said. He'd planned on taking Millie too. We found a kit of sorts in his car, with nappies and baby formula. I'm sure you'll understand, given the circumstances, we need you to come in straight away.'

Cora's thoughts raced ahead. Had they really caught her persecutor already? Was Millie safe? Cora clutched a chair for support as her legs turned to jelly. She recalled the dreams in which she was visited in the night by a dark figure. But the encounters had been fuzzy and clouded, her memories dream-like. Had it been him all along?

'Are you there?' The detective's voice interrupted her thoughts. 'We can only hold him for twenty-four hours, so we need you in right away.'

'Yes . . . Who . . . Who is it?' She nibbled her bottom lip, unsure she wanted to know.

But the detective's words were stilted. 'I'd rather you come in and see for yourself. We don't want to influence an identification.'

'I should be able to get a babysitter. I'll be in as soon as I can.' Cora paced the room in a daze, barely able to comprehend the news. The mythical creature she'd believed to be stalking her was made of flesh and bone. But how? The police said they had a suspect. Was it her father, back from the dead? Had they really found his remains that day? There wasn't much left of him after the fire had taken hold. Or was it someone else from her past? She blurted a gasp of relief. Either way, perhaps she and Millie really were safe. And the nightmare would soon be over. Her vision blurred with tears as she stared at her precious little girl, who had stirred but not yet cried out from her cot. Her heart swelled with love. Cora didn't deserve a second chance, but she would take it.

She slipped her phone from her pocket. Timmy wouldn't mind coming over. He'd been her rock since this began. She glanced around the room for her shoes. The sooner she sorted this out, the sooner her life could begin again.

Chapter 31

Cora drew in a breath to steady herself as she stepped outside. Timothy had come straight over, and it made more sense for her to walk the short distance to the police station in town. Besides, she couldn't focus on driving, not when she was swamped with thoughts of facing her father again. It was him. It had to be. Why else were the police so cloak and dagger about the man they had arrested outside her flat? She'd never allowed herself to believe that he was truly dead. Whatever possessed him must have lingered and got him out of the bunker alive. But was he really dead? How had he visited her as she slept?

She strode down the wide street, past holidaymakers and drinkers still hanging around outside cafés and bars. Isolated by her thoughts, she recalled her last memories of her father, the highly respected Dr Osmond. Once a day, he visited to change the bucket she used as a toilet. He brought food, clothes, toiletries, and even marked the homework he set for her. But her sanity was preserved by the printed word. The stories in the books he brought were her saviours, transporting her from her underground world. She became at one with the characters on their adventures through magical worlds.

Her father's care of her in captivity had gone steadily downhill. By her last day in the bunker, her hair had grown long, and her skin had broken out in pimples which she couldn't help but pick. Her nails were jagged and dirty, and she couldn't bear the slimy coating of plaque that coated her teeth. Her father had become distracted, and his visits became sporadic as he forgot to bring much needed supplies. Instead of providing her with home-cooked meals, he gave her tins of food. Then he dragged down the camping equipment that would change everything – a small two-ring stove and a gas canister.

'It's like camping,' he said one day, as he installed the cooker next to her bed. He gave her a kettle for the pot noodles, tins of baked beans, bread, bottles of water, pasta and sauce. At ten years of age, she'd had to learn how to fend for herself. Her father's expensive-smelling aftershave told a story, and she couldn't help but notice his new clothes. He'd recently had a haircut. He was seeing someone else. The shine of keeping Cora as his pet had worn away. The dark voice that whispered in his ear was being listened to now. She knew he was building up to something. She'd seen it in his eyes.

Cora no longer cried. She didn't wail. Didn't scream to be free. Her father's will was a twig bent as far as it could go. He was hanging on to a normal life in the outside world, but one wrong word from her and he could snap, just as he had before.

Cora had kept track of the date. Her birthday was coming up. It was a special day in more ways than one.

Her sense of self-preservation intensified her senses as she monitored her father's moods. She knew exactly where to listen at the gap in the door when he spoke to the walls of the bone house. Accustomed to the cadence of his voice, she responded accordingly.

'I've got a surprise for you,' he'd said, the day before she turned eleven. 'We're going to celebrate your birthday. There will be a cake, presents. I'll even bring you flowers.' He'd looked away, but not before she caught sight of wetness in his eyes. Cora's spirits plummeted. The dark side had won.

She didn't sleep the night before her birthday. She could hear activity overhead. It wasn't just her father's footsteps. Things were being moved in his shed above. This was going to be her last birthday. She could feel it in her bones. But he wouldn't nail the trap door shut. He'd silence her first.

That night her mind turned over options that shouldn't enter the thoughts of a young girl. Her father was a doctor. He could put her down, as you would a dog. There were many ways he could end her, and she was powerless to stop him. She had gained her father's trust, doing exactly as she was told. But the day had come. She could sit back, as her mother had done, or fight for her life. Nobody was coming to help her. Just as nobody had noticed that something was wrong the day her mother and sister died. Cora thought about weapons, but she wasn't physically strong enough to use them against the respected man who lived a double life.

Cora tried to reason, even hinted that she could be trusted to live with him again. But he wouldn't have it. The threads of his story would unravel too fast. That night, without her father's company, Cora had hatched a plan.

Cora stared up at the police station, slightly out of breath. Her past was here for her, teasing, clutching, and hungry for revenge. But this time she wasn't alone. The police were finally on her side, and she would do whatever it took to keep her daughter safe. But exactly who was waiting to be identified?

Chapter 32

Sarah was greeted at Maggie's front door with a smile. She was happy to babysit Elliott, although she wasn't thrilled about Maggie dating McGuire. There was nothing wrong with her DI, and Sarah knew she was being selfish, not wanting her circle of friends to change. Elliott bounded down the corridor, a ball of energy and enthusiasm. He looked so cute in his red Benetton shorts and blue shirt. He'd come a long way from the haunted little boy who spoke in whispers when they first met.

'We've got a present for you!' He grinned, taking her by the arm and guiding her down the hall. Not that she needed to be shown where to go. The bungalow had a similar layout to her house just next door. It was a bright and welcoming space, and with her flair for design, Maggie had quickly made it her own. She had decorated it in soft, warm colours, which was a big improvement on the stippled ceilings and wood chip wallpaper that had been there before. Beading had been attached to the walls, and newly painted panelling and radiator covers made the house seem more up market than it was. Colourful soft furnishings and neutral carpets finished the look. Sarah couldn't have picked a better tenant to live in the home she had secretly gifted to Elliott in her will.

'He's been bursting to tell you, but I made him wait until the paint had dried.' Maggie laughed in unison with her son. Sarah couldn't help but smile. Being here with them both, in a house filled with laughter, was a tonic. They had all come so far in the last year.

'Here it is!' Elliott stood next to an easel in the kitchen, its artwork ceremoniously draped with a clean tea towel.

'I wonder what that could be?' Sarah was secretly thrilled to have her hands on one of Maggie's pieces of art. Her eyes lit up as Elliott pulled back the towel to reveal a portrait of Sherlock, Sarah's ginger tabby, looking regal on a red velvet cushion with a dainty golden crown on his head. His green eyes twinkled in satisfaction at finally being recognised for the royalty that he was. 'Oh wow, it's amazing!' Sarah cupped a hand to her mouth. 'I love it!'

'It took a while to capture his signature disdainful look.' Maggie smiled. She looked pretty in her black dress and heels, her hair pinned back with a diamanté clip. The scent of expensive perfume pleasantly followed her around.

'Going somewhere nice?' Sarah looked Maggie over with an approving eye. 'Must be posh!'

'Daniel's booked us in to the new French restaurant in town.'

'You look stunning, and you've nailed the painting.' Sarah stood back, taking in every facet of the image which must have taken ages to create. 'I'll put it in the hall so it's the first thing people see when they walk in.'

Elliott bent to stroke Sherlock who had joined them. 'He'll like that. Everyone will know it's his house.'

'I'm a bag of nerves,' Maggie exhaled a long breath as the conversation turned back to her date. 'I haven't felt this way since I was sixteen.' She checked her watch before Sarah could respond. 'I better go. Have fun!'

Sarah settled on the sofa, the movie *Fantastic Beasts* playing as a backdrop to her thoughts. Elliott dipped his hand into the bowl of salted popcorn that rested between them. Such was their routine. Sarah was pleased to get some alone time with him, because she had a lot on her mind. Her conversation with his teacher had not rested easy in her thoughts. The comment Miss Grogan made about Elliott being family in a former life had riled her. Had it been a throwaway comment? Or did she know about the tragic set of circumstances that had robbed Sarah of her little brother? Perhaps the woman was manipulating her or using Elliott for her own gain. Psychics were drawn to Slayton by so-called energy ley lines deep in the land. Slayton's dark and mystic reputation wasn't changing any time soon. In passing, she had seen the restoration taking place at her childhood home, now renamed The Blackhall Manor Hotel. It wouldn't be ready for months, but then people would be lining up to stay there. The elderly twins who had purchased it had fulfilled their promise of bringing it back to its former glory. The gothic mansion promised luxury rooms as well as affordable B&B. A small part of Sarah wanted to revisit and lay old ghosts to rest. Another part of her wanted to keep the hell away.

She switched her focus back to Elliott as he watched the movie, fascinated. Did he see himself in the Harry Potter franchise? Were regular people 'muggles' but he and his teacher different? Sarah had sensed Miss Grogan's need to protect the vulnerable who were out of their depth. People like Elliott. He was finally going through a growth spurt, having always been small for his age. In the last few months, he had outgrown his clothes. Soon he would be hurtling towards his teenage years. How would he manage that on top of everything else? She had mentioned Miss Grogan to Maggie but 'If Elliott's happy, I'm happy,' was her mantra. Sarah needed to delve deeper.

'Elliott, your teacher came in to see me at work.'

'I know.' As he stared at the wide screen television, his expression did not relay concern.

'How do you get on with her? I'm not sure if I like her or not.'

'That's OK.' Elliott chewed his popcorn, still glued to the screen. 'You don't need to be scared. She helps me a lot.'

'How?' A frown disturbed Sarah's face. Once upon a time she was the first person that he'd turn to.

'She helps the scary stuff go away.' Elliott did not elaborate and as he kept his gaze fixed on the television, Sarah sensed that it was something he did not want to discuss.

'Well, I'm always here if you need to talk, and I'll do my very best to understand.' She tilted her head to one side as she tried to capture his attention. 'You know that, don't you? I'm the best person to come to if you're scared. It's my job to keep people safe.'

'I know,' he smiled, finally meeting her eye as he took a handful of popcorn from the bowl. 'But this is a different kind of safe.' He nodded to himself in agreement with his chosen words.

'She showed me your drawing,' Sarah continued. 'The one with the skull on the table. Did that come from a scary dream?'

Elliott nodded as he chewed. 'There's something bad in Slayton.'

He gave a little involuntary shiver. 'It comes from a dark place and wants to do nasty things.'

'I thought Miss Grogan made the bad dreams go away?' Sarah looked at him intently.

'She does,' Elliott said. 'She showed me how. But the thing is mad. Real mad about the baby in the pram.' He shoved his hand back into the bowl of popcorn. 'Can we watch the movie now?' His full blue eyes looked at her pleadingly. There was more to this than the movie. Elliott didn't want to dwell on the scary thing anymore.

'Of course,' Sarah said with a smile. 'And don't you worry about that other stuff. I'll take care of it.' She watched him visibly relax and gave his shoulder a little squeeze. Her mind filled with questions, but Elliott clearly wanted to let it lie. Had he been watching the news about the discovery of the baby in the lake? Perhaps it had played on his mind, resurfacing in his dreams. But yet, it felt like she'd been given a warning. What did Elliott mean about something being mad about the baby in the pram? Just who had fathered Cora's child? Sarah became lost in thought as theories rose in her mind. She'd been so focused on Cora that she hadn't stopped to think how the father of the discovered baby would have felt. Had he watched the news, found out where Cora lived? Was he coming for her?

Chapter 33

Sarah muttered beneath her breath. Just minutes earlier she'd told Maggie how lovely it was, having such a short distance to go home. But she couldn't follow Sherlock inside and slip on her pyjamas and do some crossword puzzles before bed. Instead, she had to leave the comfort of her home to drive into town for milk. She could have had toast in the morning. Dry cornflakes weren't the end of the world. But there was a reason why she felt the sudden urge to buy a litre of semi-skimmed. Elliott's warning had itched like a red bumpy hive; something she should leave alone but found herself scratching just the same. It wouldn't do any harm to drive past the bookshop on her way, would it?

At least Maggie had returned from her date relatively early, and to Sarah's relief, McGuire hadn't come inside. The date had gone well, according to her friend, but Maggie had vowed to take things slowly for Elliott's sake. Sarah scanned the streets as she drove. A few stragglers were still milling around in town. The pubs would soon be issuing last orders. Lights twinkled from the restaurants which were benefitting from the stream of holidaymakers making the most of the dry spell. Sarah slowed her car outside Turn the Page. All the lights were on in the upstairs flat, a curtain flapping through an open window. She parked up her red mini, grateful to find a space.

She stood on the pavement and was locking her car door when a figure streaked out from the side alley. It was Cora. Her eyes were wild, tears running down her face as she screamed her daughter's name.

'Cora?' Sarah approached her, crossing the road in a few quick steps. 'What's wrong?' She dreaded hearing the truth as Cora stared at her with the eyes of a stranger.

'My baby . . . My baby's gone!'

'Have you called the police? Cora, listen to me.' Grabbing her arm, Sarah fought for her attention as she wriggled to be set free. People were staring from across the road, but nobody dared approach.

'Yes. I can't . . . I can't breathe.' There was blood on the tips of Cora's fingers. She held her at arm's length, examining her for injuries but finding none.

'Cora, listen to me. Whose blood is that?' Sarah thought of the flat upstairs, of the curtain billowing from the window. What had taken place up there? A prayer rose in her mind. *Please God, let the baby be OK.* Because Cora had form. She had done this before.

Sarah guided Cora to the side of the road as a police car approached, the scream of its sirens tainting the air. Its blue strobes highlighted the 'baby killer' graffiti daubed on the side wall of Turn the Page. Sarah recognised the uniformed officer as he exited from the car. It was PC Adam Gardiner, an officer with twenty years of service, known for his common-sense approach. His partner, PC Katie Lucas, paused to update control.

'My baby!' Cora wailed as he approached. He calmly offered Sarah a nod of acknowledgement. 'She's gone!' Her hand rose to her mouth, a small streak of blood staining the top of her lips. Adam exchanged a look with Sarah that spoke volumes.

'Control said a baby is missing. They also mentioned the warning marker.' Sarah knew about the flag on the address because she had put it there. The intelligence offered a snippet of Cora's history. Katie, Adam's shift partner, spoke to Cora in a soothing voice.

'Why don't you come with me, love? We can sit in the back of the car while these officers look inside.'

'But my b . . . baby . . .' Cora stuttered, before dissolving into tears.

'We're here and we'll do everything we can to sort this. But we need to get you sat down so you can tell us what's happened. You don't mind if I give you a quick pat down, do you, love? Have you anything on you which could hurt you or me?' Adam cast a protective eye over his partner as she conducted a quick search before delivering an approving nod. Search over, Cora was led into the back of the police car. Sarah had never seen Cora so out of it, which did not bode well.

'Paramedics and another unit are on the way.' Adam nodded

towards the flat. 'C'mon. We'll start in here first. What were you doing here, anyway?'

Sarah took quick footsteps to keep up with his long gait. 'I came out to buy milk and saw her running out of the alleyway, so I pulled over to see what was wrong.' It wasn't a hundred per cent true, but she was hardly going to tell him that she'd had the willies and couldn't settle at home.

'Good timing.' Adam's deep voice echoed in the corridor as they entered through the open door. 'Because God knows what's waiting for us up here.' Sarah followed him up, absorbing her surroundings. A sense of trepidation tempered her movements as she recalled the blood on the tips of Cora's fingers. There was no sign of forced entry, no jemmied door or broken locks. But there was no sound and no evidence of life. A pulsating silence pervaded the space.

'Anyone here?' Adam called out, pushing the flat door open. As she followed him inside, all Sarah could see was the blood on the floor.

Chapter 34

Oh, Cora . . . you should have seen me. The moment was glorious. Every step fell into place, reinforcing the knowledge that this was meant to be. You have no family in Slayton, and your trust in the people around you is misguided. Because I know, you see. Even in the last few days I've been able to piece together what I need. Just enough information to instil the confidence I needed to go through with my ambitious plan. I got your mobile number easily enough. Your trusted shop assistant didn't guard it very well. He greeted me with a smile, his colourful shirt patchy from sweat. He rested his phone below the shop counter as he searched out back for the first edition book that I lied about ordering in. His distraction granted enough time for me to find your number on his contacts list. I had to move quickly, because now the good people of Slayton have boycotted you, your precious shop will soon be shut down.

You thought you had everything covered, but you weren't expecting my call. I can't believe how gullible you were. I'd rehearsed all day, watching true crime programmes to produce an authoritative voice. A couple of comments about the custody clock winding down and I had you in the palm of my hand. It felt strange, hearing you speak outside of my head. Because you whispered in my ear last night, your mocking voice rebounding in my head as I tried to brush my teeth before bed. I knew it wasn't really you, but I listened just the same. But hearing you on the phone . . . solid and real, with no doubts . . . It took every ounce of my self control not to scream at you down the phone. Instead, I repeated my script that we needed you in straight away. My portrayal of DC Richardson was convincing enough to get you out of the flat. After stumbling over your words, you agreed to come. Then I watched from my vantage point as your shop assistant arrived. I knew it would be at least twenty minutes before you realised that you'd been had. Just after you left, your assistant buzzed me in.

Judging by the size of him, I knew he'd happily accept the takeaway delivery I brought to his door. He didn't recognise my features behind the motorcycle helmet, he was too engrossed in the goodies piled high in his arms. You should have seen his face light up when I said you'd ordered them as a thank you. I filled his arms with pizza, fries, Coke, chicken wings, cookies and ice cream so he couldn't close the door in my face. My adrenaline flowing, I channelled my anger. As he turned to get me a tip, one forceful swipe to the side of the head was all it took to bring him down. The pocket-sized sandbag was designed to stun him long enough for me to take control. I'd thought hard about my weapon of choice. It would have been a shame to fracture his skull. There was no time to dwell on it, as he hit the coffee table on the way down.

Thankfully, your precious baby didn't make a fuss. I stood over her cot, shaking in disgust and fury at her presence in the world. Why did she deserve to live while my baby had died? Where was your compassion then? Where was the nurturing, the love? You were so protective over this one, yet callously sent mine to her death. She could have been something special, but you dumped her like a worn-out car tyre in the bottom of the lake.

Now I'm sitting in Willow Cottage as your brat exercises her lungs. How does it feel to know you're about to lose something so precious? Your own flesh and blood. Because let me tell you something, Cora. I've covered my tracks. Do you feel the stirrings? The time of reckoning is near. But you won't find me until I'm ready for you to return.

Chapter 35

Cora sat in the police interview room, unable to comprehend Sarah's words: 'Do you understand what you've been arrested for?'

But Cora's thoughts were all bent up. She had cried. She had screamed. She'd raked her arms with her nails as panic took her in its vice-like grip. She rocked on the hard plastic chair, the air heavy with desperation and the smell of her own sweat. Her breasts ached with the need to express milk. She folded her arms tightly against her chest. If she had any hope of finding Millie, she needed to gain control. But she was stuck in this boxy room while her baby was God knows where.

Sarah Noble and the real DC Richardson sat across from her, not the fake one who'd drawn her out. His tie hung loose from his collar; the first button of his shirt undone. Cora was wearing a custody tracksuit and plimsolls because the police had bagged up her blood-stained clothes. She should have agreed to come to the station voluntarily. Instead, she was arrested by PC Katie Lucas because she'd lashed out in the back of the police car. She hadn't been trying to hurt her, she just wanted to be free.

'I didn't kidnap Millie.' Cora swiped at the tears that refused to stop. 'I should be out there, looking for my little girl. Why won't you listen to me?'

Sarah Noble spoke calmly and without reproach. As she leaned forward, her eyes twinkled with the sincerity of someone who cared. 'We *are* listening, Cora. Teams of specialised officers are searching for Millie as we speak. But the sooner we get you interviewed, the sooner Richie . . .' she cleared her throat as she glanced at the man beside her with warmth in her eyes, '. . . DC Richardson and I can get back to looking for her. Now tell me from the top, what happened tonight, from you getting the phone call to me stopping you on the street.'

Sarah had a motherly quality about her, and Cora spoke between juddering sobs as she told her about the phone call. 'The woman in reception kept saying that she'd . . . she'd spoken to DC Richardson, and he hadn't called. I didn't want to ha . . . hang around any longer so I ran straight home.'

'And you didn't think to mention your concerns to the police?'

Cora shook her head. 'Things changed after my baby was recovered from the lake. I've had graffiti sprayed on my wall, a b-bottle thrown against my window, and people have been boycotting my store. I did . . . didn't want social services to think I wasn't coping with it all.'

'So, you went straight home?'

Cora chewed her bottom lip, wishing she'd made more of a fuss at the time. 'I panicked. Timmy wasn't answering his phone. All I could think of was getting back to Millie.' She inhaled through her nose to regulate her breathing.

Sarah handed her a tissue from the box she had brought in. 'And then?'

Cora twisted the tissue between her fingers. 'Timmy didn't answer the buzzer. My hands were shaking so much that I could barely get the key in the door. I ran up the stairs and . . .' Cora swallowed the saliva backed up in her throat. 'I found Timmy on the floor. He was lying on his side. His head was bleeding.'

'What did you do?' Sarah spoke, as the man beside her made notes.

'I turned on every light, searching for Millie. But she was gone. Her crib was empty. I called the police. That's when I ran onto the street. I thought . . .' Her words fell away. Her arms felt empty, her throat scratchy from shouting. 'I thought I might catch up with him.'

'Who, Cora?' Sarah searched her face, the tone of her voice more pressing now.

'My father, of course! Or what's left of him. He didn't die in the fire. He's out there, waiting to finish what he started. The bone house still has a hold over him.' She watched as the officers exchanged a glance. Even Sarah, with her kind and nurturing nature, had turned against her now. Her male counterpart finally spoke, his brown eyes searching hers.

'Where did the blood come from, Cora?'

Horrified, she could not believe her ears. 'Where do you think?

Timmy, of course. I put a towel against his head, told him help was coming. I'd never hurt my baby if that's what you think. It's not Millie's blood.' She could recall the tacky feeling of his blood drying on her fingers, her disbelief at everything that had gone on. Her frustration was rising, but hammering her fists against the table would only make things worse.

'The thing is . . .' Sarah started. 'That's not what Timmy is saying.'

'Timmy?' Cora blinked. She'd been so consumed with fear, she'd barely given him a second thought. 'He's alright? Oh my God, I'm glad. What did he say? Did he see him? What happened?' She blew her nose, and little bits of the tissue came away in her hand. Sarah pushed the box in her direction.

'Cora, Timmy said he popped around for a visit this evening. He said you've been acting strangely and he was worried about your mental health. He also said he had no recollection of you receiving a phone call.'

'He wasn't there when I got it.' Cora pulled another tissue from the box.

'But you did tell him that's why you needed to leave the flat?'

Cora nodded, recalling their conversation. 'He must be concussed. I definitely told him about the phone call.'

'Timmy said he brought takeaway food for you both. He was putting it down on the table when he was hit from behind.'

'No . . .' Cora whispered. 'That's not right. I didn't have any food. I left the flat. You must have me on CCTV at the station.'

'We do.' DC Richardson spoke firmly. 'But there's nothing to say that you didn't assault Timmy, then use your visit to the station as an alibi before going back and calling the police.'

'You're not serious. Why would I do that?' Cora looked from Richie to Sarah, astounded. 'You really think I hurt Timmy?' But their grave expressions relayed their belief that she was capable of far worse.

'You . . .' Cora could barely speak the words. 'You think I hurt my baby?'

'It's our job to ask questions,' Sarah replied. 'And this is your opportunity to give your account. You said earlier that we weren't listening. Cora, you've got your captive audience now. Tell us everything.'

And she did relay her story. But not the cock and bull version that Timmy was coming out with. His injuries were distorting his memory. It was the only explanation. Why else would he lie?

'But there was no forced entry to your flat,' Sarah said. 'And Timothy is adamant he was assaulted while you were there. The timings don't add up.'

It was DC Richardson's turn to speak as he gazed at her with such intensity that she had to look away. 'Where is Millie, Cora? Tell us. We can help.'

As Cora dropped her head into her hands, she realised she was completely on her own.

Chapter 36

'That was intense.' Richie strode with Sarah back to the CID office. Cora had been escorted back to her cell, to be bedded down for the night. The woman was a wreck – emotionally exhausted and upset. Sarah had asked for the cell door to be left open. Given her childhood history, a confined space might not be the best place for her. A uniformed probationer had been despatched to sit outside the door and keep an eye on her. Sarah had put in her time on suicide watch. She'd given the young officer a bottle of Coke and a bag of crisps to munch on. Not much of a consolation prize but he welcomed them just the same.

'Do you believe her?' Sarah was still digesting their interview and was keen to hear her colleague's thoughts. Her small cold case investigation had snowballed and now the whole team were on board. Sophia Hudson's report was in and it made for grim reading as she detailed every fracture inflicted on the baby pulled from the lake. If Cora had inflicted such injuries, then she was capable of hurting Millie and no expense would be spared in finding the infant. Specialist officers had been drafted in to search for Millie, as well as the canine unit who were searching the vicinity of Cora's flat. PolSA were involved, and CCTV was being viewed, what little was available, with senior officers being briefed. It was only a matter of time before the press got hold of it.

'Seems obvious to me.' The certainty in Richie's voice was reflected in his expression as he paused at the vending machine to buy a bottle of Coke. 'Cora lost the plot with her baby then dumped her body, just like before. But this time she knew she'd have to come up with an alibi. Want one?' He raised the bottle of Coke in the air and Sarah shook her head.

'Why do you think she came to the police station?' Richie continued, before answering his own question. 'Because our front counter has a camera. She's not stupid, that one.'

'But what about Timmy? Are you forgetting about him?' Sarah held her paperwork close to her chest.

'Think about it,' Richie replied. 'We were her alibi and Timmy was her witness. She called him over to babysit, then when his back was turned, she whacked him over the head. She probably didn't expect him to recover.'

Sarah thought of Millie's pink cheeks, and the cute folds in her wrists. She couldn't bear to think of history repeating itself. Was Cora capable of such violence and deceit?

'I really hope you're wrong,' she said, her spirits sinking. Soon they would relay everything to their team. She wanted to be on the same page.

It seemed that Richie wanted that too, as he put forward his case. 'Why would Timmy lie? You heard what he said. He'd just got to Cora's when someone hit him from behind.' Timmy was lucky. The gash to his forehead would heal. It could have been a lot worse.

'She wasn't too concerned about him either.' Richie pushed his tag against the security panel outside their office door.

'She called the police.' Sarah reasoned as she followed him inside. She couldn't condemn the woman just yet. Once, she had been the talk of the town herself.

Her colleagues were busy working, their space lit by desk lamps, the fluorescent strips turned off to give their eyes a rest. Empty pizza boxes littered the printer desk, and Gabby was focused on her screen as Richie took a seat. 'Have you listened to Cora's call? She was all over the place. The first we knew about Timmy was when you found him lying on the floor.'

Sarah remembered the sight of his blood pooling on Cora's tiled floor as he lay, stunned by the fall. 'He recovered quickly enough though.' Sarah rested her paperwork on his desk. They needed to collaborate on their report. She wanted to believe that Cora was innocent, but things were not looking good.

'He said Cora kept checking on her baby, but she wasn't making a sound.'

'All new mums obsess over their babies,' Sarah snorted. 'And we do have a record of her getting a phone call.'

As Richie logged into his computer, he didn't appear convinced. 'She could have called herself from a burner phone. If Timmy had seen Millie alive, all of this would be in a different light. But he didn't. The poor kid could have been dead in her cot when he arrived.'

'Jesus.' Sarah sighed. 'That's dark.' She was bone weary from the day, but still had to write up her report. They would update McGuire when he got back.

'Dark but not impossible,' Richie said. 'Cora could be responsible for the lot. Because even if her father is alive, he's hardly going to blow his cover to take her child. This isn't an episode of *Dallas*. People don't return from the dead.'

'You're showing your age there, Richie.' Yvonne passed, catching the tail end of their conversation.

'She could have a split personality,' Sarah said, ignoring Yvonne's remark. 'The Cora everyone knows, and the traumatised girl abandoned in a bunker of bones. Perhaps she's reconstructing her father's movements when he killed her little sister and is keeping him alive in her head. Did you read the poem she wrote about him as a child?'

It had been found in the bunker with the rest of her stuff. The words were imprinted on the back of Sarah's mind.

> *It whispers your name*
> *In the dead of night,*
> *In the silent spaces*
> *Devoid of light.*
> *Keep your babies silent*
> *For it will take them too.*
> *The bone house, the bone house*
> *Is calling for you . . .*

'Yeah, it's disturbing.' Richie slid off his tie and shoved it into his jacket, which was resting on the back of his swivel chair. 'But how can a place physically manifest? I'm no psychiatrist but the Silver Cross pram could have triggered Cora. She could be using the "bone house" to take the blame for what she's done.'

'Maybe,' Sarah said, but she wasn't sure. She couldn't forget Elliott's warning. Her intuition had driven her to visit Cora's place for a reason. Someone wanted revenge, and what better way to avenge the death of your baby than to set its mother up for murdering her own? 'I'm going to do some more digging on the father. If only to satisfy myself.'

'I'll research the bunker,' Richie replied. 'From what I've read, someone went to a lot of trouble to hide it, long before Cora's family moved in.'

As McGuire entered the room, Sarah prepared to explain her reasoning all over again.

Chapter 37

Cora lay in the custody cell, staring up at the ceiling. The bed consisted of a thin layer of foam encased in hard blue plastic. There was a stainless-steel toilet in the corner, and a camera on the ceiling above her head. She pulled the blanket over her shoulder, grateful to Sarah for requesting her cell door be left ajar. The air was warm and stuffy, and some questionable smells roamed down the corridor. Her block of cells was quiet, although she could hear a prisoner shouting in the distance as he rattled his cell door. She was grateful for the noise. It was a comfort compared to the deadening silence of the bunker.

Cora's thoughts were with Millie. If the police believed she had hurt her little girl, it meant they weren't going after the monster who had taken her from her cot. Outside Cora's cell, the officer assigned to watch her had eaten his bag of crisps and was now scrolling on his phone. Cora's throat was raw from shouting, her eyes puffy from a constant stream of tears. The last time she had felt this helpless was when she was imprisoned below the ground.

She had grown tough during her time in the bunker and developed a hard outer shell. She had learned to think for herself. She hadn't wanted to hurt her daddy, but nor had she wanted to die. The only way she could escape was to take him by surprise. Her time in isolation had changed her too. Sometimes she had become so lost in her fantasy books that she no longer felt part of the real world. There was no prince coming to rescue her. That, she had to do herself. But the bravery of her fictional characters had given her hope. She was thankful for the electricity that her father had sourced from the shed and supplied to the bunker. Without light, she would have surely gone insane.

She recalled the night when death visited her in the bunker, and for a fleeting moment she considered hurting herself to make the pain go away. She had lived in a heightened state of fear for so long that she finally let the destructive thoughts in. But the darkness that settled around her could not snuff out Cora's will to live. It delved deeper, twisting her thoughts. It told her that her father was a murderer. It made her think about what he did that day. Ugly, sickening thoughts bloomed in the night which she was unable to recoil from. It told her to go into the back room and look at the pretty bones. To pick them up and examine them. To strip away the flesh. The undercurrent of violence still hummed. It was waiting. It would happen again.

Cora was small and undernourished. Her father didn't see her as a threat. But her presence in the world was. What if somebody found her? She was a tie. He could never form another relationship or move away. Cora realised that she was viewing her father's blackened thoughts. Natural life bloomed in sunlight, but whatever was in the bunker fed in the darkness on a diet of violence, emptiness and fear. Without a host, it had come to her. It was too late to save her father, so she had to save herself.

She was cooking on the makeshift gas stove when her father came home. She heard the clank of the bolt being drawn across and became giddy with trepidation. She had planned to rush past him up the steps to freedom. She clutched a plastic knife for protection, knowing that it would snap in half against his chest. Like her, it wasn't strong enough. But that day luck was on her side.

'Cora?' His voice came before his presence, as it always did. 'Are you against the back wall?'

'Yes, Daddy,' Cora said. Silently, she edged from the wall to the steps as she waited for her father to descend. Her heart felt like a toy wound up too fast.

'Hang on,' he said, a lightness to his voice. 'I've got something special for you.' There was a soft grunt of effort as he made his way down the steps. Then he began to sing. 'Happy birthday to you . . .' The words of celebration were out of place in her prison, and she watched first his shoes, then his legs descend. She gripped the plastic knife. But she was frozen, a prisoner without shackles as she bent to her father's will. She couldn't do it, no matter how much she wanted to. It was the bone house she needed to escape, not her daddy, who was just carrying out its will. She dropped the knife, a tear descending her cheek. She would die here, her remains would be left with her mother and sister and he would fill in this place. She would be left here in the darkness forever, with that *thing* . . .

You can do this. It's too late for your father. Save yourself. The memory of her mother's voice delivered a small spark of hope that forced her on. Her limbs trembled as she stared up at her daddy. He was holding a bunch of roses in one hand and her cake in the other as he descended the steps. And then she knew, she had to act now. It felt as if she was outside herself as her hands shot out from the side of the steps. Gritting her teeth, she grabbed his ankles tight.

'Happy birthday dear Cor— agh!' he yelled. The cake slipped from his grip, its candles still ablaze. He took one, two, three faltering steps down the stairs as he tried to balance, but his momentum was too strong, his weight thrust forward as he crashed down the steps into the stove. Rose petals and cake icing were smashed into his face, a groan emitting from his lips as he lay on the cooker, now collapsed beneath his weight.

Cora's movement was instinctual as she bolted up the steps. Any second, she expected her father to grab her leg and pull her back down. To take a hammer to her head just as he'd done to her mother and baby sister. But then she was outside in the air, which smelled amazing, the sunshine burning her eyes and making her blink as she ran barefoot down the garden path. She ran onwards, down the grass verge until she reached her friend Becky's house. She had been gone so long and she didn't recognise the older woman who opened the front door. This wasn't Becky's mother, or grandmother as far as Cora could tell. Cora didn't wait to ask as she ducked under her arm and ran inside.

'Close the door, please! He's coming!' Cora's words were ragged as the residue of terror remained.

The woman stood, with her permed hair and floral dress, looking like she'd never seen a single scary thing in her life. Her mouth dropped open as she looked Cora up and down, her gaze settling on her bare feet.

'You've got no shoes.' It was such a bizarre thing to say. The sort of thing you said when you were in shock. But Cora could not stop, not when she'd got this far, even if her feet were staining the woman's hall carpet blood red.

'Don't let him in!' She panted for breath, tugging on the woman's arm. 'Please! He's coming to get me! Lock the door!' But the woman stood, stupefied, her hand still on the latch of the open door.

'Do as she says, love, then lock the back door and check the windows too.' The deep voice of the man descending the stairs came as a blessed relief. Cora didn't know it, but his name was John Goodman and he was a retired Chief Fire Officer. He took one look at Cora and instinctively knew what to do.

Chapter 38

Sunday 23rd July, 2023

When it came to her job, Sarah didn't often take no for an answer. An uncompromising 'no' raised alarm bells during an investigation. Father Duffy and his wife were accommodating but when it came to their son, their defences rose. Perhaps he *was* anxious around police, or maybe he had something to hide. It wasn't as if he was a hermit. The young man worked with members of the public, so he couldn't be that shy. He even did some volunteer work helping local charities through his father's church. So why had his parents insisted that Sarah keep him out of things? It wasn't as if they had power over her movements. If she met him in a public setting, then where was the harm?

Sarah had been keeping the PNC busy as she did her homework on the families Cora had met. The police national computer revealed that Abel didn't have any markers: no history with the police, not even a speeding ticket. It had been easy enough to find out where he worked. Unusual names were a blessing in her profession. All she had to do was type the name Abel Duffy online and he came up as a member of staff at the Lincoln electronics hyperstore. It was a big flashy building with every type and brand of technology, advertising '0% Finance' and 'Buy Now, Pay Later' in bright banners around the store. Abel was tall like his father, with shaggy hair and wide-rimmed black glasses which were all the fashion these days. She watched as he engaged with his customers, demonstrating the latest Apple MacBook Pro. He was dressed in the uniform of blue shirt and black trousers, but with white trainers underneath. Sarah observed him use the same mannerisms as his father, such as the slight bow of the head and the gesticulation of his right hand. He avoided eye contact but was capable of processing a sale. Sarah had timed her visit to coincide with the Sunday closing time of 4 p.m. She browsed the selection of laptops and computers, waiting for him to come to her.

'Can I help you?'

Abel seemed to have floated up behind her, and she hadn't heard him approach. She glanced upwards. Sarah had not been blessed with the tall gene. 'Oh hello, I was waiting for you to finish talking to those people. I was wondering if I could have a word.'

'Certainly,' he said politely. 'That's what I'm here for.'

'Not here though,' Sarah smiled. 'What time do you get off?'

His eyes widened as two spots of red stained his cheeks. 'I'm sorry?'

'Oh!' Sarah giggled as she realised what she sounded like. 'Sorry. I'm not chatting you up. I'm making enquiries about someone you used to know.'

Abel seemed at a loss for words as Sarah rooted around in her bag. 'It's got to be here somewhere. Ah, here it is!' She produced her warrant card like a magician pulling a rabbit out of a hat. 'It's nothing to worry about,' she said as his face fell. 'I just want a quick word about Cora.' But Abel's grey eyes were blank, making him hard to read. 'You remember Cora, don't you? Your dad and stepmum fostered her.'

'Of course I remember her,' he said sharply but quietly as a family walked past. 'But there's nothing to tell.'

'Then it'll be a very quick chat. How about we go for a coffee? My treat.' Sarah smiled hopefully.

Abel shifted from one foot to another. 'I've got to get home to my wife.' That, Sarah had not expected. He looked too young to be married. For some reason she imagined him living alone. She caught the flash of his silver wedding ring as he rubbed his chin.

'Five minutes?' Sarah said. 'Then I'm out of your hair. I'll wait outside if you prefer.'

Abel heaved a deep sigh. 'No need. Stay here.'

Sarah watched him walk heavy footed to the customer services desk and speak to an efficient-looking woman in a blue suit. She glanced at Sarah before nodding, and in the background a tannoy announcement was made to say the store was now being closed.

'Come this way,' Abel gestured as he returned. Sarah dutifully followed. She didn't need to assert herself because this situation was best handled with kid gloves.

For all its flashiness, the superstore had a modest staffroom. It consisted of a couple of cheap leather sofas, two round tables, a fridge and small kitchenette that had seen better days. The room smelled deliciously of the pot of coffee being kept warm on the side, and the walls were decorated with health and safety posters and instructions on how to wash your hands.

'We haven't got long.' Abel's expression was taut as he pulled out a chair. 'They'll be locking up soon.'

'What can you tell me about Cora?' Sarah sat across from him. 'I'm doing some digging into her past.'

'Why?' Abel said flatly.

'Haven't your stepmum or dad mentioned her to you lately?' The response was a shake of the head.

'The remains of a baby have been recovered from Slayton's lake. They've been there for some time. Cora came forward to say that the baby had been hers. It was a little girl, a newborn.' Sarah watched his face for a reaction but as Abel stared at the table, his expression was blank. 'Unfortunately, the baby did not have a peaceful death.'

'I heard about the pram on the news.' Abel spoke in a quiet voice. 'I didn't know the baby was hers.' He began to crack his knuckles. For Sarah, it was a toe-curling sound.

'What can you tell me about your time with Cora? How did you get on?'

'We didn't.' Abel continued to work his knuckles. 'She was horrible to me, and Dad wouldn't have a word said against her.'

'Did you spend any time together? Family outings, holidays?'

'I was shunted between Mum and Dad. I usually stayed in my room.' His shoulders hunched, Abel began to close in on himself.

'Did Cora have any boyfriends? Do you know any of their names?'

But Abel had folded his arms and wouldn't meet Sarah's eye. Silence stretched between them as she waited for an answer. 'Abel?' She was met with a tight shake of the head. The colour had left his face as he stared into space. Sarah flinched as he jumped up from his chair.

'It's closing time. You should leave.' He turned on his heel and without a backward glance, left the room. Sarah stared after him.

'Rude,' she mumbled into the empty room. The encounter had been bizarre. She had watched Abel in his comfort zone, talking to customers with ease. But the deeper she delved into his relationship with Cora, the more uncomfortable he became. The mention of a boyfriend had tipped him over the edge. She left the staffroom, catching his eye as she walked onto the shop floor. A second tannoy was playing, reminding customers that the store was about to close. Abel walked through the aisles in the opposite direction. Sarah had clearly touched a nerve.

Chapter 39

McGuire leaned against the edge of Sarah's desk, a half smile resting on his face. He was tall but never imposing, and Sarah and her colleagues were getting used to him floating around. The trick was to carry on working until he spoke first. As for Sarah, spelling errors inevitably crept in as he watched her type. She was in the middle of a report for the Crown Prosecution Service who would make the final decision on Cora's case. It wasn't needed yet, but Sarah liked being prepared. There was lots of overtime available, now they had a missing baby to contend with. Finally, McGuire took a breath to speak.

'This case of yours is like a corkscrew with all its twists and turns. I thought I was giving yous a nice wee cold case, but now it's looking grim.'

Sarah tilted her head to look up at him, painfully aware that she had the least amount of service of anyone in her team. She wanted to say that she could handle it. That she'd had some good results in the past. But she couldn't blow her own trumpet. Everything she'd achieved was a team effort.

McGuire continued. 'The thing is, if this goes to court, your lack of service will be the first thing the defence team will pick up on. Everything needs to be watertight.'

Sarah relaxed in her chair. At least he wasn't taking her off the case. 'I'm investigating every avenue, time allowing, and Richie is helping too.'

'Then do me a favour and chase up this enquiry. I've had a call from the Chief Super. He's golf buddies with a chap by the name of John Goodman – I think they're in the masons together, best not to ask.' He shook his head. 'Anyway, Goodman's asked to have a chat with the officer in charge of the case. He'll be here in . . .' He paused to check his watch. 'About half an hour. Goodman was Cora's

139

neighbour. They'd only lived there six months when Cora turned up after escaping the bunker.'

'I see,' Sarah said, her curiosity satisfied. Police grew used to not having resolutions. You worked a case and you moved on. But for Mr Goodman, the incident was bound to have an effect, especially when it was so close to home. 'Cone of silence, I take it?' Sarah asked. 'How much can I tell him?'

'Very little,' McGuire replied. 'Pacify him – and get the Super off my back.' He delivered his usual wink. Sarah wanted to ask how his date with Maggie went, but she held back. 'Oh, and one more thing . . .'

Sarah forced a pleasant smile.

'Do us a favour, will you? I promised Sophia that I'd take her out for drinks, but I can't afford the time.'

Sarah's mouth dropped open. This wasn't work related. 'Boss, I'm not being funny, but neither can I. This case is taking up all my time.'

McGuire checked over her shoulder. Her colleagues were busy working, heads down. Yvonne had gone to pick up CCTV and Gabby had just left the room. 'Ah, but there's the eleven-hour rule. You started at seven this morning. You must finish by nine if you intend to come in bright and early in the morning.' His eyes twinkled as he spoke, making it hard to say no. She had to admit, the man had a certain charm. Plus, he was her boss, and he had a point. The rule of eleven hours rest was invoked so officers didn't fall asleep behind the wheel on their way home. 'She likes you,' he added. 'And I'll give her my credit card, so drinks are on me.'

Sarah heaved a sigh. She was so in awe of Sophia Hudson, she was sure the woman would find her a bore. Still, alcohol helped. And they couldn't get into too much trouble if they only started drinking at nine. 'Alright. I'll take her to the hotel.'

Once, she would have been thrilled to spend time with her favourite author, but Cora's case was getting under her skin. It felt disrespectful to be out drinking with Millie missing. But then not all policing took place in a formal setting. They would probably spend their evening discussing the case.

Sarah logged off her computer as the tannoy called her name. While she was speaking to Mr Goodman, a team of officers would be viewing CCTV, making door-to-door enquiries and chasing up leads. The search team were still scouring the area, and sniffer dogs had been brought in. They'd even managed to get the chopper to do a flyover of Slayton, although the only thing they'd picked up was thermal imaging of a cannabis farm in someone's loft.

Mr Goodman extended his hand as Sarah entered the witness suite. He was a heavy-boned man, with a low, domed forehead taken up by a set of bushy white eyebrows. Grey suit, polished black shoes. Here was a man used to being in authority.

'Thanks for taking the time to meet with me, Detective. Your boss speaks highly of you.' He spoke with a Yorkshire accent, and his eyes crinkled as he smiled, changing his persona into that of an entirely approachable man.

Sarah doubted her boss had said any such thing but reciprocated his smile as she shook his hand. 'No problem, Mr Goodman. I'm doing some background work on Cora's past so I'm happy to oblige.'

He chuckled. 'Call me John.' He took a seat, made himself comfortable and folded his arms. 'I need to talk to you about Cora.'

'I'm all ears.' Sarah was warming to the man before her. He also had friends in high places. It wasn't in her interest to screw this up.

'I'll never forget the day that poor lass came to our door. It was strange, because Chester had been unsettled all day. He could sense things, you know?' John mused. 'The missus and I were going out. We'd planned on spending the day in Skegness . . . thankfully, we were running late. Then this little girl, half-starved and stinking, ran into our home. The sight of her, eyes wild and clawing for safety . . .' He shook his head, growing serious once more. 'I've seen some sights in my lifetime but, by God, that broke my heart.'

'It was a good thing she found you.'

John nodded in agreement. 'Me, I dealt with it, but the wife . . . she was invested. She couldn't sleep, thinking about her. She blamed herself, you see. Got it into 'er head that she should have known what was going on under our nose. So, I followed Cora's case . . . we both did, truth be told.'

Sarah understood. But John and his wife couldn't have known. It wasn't as if they lived right next door. She watched as he gesticulated, his investment in the case obvious.

'We couldn't understand why Cora wasn't found. I've got contacts in the police and I managed to pull a few strings.' He gave Sarah a knowing smile. 'I got in touch with the officer in charge of her case. Bloody useless, he was.'

'Really?' Sarah sat up. This was getting interesting. Given Cora's case was handled by a different force, Sarah didn't know the officer in charge of the case.

'The man was an alcoholic.' A frown deepened on John's lined face. 'A year later, 'e was kicked off the force. It was a catalogue of disasters from day one.'

'They brought Cora's father in for questioning after his wife went missing, didn't they?'

'Oh aye, sure enough. Several times, from what I've 'eard. They may have had their suspicions but, by God, he covered his tracks well. Then there were the appeals, and the endless searches, but it were never enough, when he'd hidden them so well.'

John shook his head. 'All these years, we've kept track of the lass. When we heard she was arrested for getting rid of her baby, we couldn't believe it.'

'At least the judge offered Cora lenience.'

'Aye, but he didn't know the full story. Justice wasn't served.'

'It couldn't bring her baby back,' Sarah said sadly.

'But we can listen to 'er now.' John pinned her with a gaze. 'You know where I'm going with this, don't you? You've read 'er file. Listened to what she had to say.'

'I . . . I have.' Although Sarah wasn't sure what he was leading up to.

'Good.' John rubbed his hands together. 'Then you agree with me. Dr Osmond is behind everything – the bastard's still alive.'

Chapter 40

Sarah stared at Slayton's lake from her vantage point of the rooftop bar. The night air was so soft and warm, she could have been abroad. She usually swerved the Lakeside Hotel's cocktail bar, but Sophia's privacy would be respected here. This was a place frequented by the wealthy, and autograph hunters would not be tolerated. The plush velvet seats were well spaced beneath the rooftop canopy, and the decorative twinkling lights did not detract from the stunning view. Tonight, the lake dazzled like black diamonds beneath the light of the full moon. It was peaceful – for now. The dredging was complete, and it was deemed fit for purpose. To think, children would once more play in the waters which had held a baby's tiny corpse.

As Sarah waited for Sophia to return from the bar, threads of worry occupied her mind. She wanted to believe that Cora was innocent, but Richie had a wealth of experience and was convinced she was some kind of criminal mastermind. Cora had lied in the past, but that didn't make the mild-mannered young woman with a passion for books a murderer. There were so many facets to this investigation it was keeping the team on their toes. But they couldn't dig forever. Soon they would reach a conclusion and move on. But would it be the right one? And would they find Millie alive? Her meeting with John Goodman had given her lots to think about. Could Dr Osmond have survived? At least McGuire had promised her full access to the original case. She tapped her foot to Nina Simone as 'My Baby Just Cares For Me' played, but it did little to ease her worried thoughts.

Sophia returned, drinks in hand. She looked glam in her navy trouser suit and outrageously high heels. 'Sorry, I'm not what you'd call sparkling company tonight,' Sarah took her drink, feeling wholly inadequate. She was a poor substitute for the celebs that Sophia Hudson rubbed shoulders with. She tugged at the skirt of the same black suit she'd worn to work that day.

'Don't worry.' Sophia flashed her a smile. 'We'll let the drinks do the heavy lifting. Then you can sparkle all you want.'

Sarah couldn't help but smile. It seemed Sophia knew her well.

'What do you think about bone collectors?' Sarah traced a trail of condensation down the side of her glass. 'Do you think it's odd to line your walls with skulls?'

Sophia considered the question as she sipped her old-fashioned. 'People see bones as dry, lifeless things, but while we're alive so are they. They bleed, they heal, they support our every movement, yet they get such a bad press. Skulls are identified as being creepy. Skeletons are associated with Halloween. So little thought is given as to how amazing they really are.'

Sarah listened, enamoured, as Sophia professed her love for her job.

'You don't think it's odd, then, a doctor having a collection of bones in a bunker?' Sarah wanted to get to know Dr Osmond. Was he a domestic abuser or did his problems lie deeper? There were obviously two sides to the man – the father who Cora had loved, and his dark side which she said was influenced by the bone house. Were they one and the same?

Sophia rested her drink on her coaster. 'When I was young, I was obsessed with The Monkees. I had a hundred posters of them on my walls. In my spare time I sketched them. I started putting their pictures on the ceiling when I ran out of space.' She smiled as she drew down her memories. 'If an obsession fulfils a need and isn't hurting anyone, I don't see the harm. I've been to one guy's house in LA. He had such an impressive bone collection that for me it felt like I was in Disneyland.'

Sarah listened as Sophia chuckled, glad nobody else was listening in.

'He had a tank full of dermestid beetles that he used to clean the bones. Wriggly little things . . .' Sophia went on to talk about Los Angeles and her love for the US.

'Wait a second,' Sarah raised her hand. 'There's a beetle that strips flesh from bone?' There was almost an audible 'click' as a piece of the puzzle slotted into place. The dreadful crawling sensation on Sarah's skin. The killer's fascination with skulls. Could he have used them too?

'They're popular with taxidermists, and some forensic anthropologists, although I've never used them myself.'

'Are they difficult to get hold of?' Sarah cradled her glass with both hands.

'I guess they're quite specialised, but not impossible to buy. Why? What are you thinking?'

But how could Sarah tell her that the enquiry was based on a hunch? As nice as Sophia was, she was in the public eye and Sarah didn't want to end up on her socials as some kind of joke. 'Nothing, I'm just interested. I've not come across them before.' She sipped her drink, which was growing warm as she gripped her glass. 'There's something about Dr Osmond that doesn't sit right with me.' She swiftly changed the subject. 'Logic tells me he's dead, but Cora is convinced that he lives on. Apparently, the case was mishandled. Who knows what's been overlooked.'

'It's a shame his body was cremated.'

Or convenient, Sarah thought.

'Still, I have the coroner's report. I've been asked to examine the photographs of the skeletal remains.'

'I can't imagine anyone better qualified for the job,' Sarah said with a smile. This was an avenue of enquiry that could not be ignored.

'So, tell me, what's McGuire like as a boss?' Sophia's eyes were alight with curiosity.

'He's not been in charge all that long,' Sarah replied honestly. 'I've always considered Gabby as my boss until McGuire took over from our last DI. Bernard Lee was content to take a back seat, which gave Gabby the leading role. We all called her boss, even though she was a DS, but that's by the wayside now McGuire's here.' Sarah thought about the birthday cake she'd made her, with 'Happy Birthday, Boss' emblazoned on top. It was hardly any wonder Gabby was struggling to come to terms with taking a back seat.

'Ah, that would explain the animosity. Although it's all one-sided. McGuire's a great guy. He doesn't hold a grudge.' Sophia crossed her long legs. 'To be honest, I never imagined him as a cop.'

'So why did he join the police?' Sarah wanted to get to know him a little better, particularly now he'd asked her friend on a date. 'You two go back years, don't you?'

'Sure do, although we drifted apart after he joined MIT. He was working long hours and I was wrapped up with my projects. Next thing, three years have passed, and we haven't spoken a word.'

But she hadn't answered Sarah's question and Sarah was curious. 'Were his family supportive of him joining up?'

'Yes and no.' Sophia smiled. 'Like me, they didn't think he was tough enough to hack it, although he's always been good with taking on responsibilities. But give him his due, he's proved us all wrong.'

Sarah nodded. She couldn't disagree with that. 'Makes you wonder why he put himself through it. Having an eidetic memory must open a lot of doors.'

'He's a nice guy. He said he wanted to make a difference in the world – all that corny stuff. But I think it runs deeper than that. It may have something to do with his sister.'

'His sister?' Sarah echoed. McGuire had never mentioned a sister. But then, there was a girl in one of the family photos on his desk at work.

'She ran away from home when she was sixteen. He's never ever stopped looking for her. If you ask me, she's the real reason he became a cop.'

'I'm sorry to hear that,' Sarah said. In a way, it made sense. Was that why he'd travelled the world? A group of young women walked past, cocktails in hand, dripping with jewellery and designer bags. There were a couple of double takes in Sophia's direction before they passed.

'McGuire's parents were devastated. It's a shame, we don't talk any more . . .' Sophia paused, delivering a wry smile. 'I see what you're doing, Missy. Getting me drunk so I'll spill the beans.' She chuckled to herself. 'I've been interviewed by journalists all over the world and I've told you more in twenty minutes than I've said to them during the whole of my career.'

Sarah felt a warm glow at the admission. 'That's because whatever you tell me won't go any further than between us.'

'Alright, I give in.' Sophia sighed in defeat. 'But why do you want to know? You got the hots for your boss?'

'Get away with you,' Sarah flapped a hand. 'It's just . . . well, we work in close quarters. I'd like to know him a little better and the best way of doing that is to ask a friend.'

'You've nothing to worry about with McGuire. He's kind, compassionate, intelligent . . . a little bit wacky but a danger to no one. But what about your love life? You must have your eye on someone.'

Sarah prickled at the thought of sharing personal information, but she couldn't question Sophia all night.

'I haven't got time for that, I spend all my time at work.'

'C'mon now, I know what cops are like. There must be someone.'

Sarah's thoughts went to Richie and her cheeks flushed.

'Aha! Who is it?'

'Nothing's happened!' Sarah protested, taking a swig of her drink. Sophia was buying strong cocktails, cheering that each drink was 'on McGuire'.

'But you want it to, right?' Sophia's eyebrows rose as silence was returned.

Sarah shook her head, feeling slightly woozy as she did. 'There's nothing to discuss.'

But Sophia wasn't so easily put off. She took a vape from her bag and pointed it in Sarah's direction. 'I'll make a deal with you. I'll tell you the juiciest, most scandalous piece of gossip about McGuire if you tell me your workplace crush.'

Sarah giggled, encompassed in an alcohol-induced warmth. 'Really? You're not having me on, are you?'

'As if I would!' Sophia laughed. 'This will blow your mind.' She drew on her vape, exhaling a fruit-flavoured stream of smoke.

'OK then,' Sarah grinned. 'But circle of trust, remember?' She tapped the side of her nose. She took a breath to speak as the gesture was returned. 'There's this guy I partner with. He's been good to me, ever since I came back to work. I've no idea why . . .'

'Have you been on a date?' Sophia interrupted.

'God no. But he comes over to mine once a week.'

'Ooh, friends with benefits,' Sophia chortled, taking another drag of her vape. The rooftop bar had quietened, now a party of drinkers had left.

'No, nothing like that! We play Scrabble, or watch documentaries about Bigfoot sightings, or UFOs.'

'You're having me on, right?'

'No, that's as exciting as it gets.'

'So how long since you've . . .' she gave Sarah a knowing look. 'Got it on.'

'I can't believe you asked me that!'

'Are we talking weeks? Months?' Sophia's eyes were alight now. She wasn't going to give up.

'Years.' Sarah sighed. 'So many years. Five, maybe six?' She and her husband had grown apart long before his demise. She had married her first love, which made the prospect of a new boyfriend daunting.

'Oh my God! Seriously? You're in your sexual prime. Get yourself out there, girl.'

'I'll think about it,' Sarah smiled, knowing she wouldn't – *sexual prime indeed.*

'It's all about confidence,' Sophia insisted. 'Walk in there like you own the room. You're pretty, behind that wild hair and those ill-fitting clothes. You've got a lot going for you. You just need to enhance your assets.' She clicked her fingers as a thought occurred. 'I've got a little black dress in my suitcase. It's too short on me, but it would be perfect on you.'

'I don't think . . .' Sarah began to say, but Sophia squeezed her hand.

'Hun, if that dress doesn't get you laid, nothing will. What have you got to lose? Call it a thank-you gift for keeping me company.'

'Go on then,' Sarah relented. She'd definitely get a kick out of wearing one of Sophia Hudson's dresses, if nothing else. She nibbled her bottom lip, wondering if she'd ever get the courage to wear it. Richie had asked her out in the past, but she'd always treated it as a joke.

'Good girl,' Sophia grinned. 'So, we're agreed? You're gonna ask him on a date?'

Mellowed by alcohol, Sarah gave in. 'Alright, I'll do it, but only if you tell me your scandalous news.'

'You've got to keep it to yourself,' Sophia warned. 'How I've managed to keep it out of the press this long, I don't know.' She paused to sip her drink. 'The reason I fell out with McGuire's parents is because I married their son.'

'Wow,' Sarah exhaled a low gasp. She *had* done well to keep that out of the press. 'I didn't know McGuire had a brother.'

'He doesn't. *He's* my husband.' She knocked back the last of her cocktail. 'Right, never mind all that. We have a date to plan.'

Chapter 41

Cora's instructions from the police had been clear after she was bailed. Don't venture out (for her own safety), leave the police work to the police, keep her appointments with social services and the crisis team, and above all, do not speak to Timmy. The only reason she hadn't been charged with kidnapping her own baby was down to lack of evidence. Timmy's concussion could have skewed his memory and it was possible she was telling the truth. But Cora *had* to speak to him. He was meant to be her friend. How could he have turned against her the way he had? But she couldn't risk breaching her conditions, which is why she called him from a burner phone.

'Yes?' The voice was guarded.

'Timmy, it's me, Cora. Can we talk?'

A pause. Time for thought. An inhalation of breath. 'Alright then. But not on the phone. Meet me in my car. I'll be parked outside the playground. We can talk in private there.' The call ended abruptly. He didn't give a time so he must have meant now. Cora's heart skipped a beat. Did he know where Millie was? He *was* the last person to see her alive. Why weren't the police looking at him? She glanced out of the window before grabbing her bag from the coat hook on the wall. Timmy had no motive to hurt her little girl. So why was he lying to the police? Cora's stomach felt twisted in knots as she drove to their meeting place.

Timmy's Fiat was parked at the side of the playground as planned. The stars shone brightly from above as Cora's footsteps echoed down the moon-washed street. The air was muggy, but not as stifling as it had been all week. Timmy wound down his window, his face like granite as he instructed her to leave her bag and coat on the ground.

'What?' she responded, feeling utterly lost. 'Why? Why would I do that?'

'Because I don't know what you've got in there. And turn out your pockets while you're at it.'

Cora almost laughed at the surreality of it all. This wasn't her Timmy talking, her right-hand man. 'Timmy, what's going on? This isn't you. I don't understand.'

'Fine!' Timmy flapped a chubby hand. 'I'll just go.'

'Wait,' Cora pulled off her coat. 'At least let me put my stuff in the boot.' She didn't care about personal belongings, but she did need her phone in case the police called. Teams of officers were still searching the local area. There was still a hope that Millie would be found.

The boot of the car popped open as Timmy activated it from inside. Cora checked her phone for messages before slipping it back into her bag. She could have cried at the sight of the blank screen.

She slipped into the car, a maelstrom of emotions inside her. She was hanging on to her sanity by a thread. 'Timmy, I don't know why you told the police what you did, but you were wrong.' She looked at the gash above his forehead and the bruise that was breaking out. How could he think for a second that she was responsible?

Timmy's lips curled in a sinister smile. A sheen of sweat had broken out on his forehead. He was clearly enjoying this. 'You really don't know, do you, Cora? All this time we've been working together, and you don't have a clue.'

Cora stared at the man before her and realised that she didn't know him at all. 'Then tell me,' she pleaded. 'Because I'm at breaking point and I don't know how much more I can take.' Her hands shook on her lap as she tried to contain her frustration.

'Looks like you're in a spot of bother alright.' He was still grinning, his face flushed pink. 'I can help you. For the right price.'

Hope flared. Did Timmy know where Millie was? 'Anything,' she said, clutching his wrist. 'You can have anything if you tell me where Millie is.'

Timmy's eyebrows shot up in incredulity as he shook her fingers away. 'What? You think I took your baby? You're way off the mark. I'm talking about the story I gave to the cops. You're heading to prison, lady. They'll be back dredging the lake, but not for crows this time around.'

'Then what?' Cora didn't care about the police. All she could think of was Millie. 'What do you want from me?' Because Timmy wanted something. There was unadulterated greed in his eyes. She'd seen his little side glances in the past, heard his snippy remarks when it came to how she ran the business. She'd put it down to him being highly strung, but it was coming together now. Timmy wanted something, and he was willing to blackmail her to get it.

He shifted in his seat, the smile returning to his face. 'I'll tell the police the truth if you give me back what's mine.'

Chapter 42

Sarah was left dumbfounded by Sophia Hudson's bombshell. She'd had no idea McGuire was married, let alone to someone easily old enough to be his mother. Then there was her best friend, Maggie. Did she know she was dating a married man? Sarah doubted it. No wonder McGuire had given Sophia a spare key to his home. But why push her and Sophia together? Was he using her, so she'd go back to Maggie and break the news? Sarah had so many questions, but after Sophia dropped the bombshell, she remained tight-lipped. Weary from socialising with such a large character, Sarah headed home. She was grateful for the bar's closing hours, although Sophia had fitted a lot in, during the short time they were out.

But her night wasn't ready to end yet. She had just fed Sherlock when her phone beeped with a text. It was Richie, keeping her updated. *Cora's bailed to sign on at the police station. Ignored safeguarding advice and gone home.*

Sarah hadn't been able to help herself. For the second time, she left the cosiness of her bungalow and headed to Turn the Page. Sarah wasn't surprised to hear that Cora had been bailed. There were too many unexplored avenues to definitively charge her now. For one thing, they hadn't found a body, or any evidence to suggest Millie had been hurt. The budget wouldn't stretch to surveillance, but again, there was no law against Sarah *happening* to be in the area as Cora left her flat.

She had hoped to be led to Millie. Instead, she witnessed an unexpected rendezvous. Living where she worked, Sarah became inexorably tangled up in each case. She could get away with knowing Cora, but unauthorised undercover surveillance she could not. Which is why she waited for Cora to return home before confronting her on the street.

'Oh!' Cora exclaimed, her face pallid as Sarah stepped out of the shadows. 'Have you found Millie?' Her voice was thick with worry, but Sarah shook her head.

'No, sorry. Not yet.' It was late. Traffic had thinned but there were a few people left on the streets. It wasn't a safe place for Cora anymore. 'Can we talk inside? Unless you're staying elsewhere, that is.'

'I'm staying here.' Cora pulled a shiny key from her bag. 'But I had the locks changed, and I'm closing the shop until Millie comes home.'

'I'm glad you're taking some safeguarding advice on board.' Sarah's voice echoed in the corridor as she followed Cora to her flat. Still warmed by alcohol, she had taken a taxi after she left the hotel. She glanced around Cora's home. Every inch of the space had been searched, although CSI had not dwelled for long.

'It feels so empty without her,' Cora's eyes searched the hollow corners, as if somehow Millie would appear.

'How about I make us both a cup of tea?' Sarah forced some cheeriness into her voice. 'You look like you could do with it. You must be exhausted.'

Sarah rested two mugs of tea on the coffee table next to the sofa and waited for Cora to join her. But the young woman stood at the open window, staring mournfully at the streets below. 'I know how this is supposed to work. I should be taking part in TV press appeals for the return of my baby, but instead, I'm on police bail. I know what you're all thinking, but I'm telling the truth.'

Sarah could feel the grief coming off her in waves. 'Cora, I joined the police to help people. Not a select few, but everyone. Because nobody was there to help me . . . at least, not until it was too late.' Sarah decided to confide in Cora about her history in the hope of building a rapport. She took a deep breath to continue. Every time she revisited the past, she felt the ache of her loss all over again.

'My family were gunned down in one night. At the time, I thought the killer was my father – the person I trusted most in the world.' Sarah spoke of her heartache of losing her little brother. 'I was locked in a wardrobe as a hiding place, then the killer took aim and fired. I still can't bear the sound of thunder because it reminds me of that night.'

Sarah watched as Cora met her gaze. 'Your bed is meant to be a safe place. But for me it was the last place I went before my family were killed. Most people don't think of how sleep makes you vulnerable, but I do. Even now, the slightest sound wakes me up.' She thumbed away the tear that she had promised herself she would not cry.

Cora moved a cushion aside and took a seat next to her. 'I'm sorry . . .' she began to say.

But Sarah shook her head. 'There's nothing to be sorry about. I'm telling you so you understand where I'm coming from.' Whatever Cora had done, Sarah meant every word. 'I followed you tonight. I won't report it, because I did it off my own back. I know what it feels like to be alone. I'm doing this because I care.'

Cora nodded, her big moon eyes filling with tears. Sarah was getting through to her at last. 'I saw you put your coat and bag in the back of Timmy's car. Then I heard you ask what he wanted before you got in. It's clear you didn't orchestrate the meeting. Is he blackmailing you? Is that what this is? Or has he taken Millie for ransom? Because there's more to this than either of you are letting on.'

Cora raised her hands to her face, her voice muffled behind her fingers. 'I don't know what to do.'

'Talk to me,' Sarah whispered. 'I'm your best chance of getting Millie back alive. Why do you think I always turn up when you need me?' Sarah was beginning to ask herself the same thing.

Cora released her hands, frustration etched on her face. 'Timmy admitted he was lying. He said that after I left, there was a pizza delivery and he let them in.'

'Go on.' Sarah recalled the takeaway boxes, and that local enquiries were being made with pizza delivery companies.

'He wouldn't tell me what he looked like, only that the delivery man knew my name.' Cora wrung her hands as she recalled her conversation. 'Timmy turned away to get him a tip and that's when he was hit from behind.' A car horn beeped outside, momentarily stilling her words. 'The thing is . . . I don't think Timmy was ever unconscious. He played dead to save his own skin. He hinted that he knew things. But he says he'll only tell the police if I gave him what he claims is rightfully his.'

'I remember his eyelashes fluttering as he lay there,' Sarah admitted. 'That doesn't usually happen when people are passed out . . . What does he want?'

Cora's jaw tightened. 'The bookshop. Apparently, he tried to buy it to begin with, but I put in a bigger offer at the last minute and begged the vendors to sell to me. In his mind, I gazumped him. He never forgave me for it. I didn't even know.'

Sarah couldn't believe what she was hearing. 'Is that it? That's why he lied to police?'

Cora nodded. 'That's it. He said if I hand over the business, he'll support my story. It was him who graffitied my shop . . .'

'And him who launched a hate campaign against you online,' Sarah murmured beneath her breath. Suddenly, it was clear. Timmy wanted Cora out of business so he could take over the store. As if she needed that, on top of everything else. 'What did you say?'

'I told him to take what he wanted. I'll do anything to get Millie back. If giving him the shop helps the investigation, then I'll do whatever it takes.'

'Then help me,' Sarah replied. 'Because there are too many unanswered questions. Who is Millie's dad? And who fathered the baby we found in the lake?'

'Millie was the result of a one-night stand. I've not seen him since then.' She looked away as she shook her head. 'I'll never trust a man enough to settle down with them.'

It was hardly any wonder, but it saddened Sarah to hear Cora say the words aloud. 'And your first baby?'

'I can't go there.' Cora grew increasingly uncomfortable, just as she had in the interview room. 'It'll break me if I do.'

But Sarah wasn't ready to give up. 'After everything I've just told you? Cora, I've been to hell too. You can and you will come back from this.'

'It's not that . . .' Cora's body tensed, her eyes reflecting the depths of her pain. 'You won't believe me. Nobody does.'

'Try me.' Sarah patted her hand. 'What have you got to lose?'

Cora pulled her hand away, wrapping her arms around herself. 'I was a virgin when I was pregnant. I'd never had sex.'

Sarah tried to disguise her surprise, needing to keep the momentum going. 'Were you seeing anyone at the time?' But Cora shook her head. 'I didn't start seeing boys until long after my first baby was born.'

'Did you go to any parties? Were you drugged? Did you pass out?' Sarah recalled a rape case she had dealt with when the victim fell pregnant after being drugged with Rohypnol. She had no memory of the night because she blacked out. It was only when she discovered that she was pregnant that she realised what had taken place.

'I was a bookworm. I stayed in my room most nights.'

Sarah sighed. 'And Abel? What about him?'

Cora's features clouded over at the mention of his name. 'I kept out of his way. His mum got remarried so he came to live with his dad and stepmum. It was always strained between them. Abel's an oddball.'

'He said you bullied him. Are you saying that wasn't the case?'

Cora's narrow shoulders bunched. 'I was upset, but I'm no bully.'

'Did any cross words pass between you?' Sarah knew she was firing questions, but she had to know.

'I didn't like the way he looked at me, so I told him where to get off. I learned a few swear words while I was in care.' A thought seemed to occur. 'You don't think he has anything to do with this, do you?'

Sarah couldn't say for sure. 'Given the timing, it's likely you got pregnant while you were under the same roof. It wasn't the immaculate conception. If you can't remember having sex, then you were raped.' She sat back, allowing the words to sink in as Cora clenched and unclenched her slim fists.

'The only two men I can think of who were in your life at the time were Father Duffy and his son.' The atmosphere became brittle as Sarah raised the subject. These were the questions Cora had staunchly avoided so far.

'I've told you, something evil touched my baby!' Cora blurted, her face twisted with disgust. 'That's why she died!'

'Cora . . .' Sarah began to say, but the young woman lashed out, just as she'd done in the police car.

'Keep your tea and sympathy. You've not listened to a word I've said!' Cora's voice rose an octave as she revealed another side to herself. Teeth gritted, she tipped over the coffee table, sending teacups and saucers crashing to the floor. 'Get out! I want you out of my flat! Just leave me alone!' She grabbed Sarah's bag and pushed it hard against her chest. 'You're a bad omen. Every time I see you, something goes wrong.'

'But . . .' Sarah began. But she could see where this was heading. If she stayed, Cora could end up inadvertently assaulting her. Her presence had backfired, despite everything she'd said.

'Get out! Go do your job and find my daughter, instead of stalking me!' Through her spittle-laced words, Cora wrenched open her door. As the door slammed shut behind her, Sarah could hear things being thrown in the flat. Cora had a temper, but how far would she go?

Chapter 43

Cora continued to stare out of the window long after Sarah had left. Her breathing had slowly regulated, but she had hurt her wrist and her flat was turned upside down. Pictures were smashed, books were splayed on the floor and tables upended. She hadn't done herself any favours, but fear for her baby had dictated her movements, forcing her to lash out. At least now Sarah knew what Timmy was like.

Her friend's betrayal had bitten deep. To think she'd trusted him with her child. All the while he'd been harbouring a secret hatred, infiltrating her business and biding his time. It reinforced what she already knew: people couldn't be trusted, not even those you regarded as friends. 'I suppose I'd better clean up,' she murmured beneath her breath. It wasn't as if she could physically look for Millie. She wouldn't know where to start.

She recalled the kindness of the couple who took her in the day she ran away. She could almost feel the soft crocheted blanket Mrs Goodman wrapped around her shoulders on the day she escaped. She'd sat, sticking her fingers through the woollen holes in the aftermath of her ordeal. After months of isolation, the world felt so big, with every sight, smell and sound closing in on her. Cora hadn't felt safe until her neighbour knelt on one knee before her and she looked into his kindly eyes. 'Now, lass, listen here. The doors are locked.' He spoke softly in a Yorkshire accent. 'Backup is on its way. As for Chester . . .' he pointed to the German Shepherd pacing the room. 'One word from me and 'e'll tear the arse from any intruder. So don't you worry your head. You're safe.'

Cora's hands trembled as she accepted a glass of squash from his wife. She forced a smile as the woman returned with a straw. 'Here you go, love. Take your time.' A plate of sandwiches was laid on the coffee table before her, along with some custard creams.

'Steady on, Betty,' her husband admonished. 'Give the girl some breathing space.' He turned back to Cora. 'Now, love, let's start with your name. Then you can tell me why you ran in here like the devil was on your tail.'

Once Cora started talking, she was unable to stop. She turned to his wife as the police entered the room. 'What if they don't believe me?' But her neighbour simply smiled.

'Oh, sweetheart, they will. We'll make sure of that.' Tentatively, she placed an arm over her shoulder and gave her a squeeze. She appeared homely by nature, the smell of her floral perfume evoking a memory of Cora's mother. 'Shh,' the woman whispered, stroking Cora's unwashed hair as the tears began to flow. 'You're safe. You're safe now, my lamb.'

Cora didn't hear about the fire until much later. She'd presumed her father was hunting for her. It was her social worker who broke the news that he was dead. No wonder the police had asked so many questions about how she escaped. Again and again, they'd questioned her account. As she poked her fingers through the crocheted blanket, she told them as much as she dared. Then they brought her to the police station, gave her a change of clothes and questioned her some more. She was too scared to admit to grabbing her father's ankles, saying he tripped on his laces on the way down.

Cora couldn't come to terms with her father's death because none of it made sense. He'd crashed against the gas cooker as he lost his footing, but how had the bunker turned into a ball of flames? According to police, her underground space had quickly filled with gas. But Cora didn't understand how it could have caught the flickering birthday candle which fell from her cake. The social worker didn't say it directly as she wouldn't allocate blame, but they believed that Cora had left a gas ring on. Given her age, it was possible, but surely the fire would have taken hold while she was there? Then there was the question of the bunker hatch which she didn't remember shutting on her way out. At night as she lay in bed, it made Cora wonder: was her father dead? The nightmares that followed seemed so lucid. Cora was told to accept the fact that the bone house was a figment of her dreams.

Now, Cora buried her face in Millie's cot blanket as she lay on her bed. Her limbs ached with tiredness. Every inch of her body hurt. She inhaled deeply, still smelling a faint trace of her little girl. 'Oh God,' she sobbed into the blanket. 'Please bring my baby home.'

At first, the tinkling ringtone felt like it was coming through the walls. It was the tune that made her sit up straight, as the song 'Here Comes the Sun' filled the silent spaces in her mind. Clambering off the bed, she followed the sound, swallowing back her tears. Was she going mad? Was it all in her head?

The cot. It was coming from Millie's cot. She pulled off the blankets, throwing out Millie's soft toys, but the ringtone persisted as 'Here Comes the Sun' played on a loop. It was taunting her. It was him. He was back, and he had been in this room. He had taken her daughter and now he was communicating with her, if only she could find the damn phone. It was only when she pulled up the mattress that she realised the phone was vibrating against the wood. Dropping to her knees, she searched underneath and found the phone taped to the underside of the cot. With shaking hands, she ripped off the tape and pressed the old-fashioned flip phone to her ear. 'D-Daddy?' Her voice cracked. She was ten years old again. 'Where are you?' She needed to take his hand. To persuade him to sit down. To keep calm. Her stomach churned in anticipation. She only hoped she wasn't too late.

Chapter 44

Elliott didn't make it back to his bed. He'd got as far as the bathroom when the whispers crept in. They weren't as loud as they used to be in their old home, but they came to him just the same. He'd woken up feeling funny today. Not ha-ha funny like when his friend Jahmelia made a joke, but a weird funny that made his stomach feel like he'd swallowed something rotten and wanted to sick it up. It was the same horrible feeling from when he stood in the shop and saw the rusty old pram roll down the street all on its own.

He thought about putting his shutters down and chasing the scary feelings away, but whatever was making it happen wasn't after him. Some things just carried in the air, like a stink bomb being let off in class. But this smelled worse than any stink bomb, because it wasn't made in a factory as part of a joke. It came from the other place. It had something to do with the missing baby. Maybe he could help Auntie Sarah get her back. He stood before the bathroom mirror, his gaze empty as he stared at his reflection.

The hollow voice that echoed came from a darkness far beyond Elliott, but he could hear it just the same. Tendrils of cold air chilled his skin as he gripped the sides of the porcelain sink. They were deep in the ground, down in the dark place where nobody came. A head with no body. Polished bones on display. Elliott closed his eyes as a soft song was hummed. It was 'Here comes the sun . . .'

The images that flooded his mind came with a level of interference that made them hard to figure out. When he opened the door to the darkness, he never knew what he was inviting in. At least now he could make it stop. He could pull down his shutters if things got too scary, just as Miss Grogan had taught him. Sometimes just listening made the voices go away for good. But now the crying was back, and the chubby fingers of a baby swiped the air. She was looking for her mother, but a pair of strong hands were gripped round her

162

body as a cold bottle of milk was forced into her mouth. This was bad. Elliott didn't like it. The light over his head flickered, and the bathroom tiles turned to ice beneath his feet.

Somewhere far away, he thought he heard his mother's voice. But the scuttling noise demanded his attention, and he peeped down the sink plughole at the movement from below. The scratching, clicking sounds grew louder as a hoard of shiny black beetles skittered up the plughole. They seemed too fat to fit, but they came just the same. First five . . . then ten . . . they kept on coming, climbing over each other, hungry and scuttling in search for food. Elliott stared in horror as the porcelain sink grew black with scurrying black bodies. They were the same ones he'd seen coming from the pram. But now he was paralysed, unable to draw his shutters down and make it go away. He shouldn't have opened the door and let them in. A scream locked in his throat as they climbed up to his fingertips and began to nibble on his skin. The air filled with a buzzing hum as they took flight around his face.

It wasn't until the warm water touched his skin that Elliott returned to himself. He gasped for breath, overcome by confusion. He was sitting in his mother's arms, both of them dressed for bed as the shower soaked them through. 'It's OK, baby, I got you. It's OK, you're safe.'

'The beetles . . .' Elliott gasped, staring around the space. But there was nothing there. He touched his face and checked his fingers. None of it was real.

'It's OK, sweetheart. There's nothing here.' Maggie reached above her to turn off the shower. 'Are you OK?'

Elliott nodded. It was scary when it happened, but just like switching off a movie, the bad feeling had gone. The shock of the warm water had made it all go away. His mother wrapped a warm towel around him, before tending to herself. Elliott was brave and now the moment had passed. The beetles weren't meant for him. He had just got in the way. He was a light in the dark, a short distraction while they waited for someone else.

Chapter 45

Sarah rushed around to Maggie's, barely giving herself time to pull on her slippers before heading out the front door. A blast of cool air threw open her nightgown. The hot weather was breaking, and according to the weather forecast a storm would soon dispel the humidity. As much as Sarah hated thunder, the weather was the least of her concerns now. Tying her dressing gown together, she slipped her spare key into Maggie's door. Her friend had been so upset when she rang, Sarah insisted that she go straight round. It didn't matter that it was the early hours. She would always be there for her.

'Maggie?' She called out, but not too loudly as she entered the hall. Had this something to do with McGuire? This was what Sarah had been afraid of. If he'd hurt Maggie . . . the thought made her blood boil. Regardless of who he was, she'd have it out with him.

But the look on her friend's face as she met her in the hall relayed it was something else. Elliott. Maggie was chalk white, her hair damp. Sarah's heart gave an unsteady jerk in her chest. 'What's wrong?'

'You didn't need to come over. Elliott's back in bed. I just . . . I just . . .' Her friend's chin wobbled, and she clasped a hand over her mouth to silence her sudden sob. Sarah followed her into the kitchen. Maggie was searching the cupboards for a bottle of wine.

'Maggie, what is it? You're scaring me.' Sarah noticed the tremble in Maggie's hand as she pulled a glass from the cupboard. She'd been doing so well, cutting back her drinking to just once a week. But as Maggie gulped from the wine glass, she couldn't get it down quickly enough.

'Sorry,' she gave an apologetic smile as a tear ran down her face. Sarah took the glass of wine from her hand, rested it on the table with the bottle and insisted Maggie sit down. She waved away the offer of a drink for herself.

'What happened? Is it Elliott?' Sarah said, firmer this time. 'I can peep in on him . . .' She knew it couldn't be McGuire, not while Maggie was like this.

'No, don't do that,' Maggie said, red wine staining her lips. 'I got a fright, that's all. I didn't know what to do. But I'm OK now.'

Sarah reached across the table and squeezed her friend's hand. 'I'm here, and I'm not leaving. Now tell me, what's wrong?'

Maggie downed the rest of her wine, colour finding its way into her cheeks as she poured herself a second glass.

'And go easy on the loopy juice, eh? Elliott needs his mum sober.'

'Oh, hun,' Maggie sniffed. 'This won't even touch the sides.' But she took in Sarah's disapproving face and screwed the lid back on to the bottle just the same. 'Two glasses are my limit. Promise.' She looked Sarah up and down. 'Oh God, I'm sorry. Were you in bed?'

'Don't worry, I wasn't asleep. But you put the fear of God in me. The nightmares are back, aren't they?'

Maggie didn't disagree. 'Elliott woke up to use the toilet. Then I heard him screaming. I found him in the bathroom. He was standing at the sink, flapping and kicking out at thin air. He said there were beetles biting and nipping his skin. It was awful. I've never seen him that bad.'

'Is he OK?'

'He is now. But I couldn't snap him out of it. He was in a world of his own. I dragged him into the shower and turned on the warm tap. I don't know why but . . . this is going to sound silly . . .'

'Go on,' Sarah urged.

'It was like I could hear his teacher's voice in my head. Maybe it was one of those "what would Miss Grogan do" moments, I mean, she's so good with him.'

'And the shower worked?'

'Instantly.' Maggie sipped her wine. 'It was strange, how quickly he recovered from it. I dried him and put him back to bed. He said that he was fine and that I wasn't to worry, because the bugs weren't here for him.' She shook her head. 'So typical of him to worry about me instead of himself. Once I'd put him to bed, I needed to hear a friendly voice. That's what I miss the most about being married, not having someone to bounce things off.'

'That's what friends are for too,' Sarah said.

'Do you know what was weird?' Maggie stared into the shadows in the corners of the room. 'When I was leaving the bathroom, I saw two beetles scuttle into the sink plughole. They were so big . . . I've no idea how they fitted. Then I blinked and they were gone. Maybe I imagined it.'

'Yes, that must be it,' Sarah said, but she wasn't so sure. All week, her skin had itched and tickled like there were insects crawling on her skin. She resisted the urge to rub the back of her neck. 'I'm just going to peep in on Elliott. I won't wake him if he's asleep.'

Maggie didn't try to stop her this time.

Elliott was sitting up in bed, expectantly. He smiled as Sarah entered the room, putting his book aside.

'Hey, how are you?' The mattress bounced slightly as Sarah sat. She couldn't say he'd had a bad dream like usual, because Elliott had got up to use the loo. Also, how could it have been a dream when Maggie saw beetles too?

'I'm OK.' Elliott exhaled a very grown-up sigh. 'Is Mummy alright?'

Mummy. Elliott rarely used the term.

'She's fine, but what about you? What happened in the bathroom?'

Elliott shrugged. 'They're gone now. They weren't for me. I got in the way.'

'What's gone? Who?'

'They showed me the bugs. I shouldn't have looked. Miss Grogan taught me how to keep the bad things away, but it was my fault. I let them in.'

'Why did you do that?' Sarah was trying hard to understand. Usually, she tried to help him reach a rational explanation, but she didn't want to shut him down.

'Because I wanted to help the baby. It's about the pram. It's all been about the pram.' He turned his eyes to her, wide and enquiring. 'Will you find the baby? I don't like the bugs.'

'What baby?' Sarah asked but the creeping sensation of dread already brought the answer. She knew who he meant.

'The baby from the bookshop. Can you find her before the bugs do?'

'I will, sweetheart, as soon as I find out who's taken her.' But Elliott didn't have the answer to that question, and she didn't want to push. He could have heard about the baby from Maggie. Her whereabouts was the question on everyone's lips. 'Try not to be scared,' she added. 'Your imagination could have been playing tricks on you after some bugs climbed up the plug. I'm not saying it didn't happen, because you're a very special little boy. But it's also important to keep a sense of . . .' she searched her mind for the right word. Tonight, she was tired and not on the ball.

'Per-spec-tive,' Elliott said with a smile. 'Miss Grogan taught me that too.' He stretched his arms in a yawn, seemingly no worse for his experience. It seemed that Elliott was growing up.

Sarah pulled up his duvet as he snuggled down in bed. Not for the first time, she thought of her little brother. She missed him every day.

'I'm going to sleep now. You can go home.'

Elliott's bluntness brought a smile to Sarah's face. He blinked a couple of times. 'But Sherlock can stay – if he wants to.'

'That sounds like an excellent idea. He can sleep on your bed.' Sherlock was wandering Maggie's hallway, equipped with the uncanny ability of knowing where he was needed the most. Sarah opened the door wide and watched as he jumped up on Elliott's bed. Elliott reached out to stroke the cat, a sleepy smile warming his face. He closed his eyes, his nightlight illuminating the room, and Sherlock's comforting purrs dispelling the silence. Sarah had been naive to think that moving house would chase his visions away for good. She quietly left the bedroom door ajar. She walked down the hall, pausing at the bathroom. A wet towel lay splayed on the ground. The sink was sterile white, with no signs of any nocturnal visitors. Tentatively she pushed the plug into the sink, shuddering at the thought of what had taken place.

Chapter 46

Sometimes Sarah wondered why she gave so much of herself to the people of Slayton. Revealing her past to Cora had breathed new life into the grief she'd worked so hard to repress. Not that it had done her any good. She could not force Cora to open up to her but being thrown out of her flat after she'd bared her soul had felt like a slap in the face. She'd thought she was beginning to understand the quiet young woman who ran the local bookshop, but she didn't know her at all. It was time to move forward with her life. She would not wear her heart on her sleeve again.

Parts of Slayton were beautiful, such as the lake and surrounding woodland. Upper Slayton drew in yearlong tourists and the pavement restaurants and coffee shops carried a café-chic vibe. But there were darker sides of the town which had a life of their own. The old, abandoned buildings, such as the derelict asylum, would make the hairs stand up on the back of anyone's neck. But that was Disneyland compared to Blackhall Manor. Every time Sarah drove past it, she felt like she was being watched. No amount of renovation would make the looming gothic building any less intimidating in her mind. Could buildings really have a life of their own?

There was something about Slayton that kept her here. As much as they frustrated her, the residents were special and she was grateful to have been taken into the fold. Lower Slayton had a negative vibe and many of its inhabitants had experienced a tragedy of some kind. But it was the sense of community that kept them going, as well as a quiet mutual respect. Elsie had once been a shut-in, but now she was one of Sarah's most trusted friends. Maggie had a harrowing past, but she was more like Sarah's sister than a best friend. As for Elliott . . . Sarah smiled at the thought of him living next door. The once shy, troubled little boy was becoming strong, putting the needs of others ahead of himself. The least Sarah could do was to protect them in return. Something had followed Cora to Slayton, of that she was sure. But how much of it was in her own mind? As she waited for Sophia Hudson, Sarah and her team were about to find out.

As they sat in the briefing room, the pressure was on. It felt odd, sitting in a wide circle, with rows of chairs behind her and the remaining officers standing behind. It was McGuire's idea, something about inclusivity and every officer's opinion being important, so nobody felt left out at the back. It was a world away from Sarah's previous detective inspector. Bernard was as old school as they came.

The case was snowballing into something large and complex, with enquiries being chased as far as budgets would stretch. And it had provided KCom news with some juicy headlines now that details had leaked online. Timmy had claimed memory loss due to concussion during the police interview; Sarah wished the interviewing officer hadn't informed him of the seriousness of perverting the course of justice before he began. Sarah wasn't finished with him yet.

McGuire and Gabby sat in the circle as officers took turns in updating the results of their enquiries. But it was Sophia Hudson who stole the show. Even while dressed modestly, she was a five foot eleven glamourpuss who basked in the limelight as all eyes turned on her.

'It's a shame that the body was cremated . . .' she said in her usual forthright voice. She was talking about Dr Osmond, who had left strict instructions with regards to his disposal in his will. 'But I've spent considerable time assessing reports on the skeletal remains.' She swept a gaze over her audience. 'If the measurements are to be believed, the remains that were found in the bunker did not belong to him.'

A low but audible gasp rippled throughout the room. Sarah almost expected to hear the dramatic cliffhanger music that played at the end of each episode of *In the Bones*.

Sophia rested one hand on her hip. 'The remains were identified as wearing Dr Osmond's clothes. He also had a wedding ring which was inscribed on the inside. A DNA sample wasn't taken as there was nothing from his house to compare it against. He was stepdad to Cora from an early age, so they weren't blood related, and no relatives' details were found. The man was an only child, as were his parents. To the officer in charge, it was enough to close the case.'

She glanced at the whiteboard that she had assembled, which displayed images of the grizzly remains. The crime scene photos of that bunker made Sarah shrivel up inside. Not to mention the remains of Julia Osmond and her newborn child. It was of horror movie proportions, and hardly any wonder that Cora was on edge.

Sophia glanced at DI McGuire, who stood on the other side of the board. Only now could Sarah see the connection between them. She had yet to broach the subject with Maggie. She returned her attention to the case. 'Thanks to some sterling teamwork, we delved deeper with our enquiries with regards to Dr Osmond's wife. She had reignited her relationship with an old flame, Michael Georgiou. His sister, Constantina, lives in Cyprus and hadn't seen him in years. But he did telephone sporadically, and it was through those phone calls that he told his sister that his girlfriend was pregnant, and he was the father of her child. Michael moved to the UK when he was a teenager, and that's when he and Julia first met. They were childhood sweethearts and planned to marry one day. But then Michael's father took ill, and Michael went back to Cyprus. He and Julia were reacquainted a year before Julia died.'

Sarah exchanged a glance with Richie, who was sitting two seats down.

Sophia took up the reins again. 'It was difficult to track Constantina down as English isn't her first language, and she lives with her husband out in the wilds. We eventually spoke, thanks to LanguageLine, and she told us that she reported her brother missing eighteen years ago. The last time she spoke to him was when he rang, three weeks before Cora escaped from the bunker. He said his girlfriend was in trouble, and they'd been planning on getting her out of an abusive relationship. But then she stopped taking his calls, and instead sent texts telling him to keep away. He mentioned the wording of the texts and felt something was wrong. That was the last time Constantina spoke to him.'

Sarah imagined the scene as she absorbed the words. Michael had no idea who he was dealing with when he turned up at Dr Osmond's door. Had the doctor drugged him? Or kept him a prisoner in his home? Or had his death come quickly, as Osmond tied up his loose ends? Sarah crossed her legs as her thoughts ran away with her. A love triangle involving a murderer was a very dangerous place to be, particularly one where the murderer had no qualms about killing a child.

'Now, I can already imagine what CPS would say . . .' McGuire appeared calm and in control as he looked around the room. 'That this is all circumstantial. Which is why we dug a little deeper into Michael's history. It's all in the bones, as my colleague would say.'

Sophia smiled, thoroughly enjoying herself. A question rose from the back.

'Why weren't dental records taken to identify Dr Osmond?'

'That's a good question,' McGuire replied. 'And part of the catalogue of errors which have been raised in this investigation. Along with the fact that Michael Georgiou was two inches shorter than Dr Osmond, which matches the measurements of the remains found.'

'That's not the only concern,' Sophia added. 'A small fracture was found on the victim's right tibia, which would have taken about four to six weeks to heal. Yet Dr Osmond didn't have a limp or any sign of injury.'

'Couldn't it have happened when he fell down the bunker steps?' the same officer enquired.

Sophia shook her head. 'This was a healing fracture, estimated to be two weeks old. Michael's sister specifically remembers her brother mentioning being injured while he was playing rugby. He mentioned being on crutches when he called.' Another ripple of chatter spread around the room. But this didn't sit right with Sarah.

'How was the case closed, given this information?' Richie piped up.

'Constantina reported her brother missing but she didn't have Julia's details, and the officer in charge of Dr Osmond's case wasn't aware of the link at the time. As for the evidence with regards the fracture, that didn't come to light. I'm not saying it was covered up, but . . .'

'No,' McGuire hastily added. 'We're not saying that, but it will be looked into. The main thing to take from this is that there's a new element to the case. But even if Dr Osmond survived, it doesn't mean that he's back. You'd imagine that someone with the intelligence to carry out such an elaborate plan would have the sense to stay out of the limelight.'

'Or he may not even be alive anymore,' Sophia added. 'He could be anywhere, above or below ground.'

Sarah scanned her colleagues' faces, taking in their reactions. Gabby was hard to read, as she stared at the whiteboard. Richie was rubbing his face, which meant he was thinking hard. Yvonne was chewing rhythmically on a stick of gum, her head tilted to one side as she listened to the officer sitting next to her. Either side of Sarah were two old sweats, who had been in the job a lot longer than her. They weren't prone to gossip or sensationalism. They took each update as it came and filed it away for later. In other words, they had seen it all before. Just when you think you've figured out a case, you are blindsided by a twist. Was Dr Osmond alive? If so, why would he return to terrorise a young mother and her child?

Chapter 47

It wasn't the darkness that frightened Cora, it was the creatures that made it their home. She tried to part her crusted eyelids, but they felt like lead shutters as she fought the drug-induced haze. A part of her wanted to sleep but an instinctive primal urge told her to wake the hell up. Because it wasn't just her life in danger – it was Millie's too.

Slowly, she emerged, drawing on each of her senses. The air was thick and warm, tainted with a sour, rotting smell. Cora wanted to turn away, but her limbs were heavy and numb. She fought to remember what had brought her here. A call. She'd received instructions. Directions to an address. She heard Millie cry and her adrenaline went into overdrive. Every part of her body physically ached for her child. A part of Cora had expected to end up back at her old address. The bunker may have been filled in, but everything about the situation felt like a cruel trick. And now she was back in the darkness, her baby crying from the next room. She'd been overcome with relief when she stumbled inside the cottage and saw her baby through the open door. For the briefest of seconds, she allowed herself to believe that she could take her baby home. That was what the caller had promised when they told her to come alone. But the voice had been distorted, and that should have been enough of an alarm bell for Cora to realise that Millie had been nothing more than bait. Then she was stung by the needle as it was plunged into her neck, its effects hitting her with the force of a bus.

As she crumpled to her knees, she knew her father had brought her here to finish what he started. She would see him soon enough.

A groan escaped her lips as she wrestled with her bindings and forced herself awake. Her sight was fuzzy at first, but enough to make out the dim light of candles as they flickered and danced. Round, white objects swam in and out of her vision. She blinked, taking slow breaths of fetid air. She recognised the stench. The rotting carcass smell. A groan escaped her lips as she tried to move her feet and she realised her ankles were bound. The chair she was on creaked and rattled as she wriggled her body left and right. 'Mmhhh,' she managed to say, in a long, dry-throated drawl as she tried to call her baby's name. But then her sight came into focus as did the skulls hanging on the wall. They stared, each one a promise. Her eyes rolled to the bloodied hacksaw on the table. To the instruments laid next to them. She blinked, bringing the diagram on the wall into focus. She needed to be quiet, because screaming was against the rules. But muffled screams came just the same. They filled the hollow spaces, making Millie wail. Cora rocked against her bindings as she fought for escape. The room darkened and the sudden creak of a floorboard seemed like the loudest sound in the world. Cora gulped for breath, spittle foaming in the corners of her mouth. The bone house was calling. But she would not go down like her mother. It would not have her baby. Not today.

Chapter 48

'I did some research on the address where Cora's mum died. Found out some interesting stuff.' Richie shifted in the passenger seat of Sarah's car. Both windows were rolled down as they drove towards Timothy's address.

'Oh yeah?' Sarah replied, appreciating the light breeze. 'How come you didn't bring it up in the briefing?'

'And be laughed out of the office?' Richie snorted. 'No thanks.'

'Well, tell me then,' Sarah replied, her curiosity piqued. 'What did you uncover? Satanic rites? Pagan rituals?'

'You're not far off the mark, actually. Did you know that between the fourteen and seventeen hundreds, over two hundred thousand people were accused of witchcraft?'

'Blimey.' Sarah flicked on her indicator as she drove into Timothy's close. 'I knew it was bad back then, but that's a big number. I don't suppose many of the poor sods survived.'

'They didn't,' Richie replied. 'Most of them were tortured into giving confessions before being put to death.'

Sarah's thoughts went to Elliott, Mrs Grogan and lastly, herself. 'I wouldn't have stood a chance back then.'

'No, you wouldn't, you big weirdo.' Richie laughed. 'If Yvonne had been alive then, she would have hung us both.'

Sarah smiled. She could imagine Yvonne as a Witchfinder General. 'What's this got to do with the house?' She wanted to move on from the subject which gave her the chills.

'A woman named Kitty Flowers used to live there in the mid-eighteen hundreds. Her neighbours accused her of being a witch, because anyone who pissed off Kitty became sick and died. She used to work as a maid in a manor house in Wragby, but was fired after she was caught stealing. One by one, the homeowners died after she left.'

'Where did you dig that info up?' Sarah eased her foot off the accelerator as she scouted for a parking spot.

'From the library. They have all sorts of old records and journals there. Apparently, the townsfolk were planning on having it out with Kitty when she disappeared. I read that the house stunk. It was filled with old bones, beetles, herbs and candles, but no sign of the woman herself.'

'Beetles?' Sarah prickled. That was a bit close to home. She waited for the rest of the story. 'And?'

'And that's it. Kitty was never seen again. Her cottage was mown to the ground, and Cora's house was built in its place. Not a lucky place to live, by all accounts.'

Sarah gave him a wry smile. 'I'd say what happened to Cora and her family was a bit more than bad luck.'

'You know what I mean,' Richie said. 'I don't know if Cora is aware of all this history, but I thought you'd like to know.'

'It's interesting, sure enough,' Sarah agreed, trying not to get paranoid about every little thing. 'But do enough digging and you'll find plenty of weird stuff. I can't see what harm Kitty can do us now.' She pulled up next to the kerb, just in time to see Timmy walking in through his front door. It was time to focus on the present. The past couldn't help her now. She had lost all respect for Timmy. Blackmailing Cora to get his paws on the bookshop was a rotten thing to do, particularly when it got in the way of the investigation involving a missing baby.

'Are you sure you want to do this?'

'We've nothing to lose,' Sarah replied. But Timmy had already been interviewed. Without new evidence to put against him, Sarah had no right to grill him again.

'Just be careful,' Richie warned. 'Timmy's a snake in the grass. I wouldn't put it past him to make a complaint.'

Sarah shrugged. 'Why do you think I've dragged you along?' They were meant to be carrying out door-to-door enquiries and tying up any loose ends.

'He's already been interviewed. He doesn't have to tell us a thing. You might not like policy but it's there to protect us all.'

'Hark at you,' Sarah laughed. 'The hairy biker is a stickler for rules.'

'I have a warning on my record,' Richie said, unimpressed. 'Trust me, you'll get no thanks for putting your neck on the line.' As he exited the car, it seemed Richie's rule-bending story would be left for another day.

Sarah trotted up the road after him, her new shoes pinching at the toes. She didn't have time to go clothes or shoe shopping and bought most of her things online. The downside was that many items were ill-fitting, and she didn't have the time to send them back. *One day*, she thought, wincing as she tried to keep up with Richie's long steps. *One day I'll go into one of those big department stores and get a personal shopper.* She returned her attention to her surroundings. She'd been surprised to learn that Timmy lived in such a quiet cul-de-sac in an exclusive part of town. Given it was in Upper Slayton, house prices were not cheap in these parts.

'Someone's done well,' Sarah said, taking in the sight of the four-bedroom home and the thirty-six-thousand-pound Mercedes parked on the drive. Timmy had closed his front door behind him, oblivious to their presence as they walked up the footpath. There was no graffiti here, no litter, or weeds poking through broken paving slabs. Each house was perfectly manicured, with generous, block-paved drives. 'How are we handling this?' Richie said, as they approached the house. He rolled up his sleeves as the unrelenting heat took its toll.

'*We're* not handling anything,' Sarah smiled, but was met with a look of concern. 'Trust me.' She liked the new-found confidence in her voice. She'd been awake half the night planning the conversation that was about to take place. She'd encountered plenty of people like Timmy in the past. All he needed was a little push.

A few determined barks drowned out the doorbell's delicate chime. Sarah raised her warrant card in the air as the door was opened. It was not Timmy who answered, but his husband. Sarah already knew that he would be at home, which is why she'd timed her visit to the hour. Mr Barker was a lecturer at Lincoln University. He was the calm and sensible side to their relationship, as far as Sarah could tell. He did not advertise their relationship, and his social media presence was private. He was older than Timmy, a tall, slender man with a strong jawline and salt and pepper hair. But he had a kindliness about him, with deep laughter lines and soft blue eyes.

'Oh dear,' he said, as Sarah introduced herself. 'Is everything alright?'

'Nothing to worry about.' Sarah pocketed her warrant card. 'I was hoping to have a word with Timmy. Is he in?'

'Yes, yes,' he scooped up a greying Dachshund before opening the door wide. 'Come in.'

'Timothy!' he shouted behind him, leading the officers towards the living room. The walls were tastefully decorated with artwork, and an expansive bookshelf took up one side of the room. There was no television here, just comfortable chairs, the light scent of patchouli and an expensive-looking rug. Mr Barker glanced at their shoes, one hand on the open door. 'Would you mind terribly . . .'

Sarah had kicked off her kitten heels before he'd finished the sentence, grateful to wriggle her toes. Richie seemed less enamoured but dutifully removed his shoes. Sarah smiled at the sight of his striped socks before turning her attention to Timmy as he entered the room.

'What are you doing here?' he said, a flush rising to his face. He wasn't angry. He was mortified. Sarah took in his expression as fear and embarrassment took hold.

'I have a couple more questions to ask you.' Sarah gave him a disarming smile.

'What's this about?' Mr Barker stood before the fireplace, his question directed at Timmy. This was exactly what Sarah had hoped for. Because Mr Barker hadn't been at the station when Timmy appeared, or the hospital where he received stitches for the wound on his forehead. Timmy had plenty to hide, and his husband, not Sarah, was the best person to prise the truth out of him. She watched the exchange with interest until Richie cleared his throat.

'I'm afraid we're unable to discuss the case due to data protection.' The simple sentence would cover them in the event of a complaint.

'That's right,' Sarah turned to Timmy. 'We can discuss this in another room, or even in the car if you prefer not to return to the station.'

Her use of the word 'return' may have been risky, but it had the desired effect.

'Oh, Timothy,' Mr Barker spoke in the exasperated tone of a teacher scolding their pupil. 'What have you done this time?' The dynamic of their relationship was clear. Sarah stood in the opulent living room taking it all in. She would have bet her wages that the house belonged to Mr Barker, and Timmy was a kept man with too much time on his hands. It was how he could afford to work part-time in the bookshop for the minimum wage.

'I didn't want to worry you.' Timmy's voice was small as he stared at the carpet, his face radish pink.

'We don't mean to intrude,' Sarah interjected. 'Timmy . . . *Timothy's* been helpful and supportive, but we were hoping to jog his memory a little more.'

Timothy's eyebrows rose. His lips parted as he exhaled a sigh of relief. Just as Sarah planned, he thought Cora had reported him to the police for blackmailing her.

'It's dreadful, this whole business,' Mr Barker tutted. 'Are you any closer to finding Cora's baby? I can't imagine she'd want to hurt her own child . . . but I suppose you never know.' He looked from Sarah to Richie. 'Please, take a seat.'

'Thanks.' Sarah sat next to Richie on the sofa. She wasn't letting Timmy off the hook just yet. 'I spoke to Cora last night. She was telling me how supportive Timmy's been.' She pinned him with a stare. 'She told me all about your chat in the car.' While Mr Barker tended to his dog, Sarah narrowed her eyes. 'She said your memory might be returning. I'm hoping you can shed some more light on what happened.'

Mr Barker returned to the room, having let the dog out. 'I didn't know anything about it until he returned from hospital.' He looked from Sarah to Richie. 'Can I get either of you a drink?'

Richie was about to decline when Sarah spoke up. 'A glass of water would be lovely, thanks.' She turned back to Timmy as his husband left the room. 'I know there's a lot of water under the bridge between you and Cora with regards to the bookshop, but let's look at the bigger picture here. Millie's life is in danger. You don't want to be seen in the Slayton Facebook group as the person who stood in our way.'

Timmy's mouth dropped open. It closed again. Then it opened once more. He was beginning to resemble a goldfish as he struggled to find the words. If the possibility of his husband finding out about his blackmailing didn't swing things, then the threat of exposure on the private Facebook group might. The sound of his husband returning to the room helped Timmy to find his voice.

'I may be able to help. But let's keep the Facebook group between us.'

Sarah nodded, the corners of her mouth lifting in a smile. She'd heard it said around town that Timmy was an incurable gossip. Perhaps his sensible husband had been trying to rein him in. As he returned with a glass of water, Sarah guessed that Timmy's memory was about to make a sudden return.

'It's funny what goes through your head in times of stress,' Timmy said, his fleshy hands clasped on his lap. 'I came to at the end, only briefly mind, but it was just as the intruder was leaving with Millie in his arms.' He glanced at his husband, who delivered an encouraging nod. 'I remember wondering how a criminal could afford a pair of five-hundred-pound designer shoes.' Sarah arched an eyebrow. Of all the things to recall.

'Right,' she said, turning the page of her notebook. 'Let's have a description of these shoes.'

Chapter 49

'You never fail to amaze me, Sarah.' Richie turned down the police radio before pulling away from the junction. 'I thought you were going in there, all guns blazing, but you played him like a fiddle.'

'To be fair, I did go in there pre-armed. I knew that he was married to Mr Barker, and that he'd got himself into trouble for snooping in the past.'

'Who told you that?'

'Another snooper.' Sarah laughed.

'Elsie?' Richie knew about her friendship group and remembered Elsie from school. But Sarah was in no rush to include him in their social events. Within minutes of meeting Richie, Elsie would be working out a romance plot for her next book.

'She's part of this private Facebook group. She knows all the goings-on.' She pulled back her sleeve to check her watch. 'I should have just enough time to write all this lot up before the briefing.' Timmy had given them a full account this time, although nothing had immediately stood out.

'Are you doing anything tonight?' Richie cut into her thoughts.

'If you're after another board game then you're barking up the wrong tree. My brain feels like cotton wool today.'

'No change there then.' Richie activated the car indicator as they turned left. 'I was wondering if you'd like to go out for a drink . . . maybe a meal, if we finish on time?' He stared straight ahead at the road, his grip firm on the steering wheel. Was he asking her out on a date? 'I know a nice Italian . . .' He swallowed. 'I was thinking we could . . .'

But his words were interrupted by a point-to-point call. Sarah activated her radio, turning it up loud. Gabby came through on the other end. 'Where are you?'

'On our way back, sarge. We won't be long.'

'Good. Don't delay. There's been a major development.' She didn't elaborate and the call dropped out.

'Where have you two been?' Yvonne greeted them in the hall as she came out of the staff toilets, drying her hands on the back of her skirt.

'What's happened?' Sarah was breathless with excitement at the prospect of another lead. 'Has Millie been found?'

'Not yet.' The click of Yvonne's heels echoed down the hall.

'Is it Cora? Has she been nicked?' Richie said, almost hopefully. He hated being proved wrong.

'Cora's gone AWOL. She didn't sign on at the station today. But that's not the big news.' A slight smile played on her face. She was enjoying the drama and Sarah couldn't blame her. She was itching to know herself.

Chapter 50

The clues were there, and officers had actively investigated them, but Sarah still couldn't comprehend the news. Dr Osmond really was back from the dead. The office was alive with chatter, and Gabby and McGuire were in deep conversation. For once, she wasn't scowling at him, which made a nice change. The briefing had been held and a team was being assembled. Sarah knew she should *want* to join the team on the hunt to chase him down, but something held her back. A deep dive into Osmond's finances had revealed a cyber-footprint which spanned years. Thanks to updated technology and specialist, trained officers, they had pinpointed him to an address in London which he had frequented nine months previously. There was no guarantee he was still there, but a team of officers were wasting no time. His faked death had evidently been meticulously planned. Thanks to Sophia Hudson's persistence and knowledge, they had tracked down Michael's dental records and matched them with the images taken of the skeletal remains. Sophia was as sure as she could be that the body in the bunker had been Michael, not Dr Osmond.

'Do you think he has Cora?' Sarah whispered to Richie. The young mother's safeguarding was at the forefront of Sarah's mind.

'She might have done a runner. Just because Osmond's alive, it doesn't mean he's taken her baby. But at least we're closing in on him.'

'So yous aren't joining us, Noble?' McGuire pressed the Velcro straps of his stab vest in place.

'I'll man the fort in case Cora gets back in touch.'

'Good thinking,' he said, before turning to leave. He had done well to get the operation organised in record time.

'Stay out of trouble,' Gabby said sternly, before leaving the office.

'I'll text you when I can.' Richie briefly touched Sarah's arm. A moment of unfinished business passed between them.

'Thank you,' Sarah mouthed. Then he was gone, along with the others on a three-hour drive. They could have requested a local unit, but McGuire had pushed for his team to go. Now it was just her and Yvonne covering the office in their absence. This was good news. So why did Sarah feel like she was caught in a gathering storm? She turned to Yvonne. 'Would you like a coffee?'

'No thank you.' Yvonne was tight-lipped, stabbing the keyboard with her fingers as she typed up a report. She was obviously miffed about being left behind. But Yvonne had wronged their sergeant in the past. Gabby was hardly going to do her any favours.

Sarah sat at her desk, absorbing the silence now everybody had left. She picked up her phone and tried Cora's number, sighing in frustration as she realised it was switched off. Perhaps she had run off with Millie and the whole story of her disappearance had been a ruse. But Osmond was alive. Cora had been right all along. Maybe he *had* returned to visit her, and the police would find her at his London abode. He had killed before. Had he done it again?

She sat, hunched over her desk as she carried out mundane tasks. It was easy to get overwhelmed by paperwork, and she did her best to keep on top of it. Everyone knew of good officers who didn't pass probation because they lacked the self-discipline to stay ahead of the inevitable admin. Standards were high for a reason. Cora's case was evidence of that. When the pressure was on, corners were cut, and evidence overlooked. Sarah imagined the officer in charge, pressured to find a quick outcome for the case because he was buried beneath his workload.

Having finished her report, Sarah checked her emails, which seemed to have reproduced. Yvonne was on the phone, having what sounded like a domestic with her other half. Usually, their telephone arguments were confined to the station loos. Sarah clicked through her emails, her attention drawn to the supplier of dermestid beetles. She had contacted several in the UK, but none had reported any interesting leads . . . until now. She read and re-read the email, which gave an address. It had been a large delivery of beetles, and the purchaser had paid with crypto currency, meaning the seller had no access to their name. But the address given wasn't in London. In fact, it wasn't that far away. Sarah's pulse picked up speed as she printed off the email. She opened her mouth to tell Yvonne, but her argument was well underway.

'I'm just popping out,' she mouthed to her colleague, but was met with a scowl. She would take her own car so as not to spook anyone. After all, the police had their suspect. It was Osmond – wasn't it?

Chapter 51

What if I'm wrong? Sarah thought, as Gabby's warning to stay out of trouble echoed in her mind. But she was simply making a house call, like she'd done a thousand times before. It could be nothing. The flesh-eating beetles weren't even delivered to this address. But they *were* delivered to a post office box in a sorting facility a short distance away. The same facility she'd seen the occupant of this house come out of more than once. It paid to be attentive in Sarah's line of work.

Another thought entered her mind. *What if she was right?* A tug on her gut had prevented her from joining her colleagues. Something niggled, just out of reach. But what did it mean? As she pulled up to the close, she hoped to find out. Upper Walk Close was a pretty location, with generous front gardens. Some were filled with rose bushes of every shape and colour. Other gardens had gnomes and flower baskets. The place held a sense of an older generation, with its tended lawns and garden furniture. Some of the bungalows had wheelchair access ramps, but not the address she was visiting today. She smiled to herself as a set of curtains twitched. Some things never changed.

She strode to the front door, head up, shoulders back. She was a lot more aware these days of the image she portrayed to the world. It had been too humid to wear her suit, but her black trousers and patterned blouse were smart enough. The sky was heavy with impending darkness and the rumble of thunder made Sarah's shoulder's rise. She tugged the strap of her tote bag over her shoulder then pressed the doorbell while mentally orchestrating her words. They were momentarily forgotten as Mrs Duffy answered the door.

It was the look on her face that did it. The expression of fear laced with inevitability that gave Sarah pause. For the briefest of seconds, she wondered if she wanted to step inside. 'Hello again. Can I have a quick word?'

'Of course. Come in.' Mrs Duffy checked over Sarah's shoulder, her words spoken through a nervous smile. 'Are you on your own?'

'Yes, it's just me for now.' Sarah stepped inside, inhaling the clove-like scent of the lilies bunched in a vase in the hall. She was led into a clean and modern kitchen, which had slate tiles and spotlights overhead. Sarah took a seat at the table as Paula calmly insisted on making a pot of tea. 'Peter's out. I'm not sure when he'll be back.'

There was something off kilter about the woman's behaviour as she stood with her back to Sarah. As Mrs Duffy hummed beneath her breath, a little piece of her felt oddly disengaged. Sarah scanned her surroundings as she rested the strap of her tote bag on the chair. At least she'd had the presence of mind to bring her police radio and update her status as making enquiries at the address. Kitchens were the most potentially dangerous room in the house. Most back doors were locked, and it took precious seconds to escape out the front. There were knife blocks and drawers filled with instruments which could be weaponised.

'Do you mind if I use your bathroom?' As she waited for the tea, Sarah couldn't resist a quick snoop.

'Down the end of the hall on the left.' Mrs Duffy didn't turn around.

The hall carpet was deep and soft, the walls brightened with mirrors and landscape art. Sarah peeped into each room as she listened for the slightest sound. The door to the last bedroom creaked too loudly for her liking as she pushed it ajar. She flicked on the light. It seemed like an innocent setting, the bed dressed in plumped cushions and a floral quilt. A pair of cream, floor-length curtains were closed. There were books on the side cabinets and a cross above the bed. Sarah tip-toed around the room. There were no secret cupboards, no collection of skulls on the wall. But as she turned to leave, she saw the reason for her earlier suspicions and her feet felt rooted to the floor. A pair of Gucci tan leather moccasins were on the floor at the end of the bed. Finally, she understood the niggle at the back of her mind. These were the distinctive shoes that Timmy described when she visited his home. 'It's strange,' he'd said, as his memory miraculously returned. 'I remember wondering how a criminal could afford a pair of five-hundred-pound designer shoes.'

Sarah recognised the detail of the interlocking G horse-bit, because Timmy had showed her the same pair online. They were the same distinctive black soled, tan leather moccasins that Father Duffy had been wearing the day Sarah interviewed him and his wife. But unlike Timmy, she'd thought nothing of it at the time. Not until Timmy relayed his description. She knew she'd seen them somewhere before. Evidentially, it wasn't enough to go on. But that, along with the nearby delivery of the beetles, and Mrs Duffy's odd behaviour . . .

'Your tea is ready.' Sarah jumped as she realised Mrs Duffy was watching her from the hall.

'Oh! Sorry. I em . . . got a bit lost.' Sarah cleared her throat.

'You're not very good at lying, are you, Sarah?' Paula smiled stiffly, as if telling off an errant child. 'You'll have to get your act together if you intend on staying in the police.' Sarah wanted to ask who the real liar was as she silently followed Paula back into the kitchen and took her seat at the table. But this was not a time to be affronted. It was time to listen, because Paula had something to say.

'Peter's not as good a liar as he thinks he is.' Paula's crockery tinkled. It was disturbing, her sense of calmness, as she poured tea from the pot. 'My husband is careless. Always has been. But it's worse when he's off his meds.' She handed Sarah the tea she hadn't asked for.

'Mrs Duffy, do you know anything about . . .' Sarah began.

'Please, call me Paula,' she interrupted. 'No need for formalities now.' She pulled out a chair and sat. 'You're here to make an arrest, aren't you? It's written all over your face.'

Sarah nodded. All the cards were on the table now. 'Where are Cora and Millie? Are they safe?'

'Of course they're safe.' But there was an edge to Paula's voice. 'Shortbread? I baked it myself.' She nudged the plate towards her as if it were the most normal thing in the world.

Sarah tried to swallow but her throat was dry. She had expected denial. Shouting. Tears. She could use her police radio and call this in, but what would she say? There was no sign of Millie. For all Sarah knew, Paula could be lying. She needed hard evidence. 'Where are they?' Sarah glanced around the room. 'Do these houses come with bunkers too?'

'Of course not.' Paula's gaze bored into Sarah. 'I'll tell you where they are. But only when you have the full history. You'll see things differently then.'

'A baby's life is at stake,' Sarah reminded her, her heart beating hard in her chest. 'He's killed before, hasn't he? He fathered the baby in the lake. Tell me where he is before he does it again.'

'I thought you would have worked it out by now.' Paula fell into a thoughtful silence as she rested her cup on the saucer.

'My husband didn't kill Cora's baby . . . I did.'

Chapter 52

Sarah wasn't buying Paula's admission. She couldn't contemplate the woman before her killing a newborn with her bare hands. 'You don't need to cover for him.' She tensed, ready to call for backup. 'I know he took Millie. Where are they, Paula?'

But Paula was determined to have her say. 'The first time Cora came to us, I fell a little bit in love with her. We both did. She was scared, desperate for any scrap of affection. I felt needed for the first time in years.' Her eyes glazed over as she revisited the past. 'Peter was so busy with his work. Always there for his parishioners. But what about me?' She turned to Sarah, her eyes burning with pain as she poked herself in the chest. 'What about *my* needs? We lived more like brother and sister than husband and wife.' The revelation was followed by a series of mumbles beneath her breath.

Sarah had the feeling that Paula's anger had bubbled under the surface for years. But she was telling it to the wrong person. 'An address,' Sarah said forcefully. 'I need an address.'

Paula's jaw set, her eyes on fire. 'Not. Until. I've had my SAY!' She punctuated the words with a slam of her fist onto the kitchen table. The crockery rattled from the force. It seemed meek and mild Paula had teeth.

'OK,' Sarah held her hands up. 'Then tell me. But please, make it quick.'

Paula settled back into her chair, her face at rest again. 'It felt nice to be needed. I thought that Cora cared. But everything changed the second time she came. I didn't recognise the girl. She was out all hours, forever bunking off school, even picked up a few swear words along the way.' Paula shook her head. 'Sometimes I got through to her. She'd let me brush her hair. It was like flax back then.'

'How long have you known?' Sarah said, desperate to move her narrative on. Precious seconds were passing. Time she could not afford.

But Paula picked up the teapot and topped up her tea. 'Had I known what had gone on between them, I would have put a stop to it. But by the time I found out, it was too late.'

'Found out what?' Sarah broke through the silence that followed as Paula seemed to drift away.

'That he and Cora had a special relationship. You see, he wasn't thinking straight back then. He'd stopped taking his medication. It wasn't his fault.'

Paula sighed, stirring another sugar into her tea. 'It started with the bones. He became fascinated by them, but they led him to a dark place. His mother once told me that he liked dissecting things as a child. I couldn't equate it with the man I knew back then.' She continued to stir. 'But there are two sides to Peter. The kind, loving man of God, and the part of him that I can't reach.' The clink of her spoon against the china cup felt like the loudest sound in the world. 'When my mother was alive, I used to stay over at her place once a week. One night I came home early and let myself in. That's when I saw Peter, coming out of Cora's room. I could tell by the look on his face that something wasn't right. Later, I went in to check on her, but she was out for the count.' She paused to clear her throat. 'The voices made him do it. He has a mental illness that he fights to keep under control.' Paula absent-mindedly added another spoonful of sugar. She began stirring it so hard the tea slopped over the edges of the cup. Slowly, Sarah took the spoon from her grip and moved the tea aside.

'What did he do, Paula?'

There was conflict in Paula's eyes as she finally met her gaze. But there was thunder there too. 'You won't understand. He's not a well man.'

'Then make me understand,' Sarah encouraged. She quickly ran through a caution in order to cover herself.

'He used to put something in her hot chocolate to help her to sleep. That's when he . . .' Paula closed her eyes. She released the breath she had been holding, unable to say the words. 'I think Abel had his suspicions that something was going on.'

Sarah sat, absorbing Paula's account. Cora was so drugged during

Peter's visitations that they must have felt like a lucid dream. No wonder she had problems taking a firm hold of reality.

'I confronted my husband,' Paula continued, her chin tilted upwards. 'Made sure he took his medication. We were back on track. But months later, Peter delivered a bombshell. Cora was pregnant with his child. Then he said that it was a blessing. That we could raise it as our own. I hated that girl more than I've hated anyone in my life.'

Sarah supressed her disgust as Paula made excuses. They had fostered a vulnerable, young girl and taken advantage of her. How could Paula defend the man who had turned Cora's nightmares into real life? Dr Osmond may have lived on, but it was Peter who had carried out the most heinous crime against her. After everything Cora had been through.

'I decided to have it out with her, away from Peter.' In the silence of the room, Paula was oblivious to Sarah's disgust. 'I knew where she was because I'd followed her before.'

'Go on,' Sarah urged. She was getting to the meat of it now.

'She used to go to an old barn on a derelict farmyard. She felt safer out in open spaces. Anything to get away from the memory of being stuck in that bunker, I suppose.' Paula stared into the distance as she recalled the past. 'It was a wickedly cold and wet night. I went into the barn with my flashlight. First, I saw the pram. But it was empty, so I looked around some more. I heard breathing on the top floor of the barn and climbed up the ladder to get there. It was rickety. I almost lost my torch. Then I saw Cora, passed out on some hay. She'd rather lie in filth than in her beautiful bedroom at home.' She snorted in disapproval. 'I thought she'd overdosed. It wouldn't have surprised me if she was on drugs. That's when I noticed the blood . . .'

As she sat in the gleaming kitchen, Sarah could visualise the scene, which was a world away from Cora's account. But was Paula telling the truth? Lines of concern creased Sarah's forehead as she monitored Paula's face.

'I was about to give Cora a shake when I realised she'd already given birth.' Paula clasped her hands together, her knuckles white. 'The baby was wrapped up next to her . . . It looked like she was sleeping. That button nose. The tuft of black hair . . . The sense of betrayal stabbed me like a knife. All I could see was Peter. I was shaking with anger. Ugly words left my mouth in whispers. Ones I'd never spoken in my life. But I couldn't help it. The sight of that *bastard* child . . .' Paula's voice cracked. She took a breath. Reined in her emotions.

'Cora was out of it. There was a half-empty bottle of vodka by her side. I . . . I don't know what I was thinking, but I picked up the baby and held it in my arms. It was so tiny, and I saw straight away that its skin tone wasn't right. A part of me wanted to keep it. Another part wanted to make it all go away. I headed towards the ladder. I wanted to take something precious from Cora, just as she had taken from me. I remember the sound of the rain as it hammered on the roof. It was dark. I couldn't see. The whole place was unstable . . .'

Dread washed over Sarah, and she listened with reluctance as the scene played out. Paula exhaled a juddering breath as she took herself back to that night. 'I was climbing down the ladder when I lost my footing and I . . .' Paula broke eye contact.

'What?' Sarah felt sick as she waited for confirmation.

'I dropped the baby. She fell from my arms onto the concrete floor below.' Paula exhaled a long breath, her confession taking its toll.

Silence stretched out between them. Paula's eyes cut to Sarah, her voice low. 'I . . . I climbed down the rest of the ladder. I walked past the baby. There was blood . . . She never made a sound. I walked all the way home. I closed the blinds, lay on my bed and waited for the police to come. But they never did. Every day got a little easier after that.'

'Christ,' Sarah said beneath her breath. 'And Cora? What about her?' Paula had conveniently glossed over the young woman's feelings.

Paula's face soured at the mention of her name. 'I never saw her again.'

'And Peter?'

'We never discussed it. He was back on his meds by then. Life carried on as normal.'

'But it hasn't carried on as normal, has it Paula?' Sarah's tone was laced with bitterness as Paula failed to take responsibility. 'Cora and Millie are missing. What have you done with them?'

'I'll show you. But only you. My husband needs to be handled gently. I'm not having a load of police officers stressing him out.'

'Stressing *him* out?' Sarah exclaimed, unable to keep her emotions in check. 'What if he thinks Cora killed his baby? What's to stop him doing the same in return? He's bought flesh-eating beetles, for God's sake!' Sarah remembered how Elliott had warned of the danger Millie was in. He'd mentioned something about a bad energy being angry about the baby in the pram. She pushed back her chair, fighting the urge to give the woman a good shake.

'I . . . I don't know about any of that stuff.' Paula's skin turned pale, despite the rising temperature. 'But either we go together or not at all.'

'Then I'll arrest you.'

Like a belligerent child, Paula folded her arms. 'Then do it. But you won't hear another word from me. I married my husband for better or worse. I'm willing to give him the benefit of the doubt.'

'But this isn't Peter, is it? You said it yourself: he's not well.'

'All the more reason for us to go now. You can call for backup once I've had a chance to talk to him. I'm not having this blown out of all proportion.'

'Come on then,' Sarah said, as Paula picked out a set of car keys from a bowl on a dresser 'There's no time to spare.'

Chapter 53

Sarah told herself that she could handle this. That Father Duffy wasn't a murderer so history wouldn't repeat itself – Elliott hadn't been wrong yet. Paula's account was horrific, and she would be held to account. But right now, Sarah's focus was on getting Millie and Cora home safe. But as Paula parked her car at the side of the run-down country cottage, Sarah's sense of dread grew. Her stomach churned as she imagined what awaited her. She picked up her tote bag from the car footwell. Her police airwaves had GPS, and she would call for backup the moment she stepped inside.

As Mrs Duffy placed her hand on the car door panel, Sarah issued a warning. 'Wait here. I can't have you getting caught up in this.'

'But you said I could come with you. Please. He doesn't know that I know.'

Sarah's annoyance grew as Paula spoke without a thought for Cora or her baby. 'I said you could show me where he was. You can speak to him when he comes out. We don't know what we're walking into.'

'But . . .'

'Open that door and I'll have you arrested for perverting the course of justice,' Sarah snapped.

Mrs Duffy slumped in her seat. Now they were at the cottage, Paula had lost her leverage and had no choice but to stay put. Sarah gave her one last look. 'If I'm not out in ten minutes, call the police. Tell them there's an officer who needs urgent backup and to send a local unit right away.' She couldn't believe she was uttering the words. What had started out as a simple enquiry had escalated fast. But she couldn't take chances where Cora's kidnapper was involved.

Paula's eyes were wide as she responded with a nod. Would she report her own husband? She had led Sarah this far. Sarah hoped she wouldn't have to find out. She recalled the embarrassment when she'd acted impulsively in the past, smashing a car window to rescue a doll on a hot day. This time, she would be sensible. There was no point in sending the calvary if Father Duffy wasn't here. Paula might not know her husband as well as she thought. Sarah's footsteps were quiet as she negotiated the overgrown path, flanked by crumbling garden gnomes. To the right, a moss-lined bird bath was gripped by vines climbing up the side. A sudden strike of lightning crackled in the distance, making Sarah wince. The storm was finally breaking. She could deal with many things in life, but each boom of thunder put her on edge.

The tiny front door was locked. She peered through a grime-streaked window. The curtains were open a crack, enough to see low, beamed ceilings and a soot-stained inglenook fireplace. The space had been a living room once. Walking around the back, she gave the back door handle a squeeze. Nothing. A prickling sensation at the back of her neck told her she was at the right place. Then she heard it: faint, grizzly crying coming from inside. Sarah's adrenaline spiked. She needed to get inside, but the last thing she wanted was to break the glass and alert whoever was in there. She reached into her tote bag. It was time to call for backup. She should have had a text from Richie by now. She rooted around in her bag. A packet of tissues, a battered box of plasters, some lippy, a compact, her police issue notebook. But her fingers were yet to grip the hard plastic of her police radio – or her mobile phone. Her heart tripped in her chest as she parted the handles and peered inside. They were gone.

'Paula,' she whispered, a swear word skimming her lips. She must have taken them when Sarah went to the hall for a snoop. Another grizzling cry was all it took for Sarah to forge ahead. There was no time to waste.

She peered around the undergrowth before picking up a piece of loose sack cloth. After shaking it free of spiders, she wrapped it around a rock. Gently, she tapped it against the small pane of glass on the back door. A black cloud of blowflies buzzed angrily past as they made their escape through the broken glass. An old saying of Richie's came into mind. *Where there's buzzers, there's bodies.* That was not a good sign. Sarah held her breath as she waited for someone to come. But there was nothing, and after clearing a path, she pushed her hand in through the hole and turned the key in the lock. What was Paula up to? Was she obediently waiting outside? If she was devious enough to take her radio, what else was she capable of? Backup wasn't coming. Sarah was on her own.

Chapter 54

Sarah had barely opened the door when the smell hit her with force. 'Oh God,' she said quietly, catching sight of blood stippling the kitchen sink. She stared at the dark red pattern which had emanated from the remnants of a rat. Its body was slit open, its innards leaking into the porcelain sink. Sarah's stomach rolled as she took in the rest of the room. More angry blowflies bumped against windowpanes, their low hum providing an eerie backdrop. Her armpits were damp, a trickle of sweat rolling down the curve of her back. The hollow groan of wind emerged from another room. *It's the fireplace,* Sarah reassured herself as she got to grips with her surroundings. Richie would be trying to call her. Control could track her police radio via GPS. But it wasn't here. It was in Upper Walk Close.

She didn't have time to linger over the instruments next to the sink, or the splatters of blood drying on the surfaces. She even felt a moment of sympathy for another dead rodent, its small furry body mangled beneath a trap. But it was the stench of rotting meat that almost forced Sarah back. She dodged the long strips of sticky-backed fly traps hanging from the ceiling. This was a place of death.

Dust-coated kitchen ornaments and dried silk flowers were juxtaposed with the ungodly smell. Sarah crept through the room as another rumble of thunder filled the outside air. Most likely, Mrs Duffy was on the phone to her husband, warning him. Had he been here, he would have discovered her by now. Pulling her sleeve over her hand, she opened the old-fashioned fridge freezer. A row of made-up baby bottles gave her hope. Millie was here. She hadn't imagined her cry. Tilting her head to one side, Sarah heard the meek moans of a baby from another room. Her fingers found the handle of a blood-splattered butcher's knife. She eased her grip around the wooden handle, feeling determined as darkness closed in. In times like this, with shadows creeping around her, Sarah felt strangely at home. She had faced up to worse than this and survived. She padded into the corridor, broken glass scrunching beneath her feet. A small, cracked picture frame held a black and white photo of a couple from long ago. Evidence of the previous owner was all around, but these items clearly weren't valued by the current occupant.

Sarah's breath locked in her throat as she sensed another presence. Heart thumping against her ribcage, she followed her instincts to a door at the end of the hall.

The further she walked down the corridor, the more the sour smell intensified. She rested her hand on the doorknob. Had she heard a baby cry? Or was it a residue of the violence that had occurred in this space? Did she really want to know what was behind the door?

Chapter 55

The door was heavy on its hinges as it opened. Sarah blinked in the dim light, adjusting her eyes to the darkness. She gripped the knife, her other hand reaching for a light switch. Her heart melted at the now clear sound of the crying baby, but where was Cora? She flicked on the switch and her senses were bombarded by the scene. Cora, unconscious and strapped to an old-fashioned dentist's chair, her head lolling to one side. Millie, emitting the hoarse whine of an infant who'd been left crying for too long. Row upon row of skulls lining the walls, hollowed eyes staring down at her. Instruments on the table. Knives, drills . . . a bone saw. A bloodied apron hanging from a hook. A hand-drawn sketch of a skeleton sellotaped to a glass cabinet, with the list of steps required to strip bone from flesh. This was too much, even for her.

It took two steady breaths for her police training to kick in. She took the baby in her arms, the most vulnerable person in the room. 'Hey there,' she said, wiping Millie's tear-stained face. She rested her against her shoulder, soothing and patting as Millie shuddered and hiccupped in her arms.

'Cora!' Sarah spoke in a harsh whisper, balancing Millie while holding the knife in her other hand. 'Wake up!'

She carefully sliced at each of the leather bindings on her wrists and ankles. But Cora groaned, her body floppy as she struggled to wake. How the hell was Sarah going to get them all out? She scanned the room. There was little here to help her. Maybe if she took the baby and . . . but then she saw the dots of red pen marks on Cora's skin. The sick bastard had already planned to take her apart.

'Cora!' she said again, gently slapping her face. 'You've got to walk yourself out of here. I can't carry you both.'

'Wha . . . ?' Cora moaned, blinking as Sarah held the baby in her arms.

'That's it. Now focus. Get to your feet. We haven't got much time.' Cora's eyes widened and she parted her lips as she tried to gargle a warning. But it came too late. Sarah's head jolted to one side as it was met with sudden force. Her vision dazzled with stars as strong arms wrenched the baby from her arms. Her knees crumpled as she fell heavily to the floor. Sarah couldn't think. Couldn't focus as she was dragged to the corner of the room. She hadn't seen Father Duffy coming, but he had seen her. A stream of warm blood dribbled over her closed eye and down the side of her cheek. She was conscious, but instinct and experience drove her to make herself small and quiet. She forced her body into a state of limpness, her head falling to one side as she kept both eyes closed.

'You've killed her.' Paula's voice rose, sharp and brittle in the room. 'Peter, what have you done?'

Sarah supressed her rising anger as she realised that she had been betrayed. She listened out for Cora, but the only sound was that of Peter pacing as his voice rebounded around the room.

'She's not dead. Just out cold. Shut that baby up, before anyone else hears.'

'You don't mean?'

'I mean there's a dummy on the table. Stick it in her mouth and put her back in her crib.' His words were tempered with anger, so unlike the softly spoken man Sarah had encountered in the past.

'What are you going to do with her?' Paula's voice was trembling. She must have warned him of Sarah's presence, but now she was in over her head. Sarah's head pounded from her injury, the ground hard beneath her outstretched legs.

'I'm going to finish this,' he said sharply.

'But, Peter . . . think about what you're doing. You . . . you're not well.'

'You brought her here!' Peter growled. 'What were you thinking?'

Paula whimpered as her husband turned on her. 'I . . . I don't know. I just wanted it all to stop.'

'And it will. Soon. Nobody else knows she's here?'

'I got rid of her radio. She even told me to call for backup if she didn't come out.'

'Good.' His deadened voice was chilling.

Sarah cautiously opened one eye as the noise of metal against metal rose. He was sharpening his tools. A cold sense of dread washed over her as she tried to figure a way out. She was outnumbered and not physically strong enough to fight them, so how were they going to get out of this alive?

Chapter 56

Oh, Cora, what a troublesome girl you've turned out to be. I thought we were destined to be together, but now I don't know. Surely it was more than coincidence that I bought your father's collection of bones all those years ago? Something changed when I came into contact with my favourite piece, Charlotte, the human skull. When I heard about what had happened, and your subsequent escape, I felt compelled to track you down. It felt like fate when we were accepted to take you into our home. If I'd have known of the heartache you'd cause us, I would have left well alone. But all I could do was follow my instincts and bring our relationship to an end.

I was shopping for supplies when the phone call from my wife came. My mind was so filled with thoughts of you, that I almost let it go to voicemail. But guilt rose and I pressed the phone against my ear. Paula has her own special ringtone, you see. She has struggled to accept this part of me, which grows stronger by the day. But as much as I enjoy my separate life, she is my bedrock.

Seeing you again rejuvenated my senses. Watching you fret over your offspring made me feel alive. My plan has always been for retribution. But the more time I spent with your baby, the more I thought of how much Paula wanted a child of her own. She loved you, Cora, and was rewarded by betrayal in return. It wasn't my fault that we had sex. I knew there was a reason you had come into my life and I was helpless to resist. Drugs softened the edges of our moral constraints. You know, for a while I fooled myself that we could be a family after our baby arrived. Then you disposed of her like she was nothing, not even giving her the courtesy of a Christian funeral.

An eye for an eye . . . I vowed to repay your malevolence. When all those crows dropped dead it was a portent of what was to come. Today, I told myself, I would dispose of you both. But then Paula called, and my world shifted once more. Everything I thought I knew about my wife was wrong. It turned out that she loved and accepted me just as I was. Her voice was breathy and urgent as she told me to get back to the cottage that I presumed she knew nothing about. 'The police are here,' she said. 'They're breaking into the back of your cottage.' I almost dropped my shopping basket in the middle of Tesco. Instead, I gently placed it on the ground, turned on my heel and walked outside.

'How many are there?' I asked, feeling sick at the thought.

'Just the one. Detective Noble. Nobody else knows she's here.' She was panting with panic, her breath ruffling the line. 'Get over here, before she realises her radio is gone.' Her voice continued through my car speakers as I sped to the cottage, cursing my carelessness. Above me, the skies rumbled and flashed their discontent. My fingers gripped the steering wheel as Paula said the same three words she had told me once before. 'I know everything.' I hadn't expected that, Cora, after everything we'd done. Why would she stay with me?

I told her that I could explain, but she didn't wait for me to finish. She said she didn't want me to go to prison. That we could move away. Be a family again. But then she told me to deal with the detective. 'Her and that bitch who started this.'

I couldn't believe what I was hearing. Was Paula really willing to give me another chance? That's what real loyalty is, Cora. But you wouldn't understand that.

'This is a trap, isn't it?' I asked her, dreading the answer. But Paula continued to surprise me.

As she spoke, it was clear that I was not the only person with plans. She said we could move away, take the baby and start somewhere else. And we had money. Lots of it, from all those old dears she knew I'd been visiting over the years. We'd call Millie our own. Start again. 'That's what you want, isn't it?' she said hopefully. But it all hinged on me cleaning up my mess before it was too late.

I told her I was on my way and to keep an eye on things until I got there. I'd been thrown a lifeline. I thought about all the work I'd put into the cottage. About my bone collection and how we would have to leave it all behind. But I was being granted permission to finish my greatest work, with the approval of the only woman in the world I had ever loved. Do you hear that, Cora? You were nothing but an obsession.

All my wife asked for in return was a baby to call her own. After what you did, I owed her that much. I told her to keep the detective there. To say she'd called for help – whatever it took. Then I said I loved her. She told me to hurry up. It was too soon for her to reciprocate. I prayed she was telling the truth and I wasn't walking into a trap.

I saw Paula waiting by her car as I drove down the bumpy brambled path. There were no police cars, no sirens in the distance to break the night. Nothing except the rumble of a thunderstorm overhead. Lightning cracked in the sky, and the hairs on the back of my arms rose. Quietly, Paula led me inside, but I was still waiting for the hammer to fall. It was only when I heard Sarah Noble's voice urging Cora to wake up that I realised Paula had been telling the truth. Then I saw her, with Millie on her shoulder, in my house, interfering in my plans. Hot anger surged as I picked up my sandbag and swung it at the detective's head. She crumpled, but not before I could support her, and Paula took the baby from her arms. Her eyes glittered in amazement as she held the child to her chest.

'My baby,' she said softly. 'At last.'

Chapter 57

Sarah resisted the instinct to wipe the blood that was streaming down one side of her face. She kept movement to a minimum as her sense of self-preservation kicked in. Squinting through her one good eye, she assessed the situation. A flash of lightning lit the room. Help wasn't coming. Peter had an accomplice, and the baby was her prize. She could not overpower both of them, but she could put a hairline crack through this family of three. Cora was lying back on the chair, a stream of drool trickling from her mouth.

Sarah watched as Paula turned to lower Millie in her crib. Peter was bending over the sink, mumbling beneath his breath. Sarah's glance fell on the knife that she had rested to one side. *Now or never,* she thought, launching herself up from the floor with surprising strength. Adrenaline pumping, she grabbed the knife. As Paula spun around, Sarah grabbed a handful of her hair and pushed the knife to her throat. She grunted with the exertion, turning Paula into a human shield. All she needed was her phone to get her out of this hellhole. Paula's high-pitched wail filled the room, her hands tearing at Sarah's arms as she reached for the knife.

'Back off or I slit her throat,' Sarah growled, as Peter advanced upon her. Sarah pushed the blade against Paula's skin. 'Stop struggling, or I'll do it.' The woman immediately complied, whining for her husband to do something.

Peter stared with dead eyes, his bulk looming over her. There was a slight shake in his hands, but not enough to make him any less menacing. 'You won't win. There's no way out. You'll have to get past me first.' He looked her up and down, as if sizing her up for his next macabre display. But Sarah didn't need to walk past him. In fact, she didn't need to leave.

'Stay very still,' Sarah whispered into Paula's ear, as she reached into her trouser pocket for her mobile phone. Peter's glare widened as he realised what she was doing. He took another step. Sarah blinked as the sight in one eye was coated in a film of red. Her head was throbbing, her legs weak. 'Stay back!' she yelled, stepping backwards. 'Or I'll cut her!'

Her threat stilled his movements. 'Then you'll go to prison,' he said in a measured voice. 'If you harm a hair on my wife's head, I'll tell them that you set out to hurt her from the start.'

But Sarah wasn't listening. She was too busy dialling 999. Why didn't he run? Just leave them to it? Cold realisation dawned. He still thought he could kill her, take the baby and get away. Sarah reeled off her address to the call taker, asking for urgent assistance.

'Please! Help me!' Paula screamed over her. 'The officer has a knife to my throat!'

'Come quickly!' Peter joined in. 'She's going to kill my wife!' Sarah couldn't believe what she was hearing as Peter babbled and begged for her to show mercy. 'Please don't hurt her.' A glint in his eye grew malevolent. He was trying to corner Sarah, making it impossible for her to defend herself.

Peter extended a hand to his wife, mouthing at her to join him. In the distance, the scream of sirens competed against shards of lightning as they pierced the night sky. Sarah silently thanked whatever higher power was watching over her. There must have been officers patrolling nearby, or they would never have got here this fast.

'Get back!' Sarah shouted, as Peter approached. The ground was slick beneath her feet as her blood pooled on the floor. Peter was right. She wouldn't hurt his wife. But the second the woman returned to her husband, Peter could kill them all. Sarah's limbs felt like water, her balance off kilter as wooziness took hold. Peter glanced at a motionless Cora, before daring to take another step.

Sarah's arm was locked around Paula's throat, the knife firmly in her hand. But as Paula lunged towards her husband, she lost her footing on the blood-stained floor. 'No!' Peter shouted, as his wife slid from Sarah's grip. 'What have you done?'

'What?' Sarah's head swam as Millie began to wail. Disorientated, she looked down at her weapon as Paula crumpled to the floor. The knife was wet with blood.

It took just minutes for a firearms unit to appear. Mention of a knife brought the full force of the police upon them, and soon heavy boots were trampling through the house. A light was beamed in Sarah's face as a female officer roared at her to comply. She dropped the knife to the floor, dazed, as armed officers shouted at her to get on her knees and put her hands on her head. 'It was self-defence,' she managed to utter, as she was bundled outside to a waiting ambulance. She could hear Peter being arrested, screaming and bawling that Sarah had broken into the cottage and murdered his wife. Within minutes the area was surrounded by officers and a paramedic crew were guided in. Sarah's thoughts went to little Millie and her mother. At least they were OK. But she had slit Paula's throat. Her blood was still warm on Sarah's hands.

Chapter 58

Six months later

The bell above the bookshop door tinkled as Sarah walked inside. This meeting had been a long time coming. Sarah had been unable to talk about the case while she was under investigation. It was a sobering experience, being on the other side of the thin blue line. Paula Duffy was dead, and Sarah was deemed responsible. She had not quite kept out of trouble as her sergeant had demanded, but at least Cora and Millie were safe. To think, all those years, Cora had blamed herself for her baby's death. Had Paula killed the newborn infant or had the baby already been dead when she tried to steal her away? They would never know.

Sarah's call to the police had been damning as the priest screamed for mercy for his wife. It had been argued that Sarah still had PTSD, from her experiences as a child. Her colleagues had been worried, and a suspension placed her career on hold. She had leaned on Richie heavily, as he kept her up to date with work. Maggie and Elsie had been an immense support, with Elliott telling her knowingly that everything was going to be alright. Father Duffy insisted he had no intention of killing Cora but the pen marks on her skin said otherwise. According to his interview, his wife was there to support him as they offered to adopt Cora's baby. But the young woman's witness statement told a different tale. In the end Sarah would receive a commendation for the part she played in Cora's rescue while her team had been on a dead-end trail. Dr Osmond may have survived, but their intel was outdated and he had moved on.

Sarah and Cora sat in the back of the bookshop just as they had done six months before. Millie had grown. She was sitting up today, content in her travel cot as she played with a variety of toys. She looked like a little flower, in her yellow dress and white tights. So much had happened since Sarah last saw them both. They were not the same people. A woman had died at Sarah's hands, accident or not, and she could have been charged with manslaughter, instead of being NFA'd. The police may have decided on no further action, but guilt bloomed in Sarah every day since Paula's death. The woman still visited her nightmares, her lips peeled back in a rictus grin. It would be a while before Sarah could bear to pick up a sharp knife again.

'I wanted to thank you,' Sarah said to Cora. 'Your witness statement helped my case. As terrifying as prison is for civilians, you can multiply that tenfold for the police.'

Cora shrugged. 'I was only telling the truth,' she said, but the look they exchanged suggested that wasn't strictly true. Cora was barely conscious when Paula slipped on Sarah's blood. It was ironic that Peter had been the one to sharpen the knife which would kill his wife.

Cora told the police that Paula had lunged towards Peter while Sarah was trying to keep him at bay. It was true, but how much of it had she actually seen? There was no doubt he had intended to kill – Cora had the marker pen on her forehead to prove it, as well as sketches in his book. But the priest seemed intent on bringing Sarah down as he delivered lie after lie.

Much had been made in local newspapers about the 'Killer Reverend' and his wife. 'Whatever happened,' Sarah said, 'I want to thank you. I would never have deliberately hurt that woman, as awful as she was. I was just trying to buy us some time.'

'You don't need to justify it to me,' Cora smiled. 'I know it was an accident. But she deserved it. She got what was coming to her. It's karma.'

There were still loose ends to be tied up before Sarah could relax, and she knew it was the same for Cora. Dr Osmond was on the loose, having evaded them so far.

'We're going to find him.' Sarah didn't need to put a name to the man who Cora once called Daddy.

'I'm focusing on the positives.' Cora gave her a sad smile before turning her attention to Millie, who was playing with a crinkly book. She seemed unaffected by her ordeal. 'She's beautiful, isn't she? If you hadn't tracked me down, we wouldn't be here today. If there's anything you need, you only have to ask.'

'I'd say we're all square.' Sarah gave a relieved laugh.

'Almost.' Cora slid a small package across the table. 'Here's that book you ordered. You should have had it months ago.'

Sarah had forgotten all about it. She slid the hardback from the brown paper bag, stared at the cover and smiled. *Bones Don't Lie* by Sophia Hudson.

Chapter 59

Sarah ran around her kitchen, poking her head into cupboards and clanking pots and pans. Sophia had gone full-on matchmaker tonight. She'd even styled Sarah's hair and helped her apply makeup. At least she didn't have to cook. Tonight, she was cheating, and was busy transferring gourmet restaurant food into saucepans.

'Have you got any candles?' Sophia said, obviously in her element.

'In the top left cupboard,' Sarah replied. Sherlock had been relegated to the spare bedroom and was loudly expressing his discontent. Sophia tutted loudly as she found the melted down stubs of candle wax.

'These will have to do.' She looked at Sarah. 'Go! Get changed! He'll be here soon.'

As Sarah re-joined Sophia in the kitchen, she couldn't believe the scene. Soft music was playing on her Echo Dot, a lamp had been taken from the living room and placed in the corner to soften the light. A purple throw that was once on the back of the sofa now changed the look of her living room table. Plates were set, a bottle of red wine that had been purchased from the hotel was open next to two mismatching wine glasses.

'You've been busy,' Sarah said, breathless with nerves. Sophia spun around, her eyes glittering in the candlelight.

'I've loved every second.' She looked Sarah up and down. 'Wow. You look a million dollars. Why have you been hiding those curves?'

'Because there's too many of them, that's why.' Sarah tugged on the figure-hugging black dress which came to just below her knees.

Sophia chuckled. 'Look at you, all bougie in your Fendi. That's a minidress on me.'

Sarah had to admit, the Bardot-style neckline was flattering, but it could not shift her growing level of discomfort. She didn't know how much the dress cost, but the cut and material felt a lot more expensive than what she was used to.

'I don't know . . .' she muttered. 'It's not really me.'

'Then make it you, girl!' Sophia countered. 'Confidence, remember.' She checked her watch. 'I'd better be going. You told him about dinner, didn't you?'

Sarah nodded. She'd mentioned that she would cook tonight. That was as near as she got to asking Richie out on a date.

'Hey, don't look so scared, girl. The whole rabbit in the headlights thing isn't a good look. Here.' She handed her a glass of wine. 'Drink.'

'I don't think I should . . .' But the glass was thrust into her hand. Sarah took a soothing breath before knocking back half a glass.

'Good?' Sophia said.

'Yeah. I'm good.'

'I want the full low-down tomorrow. Then we can plan my divorce party.'

'Divorce?' Sarah echoed. This was news to her.

'Of course! Didn't McGuire tell you? That's the real reason I'm over here. We should have done it years ago, we just never got around to it.' She chuckled, checking her watch. 'I'd better go. Have some mad fun!' After delivering a tinkly wave, Sophia was gone. She was a modern-day fairy godmother and it all felt very surreal. At least McGuire was free to date Maggie, now he was sorting out his divorce. Sarah turned down the cooker and turned the steak on the pan. It was Sophia's idea to take the credit for the food, and the smell was mouth-watering. A flutter of nerves bubbled up inside her as the doorbell rang.

Chapter 60

It's just Richie, for God's sake, she told herself as the doorbell rang for the second time. She'd never been nervous about him visiting before. But then she usually answered wearing her jogging bottoms and a T-shirt. Before tonight, she'd barely run a hoover over the living room floor. But now she was done up like a dog's dinner and her kitchen was twinkling with candles like a scene from one of Elsie's steamy romance books. Sophia had relished organising Sarah's long overdue date, but what if it didn't work out? How would she face Richie in the office, day after day?

Sarah glanced into the hallway mirror, barely recognising herself. She searched her mind for a word to bring herself to ground. *Discombobulated,* she thought, but she suddenly knew what to do.

'Hang on!' she shouted at the door, before darting into the bathroom. She carefully blotted away the red lipstick that Sophia had insisted she wear. 'Harlot Red' wasn't for her. She smeared a smidgen of strawberry lip gloss over her lips instead. *Better,* she thought, before grabbing another tissue and dabbing some of the eyeshadow away. At least her eyebrows looked decent, given Sophia had dragged her to the beauticians to have them plucked and shaped.

'Sarah?' Richie was beginning to sound concerned. She turned on her heel and opened her front door.

Richie stood in his chinos and short-sleeved Boss shirt, a bottle of wine in one hand and his motorcycle helmet in the other. He blinked, drinking in her form. 'Wow. You look . . . amazing.'

Sarah almost told him not to be silly, before she remembered Sophia's advice about exuding confidence. 'Thanks.' She beamed, accepting the bottle of wine. If Maggie could date, then why couldn't she?

'Something smells good.' Richie sniffed the air.

'It's steak, with peppercorn sauce, carrots and dauphinoise

potatoes.' She gave him a hesitant smile as she led him into the kitchen. *God, there are so many candles*, she thought, mildly mortified as Barry White crooned on the Spotify playlist. Suddenly it all seemed too much.

'Have I missed something?' Richie glanced at the set table, taking everything in. 'Is it a special occasion? I would have dressed up if I'd known.' He touched the new cloth napkins that Sophia had bought, chiding that paper napkins wouldn't cut it tonight.

'No. Nothing special.' Sarah turned away to dish up the food. She hated lying. Barry White sang about loving someone just the way they were, compounding Sarah's feelings. Tonight, she felt like a fraud. She didn't hear Richie's footsteps as he came up behind her.

'Sorry,' she said, head low as she stared at the pots and pans. 'You must be feeling ambushed. I am, and it's my bloody house!'

'It's lovely,' Richie smiled. 'Beats Scrabble any day. You just took me by surprise.'

'You're not the only one,' Sarah murmured.

'What's that?'

'I have a confession to make.' Sarah gestured towards the food. 'I can't cook. Not like this anyway. I didn't bake the apple pie in the oven either and I certainly didn't make the custard to go with it. The dessert is from M&S and the mains are from a swanky restaurant up the road.' She finally met his gaze, preparing for the worst. 'This is a set-up, all of it. If you want to leave, I'll understand.'

'And miss out on all this grub? You're kidding, aren't you?' He smiled and led her over to the table. 'Sit. I'll dish up and you can tell me all about it.'

Sarah was grateful to rest her wobbly legs. As they talked she felt herself relax. The steak was delicious, and only a tad tough as a result of being reheated. They managed to make room for dessert and easily polished off the bottle of wine.

'So, Sophia Hudson is a manic matchmaker. Who knew?' Richie laughed, resting his dessert spoon on the table.

'You don't know the half of it,' Sarah said wryly, remembering who Sophia was married to. 'So, what now? Scrabble? TV?' Sarah began to clear the dishes away.

'And miss dancing to Snow Patrol? Never.' Taking the plates from her grip, Richie took her to the centre of the kitchen floor and rested his hands on her hips. Sarah's hands fell naturally on his shoulders as they swayed from side to side. Alcohol had numbed her nerves, and it felt good to be held.

'You don't have to do this,' she said quietly. But as her hand crept over his firm shoulders, she didn't want to let go.

Richie gazed at Sarah with such sincerity that it almost melted her heart. 'You've no idea, have you? I've been wanting to do this for months. But every time I made a move, you brought out the Scrabble board.'

Sarah laughed. 'That's not how I remember it.' If Richie had wanted to take things further, she had been missing all the cues.

'I didn't force it because I didn't want to ruin a good friendship,' he admitted. 'But being together like this . . . your celebrity friend was right. It's the push we both needed.'

'But what if—' Sarah began, as more worries crowded in. But her words were silenced as Richie pressed his warm lips upon hers.

Chapter 61

Sarah stood in the shower, puffs of steam rising around her as she basked in the aftermath of her night with Richie. She'd been scared of upsetting the equilibrium, but Richie had evoked feelings which had lain dormant for years.

Climbing out of the shower, she pulled on her towelling robe and wrapped her hair. Richie was gone when she woke up, most likely at home to change for work where they would arrive separately. Should the powers that be get wind of their relationship, one of them could end up transferred to the opposite shift. That's if they still *had* a relationship. They'd had a lot to drink last night in between dancing to her Spotify playlist which Sophia had set up. Perhaps Richie had changed his mind and woken up sober and mortified.

She quickly dried her hair. She wasn't going to let anything ruin her day. She stood before her wardrobe, viewing its contents with a critical eye. Sophia was right. Her clothes *were* drab. Perhaps she could invest in something more flattering for work. She pulled on her suit, humming to herself as she entered the kitchen. The BBC Breakfast Show was playing, and the scent of fresh pastries sweetened the air. She hadn't remembered leaving the radio on, much less putting pastries in the oven to bake.

'Richie.' He was standing next to the oven and her heart gave a little flip-flop as he turned around. 'You came back.'

'I thought I'd return the favour.' He grinned, taking some croissants out. 'Courtesy of Greggs. I was keeping them warm until you came down.' He had also cleaned up the kitchen, and Sherlock was eating kibble from his bowl.

'I could get used to this,' she said, taking a seat. The fact that he had come back reassured her that everything was OK. She told herself not to expect too much. That last night had been so perfect, it was worth any future heartbreak. But there was something about the way Richie looked at her that suggested he wasn't going anywhere just yet.

'Right, now I really do have to go,' he said, after finishing his pastry and grabbing his motorcycle helmet from the ground. 'If Yvonne gets a sniff of this, she'll be on to Human Resources before our feet touch the ground.'

A quick kiss later and he was gone. Sarah sat, contemplating the last twenty-four hours. She had a lot to thank Sophia Hudson for. Her friends would have a field day with this when they found out.

Maggie was way ahead of her as Sarah locked her front door to leave for work.

'Morning,' her friend said, grinning at Sarah from the other side of the low fence.

'Maggie,' Sarah started, one hand on her chest. 'I didn't see you there!'

'Neither did Richie when he left,' she said gleefully, exhaling a stream of smoke. 'Dirty stop out. Did you two finally do the deed?'

Sarah's grin told her everything she needed to know. 'I want details.' Maggie stubbed out her cigarette before placing the remains in the carton.

'A lady never tells. And it's very early days. I don't want to jinx it.'

'Judging by the smile on your face he didn't disappoint.' Maggie tightened her dressing gown belt. 'Daniel's coming over to meet Elliott properly tonight.'

'I'm happy for you.' Sarah hoped it worked out between them. It turned out that Maggie had known about McGuire's impending divorce from the get-go. Elliott didn't need any more upheaval in his life. Sarah lifted her sleeve to check her watch. She couldn't afford to be late for work.

'How *is* Elliott?'

'Sleeping like a baby, touch wood.' She tapped the side of the wooden door. 'Let's hope it lasts, eh?'

Sarah agreed, before saying her goodbyes. She opened the door of her car, casting her gaze upwards as a grating caw rose from above.

A rook perched on her guttering, its flint eyes sharp. *Don't get too happy,* its caws seemed to echo into the overcast sky.

She climbed into her car, a little of her happiness crumbling away. The last few weeks had been shrouded in strangeness. After discovering Dr Osmond was alive, the police had got permission to dig down into the bunker where Cora had been held. An old, headless skeleton was discovered, face down. Sophia had dated it back to the eighteen hundreds. Thanks to an abundance of neutral soil, the skeleton was well preserved. The skull was discovered in Father Duffy's collection and an identification was made. It was Kitty Flowers, a woman who was reported in the local archives as practising the dark arts hundreds of years ago. It was a pretty name, for someone involved in devil worship.

The fact she was buried face down held further connotations of witchcraft, but there was a bigger question in Sarah's mind. How did Father Duffy come to own the skull of a body buried deep in Osmond's yard? Had its presence affected him somehow? Was it the real root of the bone house? She turned her ignition in her car as the air chilled.

Chapter 62

The only thing Elliott missed about his previous house was the stairwell. It was the perfect place to sit and listen in while other people spoke. His small body was hidden in the shadows, and if the doors downstairs were open, sounds carried up. Like the times when his mummy and daddy used to fight. There were happy times too, but he didn't have to hide in the stairwell for those.

Creepers creeping, he thought as he lingered in the corridor, his thick socks treading lightly on the floor. It was way past his bedtime and Sarah had long since gone home. He knew all about what had happened. He'd heard his mother talking to Elsie over the phone. Sarah had killed someone. She hadn't meant to, but it happened just the same. Then there was Mr Irving, who was hit by a car leaving Sarah's house the year before. Sarah *had* meant to hurt him because he was a very bad man. Now he lay in a hospital bed hooked up to a machine which helped him to breathe. Yet Sarah was the nicest, kindest, most caring person he knew. But you couldn't have night without day, and shadows only existed because light gave them form. It felt like a very grown-up thought, but when it came to stuff like this, Elliott knew a lot more than other kids his age. Sometimes when you tried to do good things, darkness slipped in. Sarah was still carrying it around. Maybe she always would.

He touched the coat hanging from the hook in the hall. It was light, slim fitting and smelled a little of aftershave. A small blue Tardis pin was on the lapel. It was a lot different from his father's bulky old combat jacket that used to hang there. Maggie had been dating Daniel McGuire for weeks now, but this was the first time that she had brought him home.

'Are we crazy?' Maggie's voice was bright with happiness. 'Getting serious so soon.'

'Aye. Definitely. Bring it on.' Elliott could hear the smile in his voice as he spoke with an accent. He couldn't help but like the man who had made his mother happy, because her brightness lit up the whole room. Now, instead of crying herself to sleep, she stayed up late painting, and the recycling bin wasn't filled to the brim with wine bottles anymore.

'I've never felt like this about anyone,' Maggie said.

'The minute we met, I knew I was lost to you,' McGuire said. 'My marriage to Sophia . . . I don't know what the hell that was. Defiance, rebellion, trying to find my place in the world . . .'

'Or a cougar taking advantage of a good-looking young man.'

'I thought yous liked her?'

'I admire her savvy and her business sense. But if someone her age tried to marry my twenty-something son, I'd eat her for breakfast.'

Elliott wasn't quite sure what Maggie meant but he drew comfort from the fierce protectiveness in her voice.

'Well, I hope Elliott likes me,' McGuire said, as silence fell. 'Especially now I've brought my toothbrush.'

'Why don't we ask him?'

Elliott pulled back from the doorway as Maggie spoke. 'It's a good thing you don't have school tomorrow, Elliott, because it's way past your bedtime. C'mon in. There's someone I'd like you to meet.' Tentatively, he joined his mother at the round kitchen table where she sat across from McGuire. Elliott didn't take his eyes off him as he stood next to Maggie.

'Hello, Elliott,' McGuire said, as Maggie introduced them. 'I hear you're a *Harry Potter* fan.'

Elliott nodded slowly. A part of him was mistrustful, and he opened his mind to read the person his mummy had brought into their home. 'Is it too early for presents?' He flicked a glance at Maggie and back to Elliott. 'Because I've been looking for a very good home for this book.'

'So that's what's in the bag,' Maggie said, as he produced *Harry Potter and the Philosopher's Stone*.

'I've already got that one,' Elliott said, nibbling on his thumbnail.

'Elliott, that's rude. You're meant to say thanks when someone gives you a present, whether you have it or not.'

McGuire raised a hand. 'No, no. He's perfectly correct. After all, who wants two of the same book?' His eyes twinkled as he smiled, and Elliott was about to apologise when McGuire turned to the first page. 'Is your book signed by the cast from the movie as well?'

A small, sudden gasp left Elliott's parted lips.

'Sophia has contacts everywhere,' he said to Maggie with a wink.

Elliott stared in amazement at the signatures from Daniel Radcliffe and his co-stars. 'My name is Daniel too,' McGuire said warmly. 'But everyone calls me McGuire.'

But Maggie was shaking her head. 'We can't possibly accept this, it must be worth a fortune.'

'It's nae good to me,' McGuire shrugged. 'I'm more of a *Doctor Who* fan now.'

'Thank you,' Elliott said, picking the book up from the table and clasping it to his chest in case Maggie decided to give it back. 'Are you on a sleepover?' he said, to break the silence. Maggie and McGuire had been looking at each other in a mushy lovey-dovey way. All Elliott wanted to do was to bring his book to bed and trace his finger over the names.

'Would it be OK with you if I was?'

Elliott nodded. 'Just don't let Auntie Sarah catch you.' He planted a kiss against his mother's cheek before leaving the two of them alone. Sometimes things just came out of his mouth before he had a chance to think them through. Sarah sometimes worried in case McGuire made Mummy sad, but now Elliott had met him, he knew everything would be OK. Because once, McGuire had been sad like Mummy too. And somehow Elliott knew that he never, ever wanted to go back there again.

Chapter 63

Cora closed the door behind her. She could finally relax, now Maura, the social worker, had left. Millie was gurgling in her bouncer, no worse for wear for her experience months before. At least they wouldn't have to see Maura again. Cora's case had finally been given the rubber stamp and social care had approved her skills as a mother. She'd been lucky with Maura. A native of Slayton, Maura had grown up with a knowledge of the community and the strangeness that surrounded them. To some, that strangeness would be off-putting, but Cora had never felt so much at home. Even when the community turned against her, she appreciated the reasons why. They had felt betrayed, because she had been accepted as one of them: a soul who came to a dark place because that was all she had known.

She smiled at her baby, pausing to look at her phone. An invitation to a private Facebook group had come through. It was reserved for residents of Slayton, according to the DM, but she had been nominated as an honorary member by Elsie Abraham, a customer of her book store. Cora clicked accept. Since the truth of her situation had spread, the bookshop had been really busy, and she had carefully vetted her assistant this time around. Timmy's betrayal had become common knowledge, and he was keeping his head down as a result.

'Who's a gorgeous girly wirly? You are! Yes you are . . .' She spoke the loving gibberish of motherese as Millie bounced in delight in the doorway. To think she'd come so close to losing her. When her tormentor had first entered the room, whistling 'Here Comes the Sun', her favourite childhood song, she had been sure her father had come back to life. But it wasn't Dr Osmond. It was the rapist father of her first child. He had cruelly used her aversion to the song as a method of torture. To think she had once trusted the vicar who brought her a hot chocolate before bed. But on the nights his wife was away, there was more than chocolate in that drink. He'd told her as he tightened her bindings and the drug took hold. Duffy had blamed her for killing their baby and sinking her tiny body in the lake. She in turn had blamed the lingering evil of the bone house as she awoke in the barn to find her baby dead on the ground. Neither of them had ever known what really happened until Sarah Noble reported the truth.

The woman risked her life to save theirs, and Cora would be forever in her debt. Lying to the police about what she had witnessed was the least she could do. She may not have seen how Mrs Duffy died, but from the moment Sarah arrived, her motives had been clear. Cora recalled emerging from the drug-induced haze as Sarah tried to shake her awake. But the relief she'd felt to see Millie balancing on the officer's shoulder had been short-lived. As the fog closed in on her once more, Cora had tried to utter a warning as Duffy sloped in from behind. The next time she came to, his wife was lying dead on the floor. Sarah's protests had rung clear as officers placed her under arrest.

Cora lifted her baby from her bouncer and held her close. She was never letting her out of her sight again. Father Duffy had shattered what little trust in men she had left. That day when she was kidnapped, the vicar had babbled on about retribution, with more than a glint of madness in his eyes. Picking up a skull from the table, he'd caressed the ivory eye sockets while talking about Cora's 'pretty bones'. There was a chilling similarity to her father, but they were worlds apart in other ways. Both men were touched by evil. Both men lived on.

As long as she had Millie, Cora could make her peace with the past. She had been so scared as a teen, that she'd even tied rocks around her baby's pram. At the time, she couldn't bear for her baby's precious remains to end up on a bunker wall. She remembered the flock of crows which circled the lake as she stood in the foggy twilight, her young heart filled with pain. Their harsh caws had assaulted the air as she'd pushed the pram off the jetty, instinctively stepping back to save herself. Her eyes blurry with tears, she'd watched the lake accept her offering, the pop of each air bubble inflicting further pain. The return of the crows to Slayton's lake was a signal that evil was on its way. After all these years . . . she hadn't been losing her mind. The men that wronged her would be brought to justice but she wouldn't taint her life with Millie by dwelling on it.

She touched her daughter's wavy hair, overcome by a love so powerful it burned like a furnace in her chest.

'See this?' Cora showed her baby a new painting on the wall. 'This is your little sister. Her name is Rose.' Finally, her first baby had a name. She glanced at the beautiful painting she had commissioned. There was something magical about the quality of the image. It seemed to have a life of its own. The woman holding Rose was Julia, her mother. She looked like Cora, apart from her hair. She was sitting on a picnic blanket spread out next to the lake, her blue dress coming just above her knees. An older child stood next to her. She held a daisy chain in her hands and was smiling down on them both. That was how Cora chose to remember her little sister, grown up enough to enjoy the beautiful surroundings she had found herself in. The picture had been painted by Maggie, a local artist who had welcomed Cora to the fold. She had a little boy named Elliott. When he looked at you with his full dark eyes, it felt like he was seeing into your soul.

Millie played with her hair. Happy tears pricked Cora's eyes as she felt her family's presence all around her. In a life filled with shadows, it felt good to stand in the sun.

Epilogue

The sun warms my back as it streams through the window of the hospital café. It's a novelty to see such good weather in Scotland this time of year. As the dust motes twinkle through the golden shaft of light, it feels like a positive omen for the future.

My newspaper is open but folded. I don't want to draw attention to the fact I'm reading the *Lincolnshire News*. After all these years, I'm well versed in fending off potential awkward questions, although it's best to negate them altogether. Seeing Cora in the news evoked a myriad of emotions, but my time with her feels like a former life. Given that I died the day she escaped, I suppose it is. I had so many plans that day. I'm glad the decision to kill her was taken out of my hands. Cora was out of that bunker with a speed I hadn't expected. I didn't think she had it in her to grab my ankles. Strength was not on her side that day, but the element of surprise was.

As I crashed into the gas hob, she was already halfway up the steps. But when I came around, I didn't have time to feel sorry for myself. I had to act fast. It helped that the prep work was already done. I'd planned to disappear that day. I'd been dating a woman who was asking too many questions about my wife's disappearance. That's when I knew I had to go away. I should have done it sooner, but I wanted to give Cora one last birthday, a memory I could take with me long after she was gone. My bags were packed, my money withdrawn and in an untraceable account. My new identity was waiting for me. Reinvention was a small price to pay to avoid prison, where I was inevitably heading otherwise.

With some surprise I read about 'the bone house' online. Journalists sensationalised our story at the time. I was a doctor. I wasn't the only person in my profession to own a skeleton and a collection of skulls. They were kept in the bunker as my wife wouldn't allow them inside the house. The papers didn't mention my medical textbooks or the journals that I pored over at night. Demons and monsters sell more newspapers than family men. I doted on Cora. How could I not? She was an exceptionally beautiful, special child. I raised her from infancy and treated her as my own. All I wanted was to complete my family with a baby of my flesh and blood. But when I discovered my wife had returned to the arms of her first love, my happy family life melted away. I admit to having issues. Spending time in the bunker brought out the worst in me. I'd never been violent in my life, but my anger was like a seed fuelled by darkness, not light. Sometimes I'd lose chunks of time. Stress does that to a man.

It was hardly surprising that I was devasted by my wife's betrayal. I could have handled it better. I should have got a divorce. Instead, I allowed it to simmer beneath the surface. It bubbled like tar on a hot day. I admit to being unkind, out of control. When Julia broke the news of her pregnancy, I thought that everything would be alright. It was, for a while, until I discovered the baby wasn't mine. By the time I picked her up from hospital, I could barely contain the buzzing in my head. I remember that silly little nurse, fawning over me. My smile was so rigid that my jaw ached.

I only meant to frighten Julia. I took the baby to the bunker knowing she would follow me there. But then she started saying all that awful stuff about leaving me. People talk about red mist. Mine was black, and it came down thick and fast. All the nights I'd spent in that bunker, thoughts swirling around my head. My wife was laughing at me, and when the truth got out, everyone else would be too. The moment I stared into the face of Julia's baby – the one she'd tried to pass off as my own – I knew I could never feel love for it. There was only hate, and the desperate need to make the symbol of my wife's betrayal go away. In the darkness of the bunker, rage and resentment shook loose inside me, and when Julia said she was leaving and taking *his* baby and Cora with her, that's when I lost control.

My clearest memory of that awful time is of Cora taking me by the hand and guiding me towards the chair. She wasn't meant to be there. It broke my heart that she was. Because I knew I could never allow her to see daylight again. I made the bunker as child-friendly as I could, putting up fairy lights and bringing her books. The reporters lied about the walls being lined with bones. I'd sold most of my collection to a vicar of all people, even my favourite piece. I found her skull face down under some slabs in the bunker. I told my wife that I bought her online. I never found out where she came from, and nor did I want to know, but I felt compelled to strip her skull clean. It was as if she wanted me to. She carried a morbid yet fascinating essence of her own.

I had only minutes after Cora escaped to accelerate my plan. I'd already killed Julia's boyfriend, whose corpse was in the back room. He had some cheek, coming to my house. I'd blindsided him by offering him a drink and telling him we could discuss things like civilised human beings. But you should never trust a doctor when you've been screwing his wife. He got what he wanted: his little family, back together again. His Cypriot family wouldn't miss him. The night I brought him into the bunker, I'd drugged Cora's food so she slept through. When I saw how well it worked, I planned to do it again after her birthday celebrations when we said our last farewell. I told myself that some things were too beautiful for this ugly world. The last thing I expected was for her to escape. When I recovered from my fall, I turned the bunker into a fireball. I didn't care what people made of the aftermath, I would be long gone by then.

I felt a strange surge of protectiveness when I read about Cora's past. None of this was her fault. I hope she finds the peace she deserves. I certainly never thought I would be a father again at my age. This time it's different. This baby is mine by blood.

My phone beeps with a text. She's ready. It's time for my new wife and daughter to come home. I pick up the bunch of two dozen roses from the table and throw the newspaper into the bin on the way out of the hospital canteen. There's a bounce in my step and a tune on my lips. One that never fails to make me smile. 'Here Comes the Sun . . .'

Acknowledgements

I'm so grateful to the team of people who have helped bring my latest book to you. Thanks to my editor Jane Snelgrove, and the wonderful team at Embla Books. I'm grateful to the brilliant copy editors, proofreaders, cover designer, audio book producers and narrators, marketers, and all the people behind the scenes who have brought this book to fruition. Thanks as always to the team at the Madeleine Milburn Literary, TV and Film Agency. A special mention to my author friends, and to Mel Sherratt, Angela Marsons and all the great authors I've been fortunate enough to meet this year. A special shout to my husband and grown-up children. I'm blessed to have such an amazing family behind me.

Thanks also to the bloggers and book club members who have read, reviewed and spread the word. Word of mouth is a great way of supporting authors. If you have enjoyed this book I'd be so grateful if you could leave an Amazon review.

I love hearing from my readers. You can contact me via email on hello@caroline-writes.com. You can also find me on Facebook @ CMitchellauthor, on Twitter @Caroline_writes, and on Instagram @Caroline_writes. Sign up to my reader's club for news, updates and a free short story here: https://caroline-writes.com

About the Author

Caroline is a *New York Times*, *USA Today*, *Washington Post* and international number one bestselling author, with over 1.5 million books sold. To date her books have been shortlisted for the International Thriller Awards, the Killer Nashville Silver Falchion Awards and the Audie Awards, and her 2018 thriller *Silent Victim* won the US Readers' Favorite Award in the 'Psychological Thriller' category.

Caroline originates from Ireland and now lives with her family in a village just outside Lincoln. A former police detective, she specialised in roles dealing with vulnerable victims, victims of domestic abuse, and serious sexual offences. The people she dealt with are a huge source of inspiration for her writing today. Caroline writes full-time.

About Embla Books

Embla Books is a digital-first publisher of standout commercial adult fiction. Passionate about storytelling, the team at Embla publish books that will make you 'laugh, love, look over your shoulder and lose sleep'. Launched by Bonnier Books UK in 2021, the imprint is named after the first woman from the creation myth in Norse mythology, who was carved by the gods from a tree trunk found on the seashore – an image of the kind of creative work and crafting that writers do, and a symbol of how stories shape our lives.

Find out about some of our other books and stay in touch:

Twitter, Facebook, Instagram: @emblabooks
Newsletter: https://bit.ly/emblanewsletter